Sweet Southern Hearts

Books by Susan Schild

LINNY'S SWEET DREAM LIST

SWEET CAROLINA MORNING

SWEET SOUTHERN HEARTS

Published by Kensington Publishing Corporation

SWEET SOUTHERN HEARTS

The Willow Hill Series

Susan Schild

LYRICAL PRESS
Kensington Publishing Corp.
www.kensingtonbooks.com

To the extent that the image or images on the cover of this book depict a person or persons, such person or persons are merely models, and are not intended to portray any character or characters featured in the book.

LYRICAL PRESS BOOKS are published by

Kensington Publishing Corp.
119 West 40th Street
New York, NY 10018

Copyright © 2017 by Susan Schild

All rights reserved. No part of this book may be reproduced in any form or by any means without the prior written consent of the Publisher, excepting brief quotes used in reviews.

All Kensington titles, imprints, and distributed lines are available at special quantity discounts for bulk purchases for sales promotion, premiums, fund-raising, educational, or institutional use.

Special book excerpts or customized printings can also be created to fit specific needs. For details, write or phone the office of the Kensington Sales Manager: Kensington Publishing Corp., 119 West 40th Street, New York, NY 10018. Attn. Sales Department. Phone: 1-800-221-2647.

Lyrical Press and Lyrical Press logo Reg. U.S. Pat. & TM Off.

First Electronic Edition: January 2017
eISBN-13: 978-1-60183-888-9
eISBN-10: 1-60183-888-3

First Print Edition: January 2017
ISBN-13: 978-1-60183-889-6
ISBN-10: 1-60183-889-1

Printed in the United States of America

For Bryan

CHAPTER 1

Good Sports

Linny's heartbeat galloped under her life jacket as they shot down the rapids of the Ocasoula River. Eyes wide, she watched as their orange raft careened toward a jagged boulder, bumped it hard, and spun them toward a patch of choppy water. As the water rushed around the three of them—Linny, her new husband Jack, and their beautiful, Ms. Outward Bound–type goddess of a river guide—they dug deep and paddled hard, straining to pull through the eddy. With a whoosh, they were pulled backward down the roaring, foaming river. Linny shot Jack a panicky glance, but he was grinning exultantly and looking like he was having the time of his life. With the flick of a braid and a pirate's smile, the guide thrust her paddle into the rapids, turned the raft around, and steered them downstream toward calmer water. Too soon to relax, though. Linny saw more rough waters ahead and tensed.

Be a shame to lose a third husband, she thought crazily and paddled harder.

The nimble-footed photographer from the outdoor center jogged along a path on the riverbank, snapping away as their raft rocketed toward the Turbinator, the Class III rapid that roiled ahead in the home stretch of the river trip. The photographer's ponytail bounced as he raced ahead of them, taking shots as their raft bucked, dove, and finally glided through the rain-swollen Ocasoula.

Soon, a shivering Linny stood at the takeout, hugging herself and rubbing her arms. She'd been splashed thoroughly and didn't want to think about how cold the water would have been if they'd flipped over. Though it was late June, the guide told them the water temperature was only in the midfifties. Linny found herself grinning like a fool as she waited for Jack to come back from the truck with his wallet to pay for their pictures. She'd been terrified, but she'd had a blast.

A white water rafting trip might not be high on most women's lists of a must-do on a honeymoon, but when Linny had seen how Jack's eyes sparkled as he reminisced about a rafting trip he'd taken when he was in his twenties, she'd said, "Let's do it!" in an enthusiastic, practically perky voice she'd hardly recognized. In this new and complicated marriage, being a good sport and flexible as Gumby were going to ease the way. Though rafting wasn't her thing, Jack had cheerfully gone on the vineyard tour with her yesterday and, on the drive up to the mountains, had tagged along, not looking bored, as she'd poked through vintage aprons and yellow Nancy Drew books at an antique store.

"Here you go, ma'am." The young man held out his camera and scratched one mesh-sandaled foot with the other as he watched her view the shots he'd taken.

In perfect clarity, the fellow had caught them at the moment she and Jack got sling-shot skyward in their raft after diving down into the roiling water of that last rapid. Linny peered more closely at the picture. The photographer had captured the Carolina blue sky day, the Day-Glo orange of the raft, the lithe young goddess at the helm, and her and Jack—the glowing, sun-drenched newlyweds. Twice coming down that river they'd almost flipped and been swept into the churning waters. Linny's teeth had chattered and she'd buzzed with adrenaline and fear, but she looked alive and exhilarated as she beamed at Jack, pure joy in her eyes. With powerful arms, he was digging away with his paddle, helping power them through. But Linny spotted two details that made her eyes well up: Jack's new gold band glinting in the sunlight and the look he'd given her just as the photographer had taken the shot was one of wonder and delight. He looked like he was thinking, *How did I get this lucky?*

"You did a great job." Linny smiled at the young photographer.

"Thanks." The young man blushed and pulled down the brim of his cap. He pointed to the visitors' center. "Just give me a minute to load the pictures and you can pick the ones you want."

"Thanks. We'll be over as soon as my husband gets back," she said.

He raised a hand and loped off.

Linny loved saying *my husband*. She'd probably said it too many times over the three days of this honeymoon. *My husband and I are from Willow Hill. My husband is a veterinarian. My husband likes unsweetened tea.* Linny smiled at herself. Yup, she was being obnoxious, but she didn't care. She was so dang happy that she couldn't stop. Well, at least for a while.

At age thirty-nine and with her streak of bad luck with husbands, the odds of her and Jack finding each other and falling in love weren't great. Linny sent up a quick prayer of pure gratefulness. After her beloved first husband, Andy, had died of a brown recluse spider bite while cleaning out a shed for Linny—an item on the too-long honey-do lists she always kept for him—she'd been lost for so many years and thought she'd never be happy again. Then Buck the charmer came along. She should have known a golden boy driving a vintage Caddy wouldn't be good husband material, but she'd married him anyway. He'd turned out to be trouble, but just as she was considering divorcing him, he'd up and died on her. When his aneurism blew while he was in bed with a woman named Kandi, he'd left her broke.

Linny had sworn she'd steer clear of men or die trying, and then she'd met Jack. Technically, she'd accidentally hit him in the head with a bourbon bottle while recycling at the dump. She smiled and shook her head, remembering. Most women would pretty up that how-we-met story, but Linny told people the unvarnished version. Maybe she just wanted to spread the word that second chances, fresh starts, and true love were all still possible, even at their ages. The happily ever after you yearn for just might not look the way you thought it would.

So, a few days ago in a backyard ceremony, Linny had married Jack. A small-town vet with a twelve-year-old son and an exquisite ex-wife who was just a little too chummy with him for Linny's taste, Jack came with complications. But so had she. And today she was buoyant and happy.

Jack strode toward her in his Levi's and the dark green T-shirt she'd picked out for him—the extralong one that that fit his tall, rangy frame and was also the exact color of his pine green eyes. Her shivering lessening, she grinned at him.

"Let's warm you up, shug." He wrapped her in one of his large and slightly doggy-smelling fleece he'd gotten from the truck and began to rub her shoulders.

She leaned in to him, enjoying the warmth and solid heft of him, and rested her head against his broad shoulder. "Okay." Hugging him always made her feel safe, like finally arriving home after a long, arduous trip.

On the way back to the cabin Jack cast her a sideways glance from the driver's seat of the truck. "Did you have a good time?"

"I did." Linny sighed. "This has been the best honeymoon ever." As soon as the words left her mouth, she felt her face flame. Why had she said that? She wasn't ranking her three honeymoons, holding up cards like the skating judges with numbers one through ten printed on them. Linny shot him a glance to see how hurt he looked, but he just patted her knee and whistled between his teeth as he adjusted the rearview mirror.

Linny shook her head. She'd drive herself crazy yet.

The tires of Jack's red truck crunched on the gravel as they pulled up beside their hideaway. Linny took Jack's hand as they walked up the front path, admiring the square-cut logs and clean lines of the two-room rustic log cabin. She'd rented it after obsessively comparing reviews on travel websites. Perched on a high ridge, their cabin was skirted by lush pink rhododendron and gave long-range views of the green and blue patchwork quilt of the valley laid out before it. She'd chosen the perfect, cozy honeymoon spot.

Linny took a quick shower, dried her hair, and slipped on a cool floral sundress. Jack was on the front porch playing his guitar, and she smiled as she heard him strumming. Padding barefoot to the tiny kitchen, she opened a beer for Jack and poured herself a glass of the crisp Pinot Grigio they'd bought at the vineyard the day before.

Pushing open the screen door with her hip, she handed Jack his beer. He sat in a rocker, cradling the guitar. A self-taught musician, Jack was still self-conscious about his mistakes, but he was coming along fast. He took a draw of beer, put the bottle on the floor, and eased into the opening chords of James Taylor's "Carolina in My Mind." Giving her a sorry-if-I-mess-up smile, he began to sing quietly in his warm tenor.

Leaning against the railing, arms crossed, she watched him and felt a wave of contentment. She held out her hand and examined her glittering ring, made from the emeralds Jack and Neal had dug out of a gem mine especially for her. Unbeknownst to her, the father-son adventure weekend they'd taken last summer was for the express purpose of finding stones for her ring. To have Neal involved in the gem hunt was a majorly smart move on Jack's part, especially because her stepson still watched her warily, worried that she'd try to replace his mother. The stones weren't particularly high quality, but Linny didn't care. She loved the ring.

Jack missed a chord and winced. Noticing her ring studying, a smile played at his lips.

Linny smiled back. Ruthie, the office manager in Jack's veterinary practice, said that after Vera divorced Jack, some women clients feigned reasons to bring their pets in for appointments just to spend time with him. "A woman with a poodle named Precious claimed the dog had ADHD, and another time a tummy ache-toothache-itching issue," she'd said, rolling her eyes and patting Linny's arm. "So glad he fell for you."

Thank goodness he was the type of man who was oblivious to his own charms, unlike her late hound-dog of a second husband. But banish the thought. She wasn't going to allow regrets to tarnish the present. Linny slid into the rocking chair beside his and sipped her wine. After a moment she began to softly sing along with him. No volume from her. She was prone to sudden scale changes and croaks.

A phone trilled from the kitchen and Jack gave her a smile as he put down the guitar and went to take the call.

His son, Neal—her new stepson, she reminded herself—had called to talk with his dad twice each of the three nights they'd been on their honeymoon. Was that normal for a twelve-year-old? A lot of the other stepmothers in the Bodacious Bonus Moms—the online support and advice blog she'd been reading voraciously for the last few months—complained about their teenage stepchildren not sharing a word with them or their husbands because they were too busy texting and Snapchatting friends.

Linny took a sip of wine and thought about it. How much did Neal's clinginess have to do with his mother, Vera, and her new husband bickering? Petite Vera, with her little-girl voice and perfect white-blond loveliness, reminded Linny of an airy, sweet pink confection, but with her sense of entitlement and demands, she was no cream puff. Her husband, Chaz, was a trial lawyer, and no pushover either. She could see why they butted heads. And with Vera's moneyed background and silver-spoon tastes, her wealthy new husband getting into hot water and losing a lot of his—no, *their*—money probably didn't sit well with her. Linny felt a flash of mean-spirited pleasure that perfect Vera was having problems, then chided herself. Tension in that household hurt Neal and she didn't want that.

Jack came back to the porch, rubbing a spot between his brows and talking on the phone in that soothing voice he used with scared animals at his veterinary clinic. "So they're fighting nonstop. Can you just go to your room and turn on the white noise app on your phone?" He paused and scowled. "That loud, huh?"

Jack looked at her. "Can you hold on, buddy?" He put the phone to his chest, his expression serious. "He's crying and he never cries. I'd send him to the grandparents, but they're all out of town."

Linny inhaled sharply and racked her brain. "My sister loves Neal to pieces, but she's so overwhelmed with her new baby. I could call her, though . . ." she said.

Jack shook his head slowly, his face tight. "We need to go home, Lin. Neal needs us."

Linny nodded mutely, feeling bereft. There went her week-long honeymoon, right out the window. She gazed off for one last long look at the rolling land of the valley and slumped in her chair.

Jack spoke to Neal calmly. "We'll be back this evening and you're going to come stay with us for a while until things simmer down." He paused, listening, and his voice grew firm. "I don't care if your mama doesn't like it. I'll deal with her. Right now, everybody needs to just settle down." He ended the call and sent her an apologetic look. "Lin . . ." he began.

She held up a hand and tried to smile. "I understand, Jack. I really do." Rising, she trudged in to begin packing, trying to fight the disappointment crashing down on her like a great wave. She and Jack had the rest of their lives to spend together, she reasoned, but it didn't help.

Vera and Chaz were selfish, Linny thought as she thunked the milk, yogurt, and luncheon meat into the cooler she was packing with unnecessary vigor.

Gathering their toiletries and clothes to put in the suitcase, her heart squeezed for Neal. The last thing a sensitive boy like him needed was a ringside seat to the fight of the century. Going home was the right thing to do.

Jack stepped inside and gave her a wry grin. "I just texted Vera and told her the fighting was upsetting Neal and that we were coming home early to take him for a few days. I didn't ask her, I told her. That should set off a firestorm." He grimaced and held up his phone. "The furious calls should start in four, three, two, one . . ."

Linny stood with a hand on her hip, sent him a crooked smile, and waited. The phone rang, its tone sounding more shrill and urgent than it usually did.

Jack rolled his eyes, turned it off, and slipped it in his pocket.

Despite knowing that going home was the best thing to do, as they wound down the mountain in the truck, Linny fantasized about what it would be like to deal less with Vera, if just for a little while. Maybe she and Chaz would get a sudden burning desire to live off the grid for a year to fix their marriage. They'd move to a cabin with no plumbing in Talkeetna, Alaska. Normal-looking couples did it all the time on all those Alaska shows Jack and Neal watched. Vera and Chaz could rebond while chopping firewood and fixing their broken snowmobile, which they urgently needed to go into town to get much-needed supplies because a blizzard was fast approaching. For one long moment Linny imagined how serene life would be with Vera in Talkeetna. She and Jack could walk together through a field of wildflowers, each holding one of Neal's hands—something the boy would never allow them to do. Bluebirds and hummingbirds would fly around them.

Flushing guiltily, she glanced at Jack as though he could read her mind, but he was flipping down the sun visor. Linny blew out a sigh. Glumly, she stared out the window. She didn't really wish for that Alaskan adventure for Vera. Neal really needed his mother and he'd grown to love his stepfather, Chaz, too.

Linny and Jack were quiet for much of the long drive home from the mountains to Willow Hill. Even her Technicolor daydream of Vera battling icy winds as she trudged to the outhouse in fifty below weather didn't cheer her up. Linny was just too disappointed to make conversation. Jack looked pensive, the muscles in his jaw working.

Her phone rang and she glanced at the screen. It was Ruby, one of her mother, Dottie's, two best friends. Had something happened to

Mama? Her stomach tightened as she pictured her mother lying on the floor like that woman on the TV commercial who lived alone and didn't have the emergency clicker necklace.

But Ruby sounded cheery. "Hi, sweetheart. Hope you're just walking on air now that you're freshly married. You tell that handsome hunk of a husband of yours that I said hey." Ruby had been a looker in her heyday and still had a flirty streak.

Linny breathed out. This wasn't a meet-me-at-the-emergency-room call. She called to Jack, "Ruby says *hey, you handsome hunk of a husband.*"

Jack shook his head, but his mouth crooked up.

"We're at your mama's house and you need to talk to her," Ruby said. "For weeks now we girls have been planning to go to the RV show at the Civic Center to make a final decision about what kind of camper or RV we want to rent for our trip. We're fixing to get in the car to go and now she's making all kinds of excuses for staying home. This is the last day of the show," Ruby said, sounding exasperated.

Since coming to terms with learning that her late husband had had a longtime mistress, her mother had shaken off her dour, church lady demeanor and blossomed. She'd given up the yard sale habit that bordered on hoarding, taken a two-week Caribbean cruise with her girlfriends, and was now seeing a charming older man named Mack whom she'd met on the ship. Oh, and Dottie—a card-carrying Baptist and member of the Sisters of Dorcas ladies' prayer circle—had won $250,000 on the nickel slots on the ship. So, emboldened with her first big vacation, Mama and her two friends had cooked up this RV adventure they called their "trip to see the US of A." It was all the three of them had talked about for months.

"Let me talk to her," a woman's voice said insistently. Linny heard a fumbling as the phone changed hands. "Dessie here," said her mother's other best friend, in her usual brisk tone. "This is the second time she's backed out of the RV show. Yesterday she said her feet were hurting her and today she's claiming her sugar's high."

Linny paused a beat, baffled. "She doesn't have bad feet or sugar problems."

"We know," Dessie said drily.

"Can you put her on the phone?" Linny asked, rubbing the spot on her temple that had begun to throb. What was going on?

More fumbling sounds, and the phone clattered as it dropped to the floor. Dessie picked back up. "Your mama doesn't feel like talking right now. She and Curtis are going in to take a little lie down."

Linny wondered again how her mother could get any sleep at all sharing her bed with Curtis, her 170-pound Great Dane. But maybe Dottie really wasn't well. "Dessie, does she seem sick? Should you run her by the urgent care?"

Dessie said, "We ate lunch at Captain Finn's Seafood and she had the First Mate's Special with an extra order of shrimp and lemon chess pie for dessert." She chuckled. "So her appetite's fine and her color is good, too. You ask me, I think she's just got a case of nerves."

"Nerves about what?" Linny asked, coming up empty when she tried to think of any stressors in her mother's peaceful life and remembered all the unexpected happiness that had been showered upon her over the last year.

Dessie's voice was back at a normal decibel level and extra bright. "Well, we're real glad you had a good visit to the mountains and we can't wait to hear all about it."

Her mother must have come back within earshot. Scanning the highway for signs, she saw they were almost to Greensboro. "Dessie, you and Ruby go on to the RV show yourselves and do reconnaissance for your trip. Jack and I are coming back early from the mountains and we'll be home in two hours. Tell Mama I'll stop by to see her this evening."

"I will, honey, and you two drive safe." Dessie ended the call.

"What's wrong with your mama?" Jack asked, his eyes lit with concern.

"Not sure. The girls don't think it's anything serious, but I'll run by and check on her. Dessie said it could be nerves." She turned her hands palms up. "About what I don't know, but I'll find out."

Back home, after they'd unpacked Jack left to pick up Neal at his ex-wife's house and Linny hopped in her trusty old Volvo to drive the ten miles from their farmhouse to her mother's house. She bumped down the long gravel road lined by rows of bushy tobacco plants thriving on the land her mama owned and leased out to other farmers. Rolling down the window, she breathed in the country fragrance of loamy earth, mown grass, and honeysuckle. She caught a whiff of skunk and it didn't bother her a bit. It just smelled like her childhood.

Slowing, she approached the driveway of the aqua blue trailer—the one her mother had let her stay in for free when Linny's second husband had stolen her money and then died on her. The trailer had become such a haven for her while she'd rebuilt her life. She peered down the driveway, but it was too overgrown for her to see much. She spied a clothesline strung with brightly colored T-shirts and dresses that danced gracefully in the breeze and felt better. Mama said the new renters were *a real nice young couple* who adored the trailer Linny had turned into a little jewel box with new drywall, fresh paint, and reclaimed wood floors from Habitat Re-Use Center.

Linny pulled in to the driveway of her mother's tidy ranch, right beside the carport that housed her mother's Buick. Trotting up the front walkway, Linny knocked on the screen door and looked inside. "Mama? Mama?" she called. In the background she heard a man's voice on the TV, which was turned up to her mother's usual blare level. Linny rapped harder and peered in the crack between the door and the frame. Her mother had a hook and eye holding the door shut, her version of home security. Linny pulled her cell from her purse and dialed Dottie but heard the ring and ring of the phone from inside the house. No one picked up. Her heart fluttering faster, Linny cupped her hands and called more loudly, "Mama! Mama!"

A clatter sounded and Curtis barreled down the hallway, woofing a baritone bark that would have sent burglars straight into cardiac rehab at Raleigh Memorial. Her mother followed, cooing to the dog, "Now, sugar, you just hush. That's just our Linny."

Breathing a sigh of relief, Linny broke into a smile. Though she'd always loved Mama, she'd only recently begun to really *like* her. Once Dottie shared the truth about how empty her marriage had been to Linny's father, some weight had been lifted from her. Dottie had become sunnier, warmer, and more real—and Linny wanted all the time she could get with her. So if Dottie had a cold, Linny worried it was budding pneumonia. If she had a headache, it was a sign of an impending stroke. Dottie was a fit fifty-nine with no real health problems. And ever since she'd met the dapper Mack and begun to play pickle ball and dance the tango with him, she'd lost ten pounds and started doing a Jane Fonda DVD every morning. She could probably lap Linny in a 5K. Trying to hide how rattled she'd been, Linny waved too animatedly and made a big show of fussing over Curtis whose face was now pressed to the screen. "How are you, baby dog?"

Curtis began to wag his long, thick tail—the one that could clear side tables and buckle you if he clipped your knees.

"Sorry for not hearing you sooner, honey. I was snoozing with that Inspirational Living channel on in the background to keep me company," Dottie said.

Linny tried to be surreptitious in sizing up Dottie as she shooed away the dog and unlocked the door. Her hair was bunched up on either side like she'd slept on it funny, but she was steady on her feet and her eyes were bright. "Hey, Mama." Linny wrapped her mother in a hug, comforted by the familiar smell of Jergens hand cream and baby powder with a hint of Aqua Net.

"How are you, shug?" Dottie asked, motioning Linny to follow her back into the living room. "How was your trip and why are you back early?"

Dottie sank into her velour chair and reclined and Curtis gracefully curled into a loop on the carpet beside her. Linny filled her in on the honeymoon, omitting the part about Vera's dramatics and talking instead about Jack needing to get back for a work issue. As her newly tech-savvy mother scrolled through the trip pictures on Linny's phone, Linny noticed she was wearing a faded, polyester pink zip-up housecoat and those awful white Velcro-shut sandals that she thought had been relegated to the Goodwill box. Those were remnants of the bad old days when disappointment had made Dottie dress like a frumpy woman twenty years older than her actual years.

These days, Dottie had a nice lady at Belk who helped her pick out sassy but age-appropriate clothes. So why was the frumpiness back?

After her mother's final *so pretty!* and *that looks so sweet*, Linny settled back on the couch and cocked her head. "How are you feeling, Mama?"

"Oh, I'm bumping along," Dottie said, not meeting Linny's eyes.

Trying to sound casual, Linny persisted. "So you didn't feel up to going to the RV show?"

"It'd be real crowded, plus my stomach was bothering me." Dottie picked an imaginary piece of lint from her housecoat.

"I thought it was your feet and your sugar," Linny said, raising a brow.

Flushing guiltily and probably trying to remember her original ailments, Dottie nodded her head vigorously for emphasis, "It was all three. Stomach, sugar, and feet."

The poofs on her mother's hairdo bobbed as she nodded, and Linny pictured Precious the poodle with the faux tummy-toothache-itching issues. Linny was such a bad person. She bit the inside of her cheeks and tried to keep a straight face. "What's really going on, Mama?"

Her mother blew out a gust of a sigh. "I don't know," she admitted. "Maybe I'm just getting cold feet about the whole trip."

"Why, Mama?" Linny asked. All Mama and her friends talked about was Graceland versus Dollywood, interstates or secondary roads, and how to find the most accurate reviews of campsites on the internet.

Dottie paused and blurted out, "I'm scared. What if we have a flat tire or pick up a murdering hitchhiker or fight with one another the whole way? What about beavers with rabies coming after us? That happened in a campground in Arkansas just last weekend. Dragged the man under while he was swimming at the lake. What if we drive over a steep ravine?" She made a swooping downward hand motion to simulate driving off a cliff.

Linny hid her smile. She'd had the same awful visual of the motor home flying off a cliff when she'd first heard about the US of A trip. Clearly, Mama was the genetic link to her own worrywart streak. "Anything else on your mind?"

"Well, none of us are world trotters." She glanced at Linny and smoothed the lace doily on the arm of the chair.

Linny suppressed a grin. World trotters. Globe travelers. Dottie could mix an idiom, mash a metaphor. But it *was* a big deal that Mama and her girlfriends, who had been homebodies for most of their lives, were taking this trip. Travel could be daunting, especially when they were all in their late fifties and early sixties and planning on driving a giant bus of a motor home/camper thingy.

Her mother went on, her words rushing as she let them go after penning them up for so long. "I'd never been out of the state before the big cruise and the girls had only been to South Carolina. Ruby went to Myrtle Beach once and Dessie went to Dillon, South Carolina, because she was underage and wanted to marry her first husband, who . . ."

Linny raised a hand to try to head off the inevitable spelling, but it was too late.

". . . turned out to be G-A-Y." Her mother nodded, looking proud of herself for being so wildly progressive as to know a G-A-Y person. "Anyhow, what if we can't handle it? What if we get lost? What if Mack finds another lady friend while I'm gone? What if Curtis forgets all about me?" Looking stricken, she leaned over to scratch under the giant dog's chin and stare at him soulfully.

"You've been worrying about this a lot, Mama," Linny said softly.

Dottie nodded, poodle poofs bobbing again. Linny felt like reaching over and gently smoothing them down but didn't. Dottie was feeling inadequate enough right now, the way her husband Boyd had made her feel for most of their marriage.

"All of you are smart, competent women, and you did so well on that cruise," Linny said in a soothing tone. "And you went to all of those islands and had different languages to deal with, and you flew in and out of some of the busiest airports. That's pretty impressive." Linny didn't think she needed to mention that none of them had ever even flown before.

Her mother considered this, a little smile playing at her lips. But after a moment doubts must have crept back because she threw up her hands and shook her head wearily. "I don't know, sugar. I don't think I'm up for this."

"What could make you feel more comfortable about taking this trip, Mama?" Linny's mind was in high gear, sifting through options. Was there a Triple A deal for RVs or campers? Could the three women pool their money and hire a driver or . . .

Her mother didn't miss a beat. "I'd feel better if you came with us on the first week of the trip." Dottie's gaze was steady. "You can help us learn the ropes."

Linny opened her mouth and closed it again. Her big mouth. But she watched her mother patting Curtis and saw the thin gold band she still wore despite her husband's betrayal. Linny understood every one of her mother's fears and was so proud of her for all her courage. But Linny'd been married less than a week. She breathed out a sigh.

"I can't, Mama. Jack and I are just getting settled in and Neal's coming to stay with us for a while."

"I shouldn't have even asked." Her mother nodded, but her lower lip trembled and she looked as though she might cry. "I'm afraid I need to cancel on the girls, then."

CHAPTER 2

Big Plans for Grand Adventures

At the farm, Linny walked in and saw Jack and Neal sprawled on opposite ends of the huge L-shaped sofa in the living room engrossed in their binge favorite, *Wicked Tuna: Outer Banks*. Neal's big tennis shoes and socks were in the middle of the floor. Sharing the couch with the Avery men were three of their six dogs, including Roy, the lab mix rescue dog Linny had brought into the marriage. Wedged in between Jack and the arm of the chair, Roy looked at Linny coolly and didn't even bother to get up. He was so smitten with Jack that Linny was old news. She looked at the traitor reproachfully but gave his silky black head a quick scratch. "Hey, men," she called. Still nursing some irrational resentment toward Jack for the abbreviated honeymoon, she didn't go to him for her usual kiss, just stood there with her purse still on her shoulder, feeling like a guest.

"Hey, Lin." Jack sat up, muted the TV, and gave her a smile. He shot a glance at Neal. "Son, Linny said hello."

Neal glanced at her as coolly as Roy had. "Hello."

Though she was tired of trying to be so mature all day, Linny still decided to ignore the boy's standoffish behavior and leaned over to kiss the top of his head. "Hey, buddy. We missed you."

"Me too," he mumbled. Neal scratched the ears of Wilbur and Orville, their Border Collie mixes, who were snoring on his knee, and turned his gaze back to the television as the wind-buffeted crew members baited hooks.

Linny perched on the ottoman, took her purse off her shoulder and looked at Jack. "Mama's getting cold feet and is talking about calling off the whole trip."

"Whoa. That would be a shame," Jack said, raising his brows.

Linny gave herself a mental shake, trying to dispel the guilt she felt for her mother's adventure possibly falling apart. "What's new around here?"

"Oh, not too much," Jack said but had a hangdog look about him.

"Nothing except our trip." Neal pushed the glasses up his nose, his eyes still on the television screen. "Chaz was going to take me out to Tucson for a few days on a camping and astronomy trip, but he might cancel. Mama asked Dad if he could take me and he said yes. Tucson is called the astronomy capital of the world. Did you know that?"

"I did not." Linny gazed at Jack and crossed her arms. Without even bothering to run it by her, he'd agreed to pinch-hit for Chaz and take off with Neal just because Vera crooked a finger. And Linny hadn't even let herself seriously consider riding along with Mama and her friends for a few days.

Jack gazed at her, his eyes lit with worry.

Neal pulled his eyes away from the screen and looked at her. "We're going to see the Mt. Lemmon SkyCenter and the Whipple Observatory. It has the eighth largest reflecting telescope in the world and the research on black holes is done there."

"Sounds like you all have the whole thing planned out nicely," Linny said evenly.

Lulled into a false sense of security by her calm demeanor, Jack looked proudly at his little astronomer. "We thought it'd be cool to camp in those high mountains and see the stars under the open sky, right, buddy?"

"Right." Neal's eyes slid back to the screen as a woman fisherman in a fighting chair almost got jerked overboard as she struggled to reel in a big fish.

Abruptly, Linny stood and walked into the kitchen, her shoulders hunched and her pulse raucous.

Jack trailed along behind her. "I'm sorry, Lin. I should have talked this over with you beforehand."

"I wish you had." She leaned against the kitchen counter, crossed her arms, and eyed him. "It seems like Vera can say *jump* and you say *how high*."

"It's not like that," Jack said, his eyes flashing. "When I got to the house she was still crying, and Neal was upset." He shook his head, looking grim. "I just wanted to get his bag packed and get him in the truck. Then Vera announced Chaz had gone to stay with a buddy. Said he needed some time. Neal started to cry and talked about this astronomy trip the two of them had planned." Looking weary, Jack scrubbed his face with his hands. "So I told him I'd take him. It's only four days."

Linny softened but was still bugged by his tendency to rescue Vera and clean up her and Chaz's messes. "You wanted to keep Neal from being disappointed. I get that. But maybe we should talk things over before we commit to time away from each other." Over and over, guest bloggers to the *Bodacious Bonus Moms'* blog wrote about how the first year of marriage in a blended family was always the hardest, probably even for someone who'd been married as many times as Linny had. *Negotiations and compromise*, she reminded herself. She cocked her head and gave him a crooked smile. "We're a team, right?"

"We are. Sorry, Lin," he said ruefully and touched her arm.

"When are you going?" she asked, making herself uncross her arms.

"With your okay, week after next," he said. "Chaz already lined up tickets to the observatories and made reservations at the campground."

Linny's thoughts began to click away. "Mama and her friends are leaving a day or two before that on their trip. What if I go for a week with them? I can get Mama all calmed down for the road."

"That works," Jack said, nodding and looking relieved. He leaned over and gave her a short but smoldering kiss.

Linny smiled at him. Though he'd misstepped, he was just trying to do damage control for his son, and she shouldn't blame him for that. "Who's up for pizza? I'm calling in supper."

"We were talking about how starved we were just before you came home," Jack said.

"Let me see what strange topping Neal wants to try this time. The number for Gino's is on the refrigerator." He stepped into the other room.

Linny switched on the light in the kitchen and smiled when she saw that Jack had stuck the picture from their whitewater rafting trip on the fridge door under the *Buy Pizza and Get Gas at Gino's Gas and Go!* magnet. She grimaced. The best pizza in Willow Hill, which just happened to be located in a gas station, needed to change their motto. Neal had probably stuck that magnet up there. Typical twelve-year-old-boy humor. Linny was learning how to be a good sport about that and a lot of other things: rooms strewn with dirty laundry, dishes under the bed, and bags of chips that disappeared as soon as she brought them home from the store. She slipped the photo out from under the magnet, moved to the light of the kitchen window, and looked at it again. Even though the trip had been cut short, what a perfect four days they'd had. But that river trip was like her new marriage: Every time she began to relax and glide along, thinking they were finally in calm waters, they'd go around the bend and hit the rapids.

Linny pushed her shoulders back. Nothing the two of them couldn't manage. She stuck the picture—and that magnet—back into a central spot on the fridge, reminding herself to add an action shot of the three of them doing something fun together. Also, she'd put up a shot of Jack and Neal doing something manly, like rock climbing or caving, maybe a photo from their upcoming Tucson trip. The pictures would serve as reminders to them that they were a new little family. Linny was determined to make sure Neal knew he was loved and that nobody was leaving him out or going anywhere—like Chaz might.

After supper Neal and Linny had dessert together while Jack went into the other room to work on the computer. Linny dipped into her bowl of mint chocolate chip ice cream and looked at Neal gravely. "I never understood butter pecan."

"Me neither. It's a mystery," Neal said, his expression as serious as if they were discussing evolution. "Coffee is a strange flavor, too." He took a too-large spoonful of his chocolate ice cream and worked his way through it.

Instinctively, Linny knew light conversation and large bowls of ice cream were good for Neal now. The young man needed some normalcy after all the dramatics he'd witnessed. She patted her mouth with a napkin, realizing they'd exhausted the topic of ice cream flavors. And then it came to her. Even though she was bored silly by the sport, Linny knew he was a Caniac: a rabid fan of the North Carolina

Hurricanes ice hockey team. She tilted her head. "Tell me how the Hurricanes look this year."

Neal's eyes lit up and, in the know-it-all voice he'd recently begun using with her and Jack, told her.

The following Monday afternoon Linny finished her assigned task of setting out napkins and utensils and sat sipping ice water at her mother's kitchen table. She glanced through the travel brochures and information about various models of RVs that were fanned out on the table in front of her while she waited for the peach-cobbler-eating and final-trip-planning meeting to begin. Linny eyed Dottie. She'd sprung back fast. Once Linny had agreed to join the women for the start of the trip, her mother's symptoms had disappeared and she was back to the newer and happier Dottie: bright-eyed, bustling, and organizing everybody.

Linny glanced at the others. These were the women she was going to spend almost a week with in very close quarters. She'd known her mother's friends from the time she was a girl, but Linny examined them more closely now, wondering how much she *really* knew about them. What kind of traveling companions would they be? She narrowed her eyes. And why did their hairdos all look so normal? Dottie's ashy-blond gray hair, Ruby's auburn curls, and Dessie's salt-and-pepper pixie were all missing the unfortunate pink tint their beloved hairdresser, Joseph, gave to all his clients. "Y'alls' hair looks so pretty. Is Joseph doing something different?"

"He's gone," her mother said mournfully and heaved a heavy sigh.

"Oh, I'm so sorry." Linny put a hand to her chest and, even though she hardly knew the hairdresser, felt bereft, remembering what it was like to have a man up and die on you. "He was too young to pass."

Dottie cocked her head and peered at her. "He moved to Wilmington to be closer to his mama. She's ninety-eight." She gave a satisfied little nod. "She still drives to the Harris Teeter every Thursday for senior discount day."

Linny just shook her head.

Dessie gave Linny a quick eye roll. Looking sporty and patriotic in a red-and-white-striped blouse, navy blue slacks, and bright white sneakers, Dessie poured a generous dollop of cream in her decaf and peppered Linny with questions about her and Jack's mountain trip. *What was the cabin like? Were there a lot of motorcycles on the Blue Ridge Parkway? Did you eat any mountain trout? Is that little homemade candy store still there?*

As Linny answered, she tried to think of exactly what she knew about Dessie. When she was young she'd been married briefly. She'd divorced and married Del—a photographer who was the love of her life—and had a son, a daughter-in-law, and a grandson in California. Del had passed a few years earlier from cancer. On the cruise Dessie had met a man named Perry, a divorced scrap-metal dealer from South Carolina who wore a fedora with a feather.

Ruby wore a gauzy coral dress as she took tin foil off the dish of the peach cobbler she'd made and chattered to Dottie about wishing she had grandkids. Linny knew she had a son and daughter-in-law in Colorado and a daughter in Oregon and reminded herself to find out their names and ages and ask about them. Linny noticed her jeweled sandals and the apricot of the polish on her toes. Ruby kept herself up. Did she have a man in her life? If not, did she want one? Linny remembered that Ruby's husband, Pete, had died of a heart attack a long time ago.

Linny examined her mother more closely. Dottie had fresh honeyed highlights in her hair and wore a canary yellow linen blouse over black leggings. Linny tried not to stare. Yup, her mama was wearing very cool-looking leggings. She was looking youthful and pretty—or *sassy*, as her personal shopper friend at Belk would say. She'd ditched the white velour clunker sandals and was back to wearing cute shoes. She was chirping to Ruby about her new man friend. *So Mack and I are going to try Chet's Barbecue tomorrow night; they have a bourbon pecan pie that . . .*

All the women looked pretty, and they'd put effort into their appearances. Maybe Linny needed to step up her own game. She glanced down at her khaki shorts. They were flecked with small spots of the yellow paint she'd applied to the kitchen walls. She wore her favorite sage green scoop-necked T-shirt that was now shrunken but still wearable. Neither Avery man understood that you couldn't throw everything in the dryer on the cotton setting and just waltz off. While she thought no one was looking, she pulled at the hem of the shirt with both hands, willing it to stretch.

"What are you doing, Linny?" her mother asked. Three sets of eyes turned to look at her.

"The men keep shrinking my clothes in the dryer," she muttered, and Dessie and Ruby chuckled.

Her mother just pursed her lips and shuttled the bowls of cobbler to the table. Linny paused to stare at her bowl. Her mother had served her a fourth of the size serving of the cobbler and ice cream she had the others. Even though she was no skinny minnie herself, Dottie was always vigilant about Linny's weight. She might be five or ten pounds over her fighting weight, but Linny was still fairly trim. With a pointed look at her mother, she rose from the table and filled her bowl to the rim with cobbler and topped it with a giant scoop of ice cream. She wasn't hungry and didn't even intend to eat it, but still . . . Her mother raised a brow but said nothing.

Around the kitchen table, Dottie had laid out four legal pads and four freshly sharpened pencils. The women slid into chairs.

Linny felt the familiar surge of excitement and possibilities she used to feel every late summer when school started again. *Crack.* She jumped as her mother smacked the table with a meat tenderizing hammer.

Dottie called out, "Let's pipe down, ladies. We've got work to do. I officially call this meeting of SWAT Team to order."

Linny glanced from her mother to Ruby and then to Dessie. "SWAT Team?" she asked.

Dessie chuckled and Ruby grinned as she nodded. "Southern Women's Adventure Travel. We thought of the name ourselves," she said proudly. She reached in a plastic bag on the floor beside her, pulled out white T-shirts that had *SWAT Team* emblazoned on them in black lettering, and handed them out.

"These turned out so pretty," Dottie said, holding the shirt up to her shoulders. "Ruby tried to get pink lettering, but they didn't have it."

Linny examined hers. The shirts looked pretty darned official, like the wearer should be skilled at breaking down doors using a battering ram. "Nice," she said politely. She glanced around at the others and asked tentatively, "Are we supposed to wear these when we're on the road?"

"At all times," Dessie said in a stern tone, but then cackled with laughter. "No, honey.

The shirt is optional. We just wanted to get into the spirit of the road trip."

"I'm wearing mine at all times," Dottie said stoutly.

"Remind me how long you all are planning on being gone and what's your itinerary?" Linny asked, her pencil poised over paper.

"That's item one on the agenda." Dottie glanced at Dessie. "Will you please give your report on the best way for us to get from here to there?"

Dessie tapped her pencil on the legal pad and looked at Linny. "We've made reservations and plans to visit the sites we don't want to miss, but we also want to get off the beaten track and take some days to just go where we please."

Ruby nodded emphatically. "We don't want to miss the whole freewheeling RV experience." As the women's heads swiveled toward her, she tapped the brochure in front of her. "Right here. That's what they call it—'the freewheeling RV experience.'"

Dessie hid a smile and looked down at her notes. "I've been looking at possible routes. From Willow Hill we'll take it nice and slow while we check out the RV, but our first stop is outside Dollywood...."

"My girlfriend went last year. She said the arts and crafts demonstrations were fabulous and the shows were great." Ruby put a manicured hand to her chest and looked reverent. "And what if we actually met Dolly? Can you imagine the thrill of that?"

Dessie waited a moment to make sure Ruby was done and went on. "Then, we motor on to Nashville, swing by the Ryman, the Opry, the Johnny Cash Museum, and it's on to Graceland. We'll drop Linny at the airport in Memphis so she can go home and head to Branson. We'll take a few days to tool around with no agenda and end up at Mount Rushmore and the Badlands. On the way home, we'll deliver the RV to my nephew and his wife, Brent and Lisette, who have volunteered to drive it back to North Carolina if I buy their tickets back to Nebraska." She glanced at her two friends. "We girls will fly home from there. None of us can be away more than a month and a half, and Brent and Lisette are thrilled to pieces at the opportunity to travel across part of the country. They're both good drivers," she assured them.

"No Niagara Falls or Canadian Railroad?" Dottie asked, her mouth drooping. "No Canadian Mounties?"

"Sorry, shug. We're not going to have enough time, and we don't want to be racing from one site to another," Dessie said.

"I agree," said Dottie with a regretful sigh. "If this trip goes well, maybe we'll do a northern circuit next time."

"We could see the lighthouses of New England," Ruby suggested, a dreamy look coming into her eye. "Maybe I'd meet a sea captain or a rugged lighthouse keeper."

"What kind of camping rig did you girls decide we should rent?" Dottie asked.

Ruby pulled a piece of paper from her purse. "I took notes at the RV show. The motor homes are the big ones that look like fancy buses." She pointed to a brochure that featured a couple who looked like Brad Pitt and Angelina Jolie driving a sleek, tan and gold motor coach beside what looked to be the Pacific Coast Highway, their two darling Cavalier King Charles Spaniels asleep on the broad dashboard. "Even though I used to drive a school bus, and Del and Dessie had that camper, these seem really big. Too much for me to want to drive," admitted Ruby with a delicate shudder. "The pull-behind campers looked fine, but we decided on a Class C. It looks like a moving truck but it's smaller and . . . well . . . cuter."

"Sleeker. More streamlined," Dessie clarified. "It'd give us all more room, some privacy, and we both thought it'd be easier to maneuver."

"Class C it is," Dottie said, slamming the meat tenderizing hammer down on the table so hard that the cobbler bowls jumped and coffee sloshed in the mugs.

Still wincing, Linny reached over and took the hammer from her mom. "Good job leading the meeting, Mama," she said with an encouraging smile.

Dessie made a show of pulling the Class C brochures from her purse and the four of them slid their chairs in closer to look as she spread them out on the table. "I talked to the RV rental place. These are similar to the Class C models they have available."

Ruby touched the picture on the brochure with her peachy nail. "Enjoy all the amenities of home! Ideal for ACC football, NASCAR race weekends, and hunting trips!"

With assorted brows raised and heads cocked, the three women studied Ruby.

"It says right here, sillies." Ruby pointed to the six-point font of the copy beneath the photo of the unusually attractive group of sporty-looking friends, grilling and chuckling beside their gleaming rental RV. "And look," she jabbed at another photo. "Look at that darling hot tub."

"Ours will be a more basic model unless we pay an arm and a leg, but see how these walls slide out and give you so much more room?" Dessie pointed to a picture of a living area expanded out much wider than the sides of the RV.

Linny peered more closely at the photos. The bed space tucked neatly above the cab reminded her of the cozy fun of sleeping in blanket tents in the living room with her sister Kate when they were girls. She looked at the other members of the SWAT Team, chattering with excitement as they pointed out the small washer/dryer and clever bed that pulled out from under the dining room table. She felt a frisson of excitement and grinned. The road trip she'd thought of as a daughterly duty might just shape up to be a heck of a lot of fun.

The next morning Linny met her best friend, attorney Mary Catherine, at Jumpin' Joe's, one of the area's only coffee shops and a hot spot for morning commuters. Her friend was waiting for her at a booth in the back. Looking sharp as usual in a crisp white high-collared blouse and a double-breasted black blazer, Mary Catherine frowned as she stared at the phone on the table in front of her. She moved the salt and pepper shakers around.

Linny caught Mary Catherine's eye and gave her a little wave.

Her friend broke into a smile, rose, and gave her a hug that smelled faintly of lemon verbena. "Hey, married lady," Mary Catherine said as she plunked back down in her seat.

"Hey yourself," Linny said, smiling and picking up the menu to give it a quick glance.

Mary Catherine waved a hand. "I already ordered for us."

The pink-cheeked waitress in the bell-skirted vintage dress slid two coffees, a bowl of fresh fruit, and a basket of muffins on the table. "Muffins are hot," she cautioned.

Linny's mouth watered as she eyed the supposedly healthy lemon raspberry muffins she and Mary Catherine loved. "Ah." She breathed in the rich aroma of butter, cinnamon, and freshly baked bread. She dumped cream in her coffee and took a swallow. Heaven.

"We need to talk fast." Mary Catherine pointed at her watch. "I have to get back to the office to get people lined up to interview." She slumped in her seat. "Before we talk about your marital bliss, my office manager quit yesterday. Left at lunch and never came back."

"Resigned via text," she groused, holding out her phone for Linny to read.

The office manager had simply written *I'm not coming back.*

"Oh, dear." Linny took another sip of coffee and tried to look surprised. Her best friend since fourth grade, Mary Catherine could be brusque. But she did more than her share of pro bono work, made quiet donations to the Boys and Girls Clubs, and was a champion for victims of domestic violence. Mary Catherine had a heart the size of the Atlantic Ocean.

Her friend nabbed a muffin from the basket and peeled off the wrapper. Sounding plaintive, she asked, "So why does my staff keep leaving me?"

"Because you don't say hello to them in the morning?" Linny suggested.

"I do too," Mary Catherine said, looking injured.

Linny shook her head. "No, you don't. James, that nice young paralegal who used to work for you, said he'd say *good morning* and you wouldn't say a word back. Regularly."

"Huh." Mary Catherine paused for a moment and then looked rueful. "Sometimes I think *good morning*, but maybe it never makes it out of my mouth."

"Maybe," Linny said, taking a bite of the warm muffin. *Yum.*

"When I've got a case on my mind, my own husband says he can say something to me and I don't even hear him. I'm not ignoring him, just don't hear him." Mary Catherine took a too-large bite of her muffin and had to swill some coffee to help slide it down.

Linny measured an inch of space between her thumb and forefinger. "Could you be just a tiny bit more personable with your next office manager?"

"So I need to walk around smiling like this?" Mary Catherine gave an awful toothy-looking fake smile.

"Maybe not that smile, but smiling once in a while wouldn't hurt you." Linny nodded encouragingly and slathered butter on the muffin to make up for its supposed healthiness. "Ask about their weekend, how their kids are—that sort of thing."

"I don't care about their weekends or their kids," Mary Catherine grumbled. "I just need them to excel at their work."

"But you want them to stick around," Linny said quietly.

"Stupid interpersonal skills," Mary Catherine said darkly. "You know how I am."

Linny did. A childhood spent in trailer parks with a beer-drinking, party-girl mama and no father on the scene, the family would stay in a place for a few months and have to slip out in the middle of the night because the rent was due and the money was gone. Her friend trusted only a few people, but if you were lucky enough to be one of them, she'd take a bullet for you. Linny speared a piece of melon from the bowl. "Maybe you could warn the next person you hire. Let them know what to expect and not to take it personally."

"Ah, a disclaimer. Good idea." Mary Catherine put her elbow on the table and her chin in her hand. "What about you, girl? What's new? How was the honeymoon?"

Aware of the gossipmongers in Willow Hill, Linny leaned forward and spoke quietly. "The honeymoon was wonderful, but we had to cut it short because Vera and Chaz were fighting so badly that Neal was upset."

Mary Catherine raised her eyes to heaven. "Gracious. Two big babies."

"Uh-huh," Linny said, absurdly grateful to be understood so quickly. Her friend knew all about the divorce wars because of her family law practice. "And without running it by me, Jack told Vera he'd pinch-hit for an MIA Chaz and take Neal out to Tucson to see an observatory."

Mary Catherine patted her mouth with the napkin. "So Neal's staying with you until . . . ?"

"Until things over at that household simmer down," Linny said with an inward shudder, remembering how the boy could be when he was in one of his moods.

Mary Catherine raised a brow. "If they do."

Linny grimaced. What if the fighting continued? Jack might end up having to take legal action. Her stomach tightened, knowing from Mary Catherine just how ugly a custody battle could get. And Chaz was an attorney, so he'd likely be a bear of an opponent. And what if Neal did end up staying with them? Was she really ready for a full-time, sometimes openly hostile stepson? She looked away. "Neal was sweet as pie when Jack first picked him up, but he's started acting up. Last night Jack got a work-related call after we'd just finished supper. Neal's regular chore is to clear the dishes and load the dishwasher, but because his dad wasn't there to tell him to hop to, he just sat there at the kitchen table and started playing games on his cell. Jack stayed on the phone and I was putting away food, so I asked Neal to help. He ignored me." She felt a hot flush of anger just thinking about it. "Just pretended he hadn't heard. I asked again and he just looked at me and said, 'No.' When Jack got off the phone, I told him about it. Neal interrupted me, shouting, 'She can't boss me. She's not my mother,' and ran to his room and slammed the door. And Jack just . . ." She trailed off, shaking her head.

"Let him," Mary Catherine finished Linny's sentence

"Yup," Linny said, sounding more hurt than she wanted to. "I talked to Jack about backing me up, but he reminded me of how rough things had been for Neal lately."

"Things are rough for him now, but you basically just need Jack's backup and you need to toughen up." Mary Catherine gave her a shrewd look and popped a last bite of muffin in her mouth. "The mess with Vera and Chaz is likely to stir up bad behavior in Neal, but in general teenaged boys are like jackals. They'll turn on you with bared teeth, tell you they hate your guts, and then they'll ask you to fix them a grilled cheese sandwich."

Jackals. Wow. Linny nodded, discouraged.

Her friend eyed her as if she was trying to decide if Linny was ready for more stark truths. "Not sure if you remember all this, but Dare liked to pee out his bedroom window, crashed our car when he took it for a spin at aged thirteen, and accidentally sank Mike's brand-new bass boat." She gave a matter-of-fact nod. "I think Neal is a more sensible boy, though."

Linny groaned. "What have I gotten myself in to?"

"He's got stability with the two of you, and that will go a long way." Mary Catherine took a last sip of coffee. "Just don't take it personally. You need to muddle through and it will all work out."

But she wasn't sure it would all work out, she thought, rubbing her forehead with her fingers. She was also still off-balance from Jack's guess-who's-going-to-Tucson announcement. She gave herself a mental shake. Enough about her drama. "Oh, and I'm going on an RV trip to Dollywood and Graceland with Mama and her girlfriends."

"Fun," Mary Catherine said, looking thoughtful. "Might be a perfect time for a getaway. They'll appreciate you all the more when you get home."

Linny nodded and rummaged in her purse for her wallet. "How's my favorite godson?"

"Dare is well." Mary Catherine signaled for the check. "Sent me pictures of a new girlfriend. Her name's Breeze and she wears long, flowing dresses, nothing like his usual preppy girls with snooty names like Sloane or Teague. Last one was called Atherton. Thank goodness she's gone." Mary Catherine wrinkled her nose as she pulled bills from her wallet.

Linny decided not to point out that Dare's name sounded snooty, too, even though he was just named after the only normal man in Mary Catherine's rip-roaring family: a music teacher uncle. "Send that fellow of yours a big ole hug for me," Linny said as they rose.

"I will," Mary Catherine promised. "And pat Jack and Neal for me."

Linny grinned at her friend and they walked to their cars.

CHAPTER 3

Back in the Saddle Again

The next afternoon Linny glanced at the time on her phone as she pushed open the door with the sign that read "Green Sage Information Technology Solutions." Good. She was a few minutes early for her one o'clock meeting with the owner. Glancing around the waiting room of the old cotton mill that had been converted into office space, Linny glanced up and spotted the rusted-out body of an old Chevy truck that was suspended—by good, stout wires, she hoped—above her head. One wall was lined with old gray boards and a semblance of a red tin roof: a nod to the old tobacco barns that were starting to collapse and disappear from the North Carolina countryside. The floors were honey-colored, wide-planked boards and looked to be original to the mill. She liked the feel of the place.

Surreptitiously, Linny tried to rub the knots out of her tight neck. Her business account was running on empty and she needed to pick up some work to write herself a paycheck. Too much time planning a wedding and mooning over Jack Avery, Linny decided, and felt a flood of happiness, remembering the wedding that had featured her and Jack riding to the altar on horseback and Neal flying in on a zip line. She loved her new life, but it was time to get cracking. Linny was proud of her less-than-a-year-old consulting business, but if she didn't start shaking the trees for work, she'd be in big trouble when quarterly taxes came due. She knew Jack would gladly let her pay taxes from the household account, but she never would. This was her business and she'd pay her way.

The owner of a small IT consulting firm, Chanel Green had called to arrange this morning's meeting after a business colleague—a happy former client of Linny's—had recommended her. When she'd phoned, Chanel had mentioned *personnel issues* she might want help with but had been vague about the specifics.

Linny tried to be surreptitious as she eyed the cable on the truck chassis and skooched her chair to the right. She'd heard Chanel Green was a rising star in the thriving local high-tech start-up scene, but what would she be like? Way younger and smarter than Linny was? She shuddered inwardly and prayed she wasn't one of those young business hot shots she read about in *Forbes* and *Fast Company* magazines: the ones wearing hip glasses on their unlined faces, smiling smugly and standing with their arms crossed in that master-of-destiny pose.

A pin-thin young woman stepped into the waiting room wearing red aviator glasses, a plaid skirt, and a T-shirt printed with some ironic statement about string theory and quantum physics, things Linny didn't even pretend to grasp. "Linny Taylor?" the woman asked, unsmiling. "I'm Chanel Green."

"Chanel, so pleased to meet you." Linny rose, smiled, and shot out a hand, fighting the urge to reread the shirt to try to decipher it for clues about its wearer. Staring at a client's chest—male or female—was never a good idea.

Chanel gave Linny a firm handshake and beckoned her to follow as she strode toward an office in the corner of the two-story building that had been retrofitted into an open work space. Passing partitioned areas where employees in jeans and T-shirts talked on phones and worked on laptops, Linny enjoyed the buzz of activity and liked walking on the sloping old pine floors. A young man whose blond hair was cut in a Doris Day kind of bob popped up athletically from a red slide: a speedy route from the second floor to the first. Peering down to the other end of the building, she saw a lithe young woman slide down a fire pole, a speedy exit for the other side of the building. She grinned at Chanel. "I've always wanted to slide down one of those poles."

"We could arrange for that," Chanel said, her coolness warming a bit as a look of amusement flitted over her face. "We had a king-of-the-jungle type rope swing but had to take it down. People kept doing that Tarzan call. Distracting."

Linny nodded, hiding a smile.

Chanel walked briskly. "We have healthy lunches brought in

every day, thanks to the Culinary Institute at Worth County Community College. The budding chefs get experience and we get to be tasters. My people love it so everybody wins. We have a yoga and meditation class here every day. You're welcome to stay for that after our meeting." Her eyes swept over Linny's black pants suit. "We could find you some shorts and a T-shirt."

Wincing inwardly as they walked by a woman wearing what appeared to be knickers, Linny realized she'd dressed way too corporate. "I can't stay today, but what a great idea."

"Helps us all shake off stress, although . . ." She slowed her pace, looking thoughtful. "Believe it or not, employees even get competitive about how relaxed they can get. They've come up with some crazy self-rating system about meditation." She shook her head and smiled ruefully. As she pointed her toward an open office door, Linny saw that Chanel's unpainted fingernails were bitten to the quick.

The young woman shut the door. Throwing open a slope-shouldered old Frigidaire, she offered Linny a drink. "Water, Revving Zinger Energy Drink, Cheerwine, or Mountain Dew?"

Hoping the energy drink was the youngest, most down-with-new-technology choice, Linny said firmly, "I'll have a Revving Zinger. I love the stuff. Drink it all the time." Hearing her own burbling, Linny flushed and firmly closed her mouth.

"Ah." Chanel's eyes narrowed, but she nodded, handed Linny the drink, and gestured for her to take a seat in a weathered-looking rocking chair that served as a seat for visitors. She slid behind a desk topped with an old oak door that had been modified to accommodate her phone and laptop.

Linny tilted her head back and took what she hoped was a long, youthful-looking pull of the drink. It was awful: some combination of cherry cough syrup and pink bubble gum. She wished she could spit it out but made herself swallow. A rustling sound came from under the desk and Linny froze.

Chanel nodded solemnly. "Sage speaks."

Linny nodded back, not sure why. Was there a young person under her desk? Nap pods or some such Googleish or Zapposish enhanced work environment thing?

"Do you like dogs?" Chanel asked in a tone that almost sounded like a challenge.

"We have six," Linny said hesitantly and gave her a smile similar to the one Mary Catherine had practiced at breakfast yesterday morning.

Grinning, Chanel raised her fist in some sort of power-to-the-people gesture and said, "Dogs rule." Gesturing for Linny to come around the desk, she leaned over and said, "This is Sage. He's retired."

Linny saw a gray-muzzled German Shepherd sleeping curled up on a gold velvet dog bed, his legs twitching. A gray muzzle on an old dog always touched her. Not wanting to wake him by patting him, she murmured, "He's so handsome." She chided herself. Of course this place would be dog friendly.

"He is." Chanel gazed at him adoringly. "He's gone deaf and he's got bad arthritis, but he's still a prince," she said, her eyes sparkling. "When I was just starting out as a one-person operation and trying to get people to take me seriously, I always mentioned my business partner to prospective clients. That was Sage. Made us sound legit, like we were bigger than we were."

Linny went back to her chair, sank back in it, and began to slowly rock. She liked Chanel. "So how can I help you?"

"Green Sage is a forty-nine-person information technology consulting firm I started after grad school. We're good at what we do and our client list is growing, but I've got two problems." She pushed her red glasses back up on her nose and winced, admitting, "Some of my employees are getting complaints from their clients. They think of the regular callers as friends and talk to them too casually or eat on the phone or don't call them back in a timely way. Others would rather text clients than talk to them on the phone or in person. If they can't talk to clients, they can't solve problems or introduce new add-ons or products." She blew out a gusty sigh. "None of them are very good at handling customer complaints. Last week I found three of my women huddled in the bathroom, hoping that one of the other employees would get stuck with a call they knew was coming from an angry client. Scaredey-cats. Oh, and they play pranks on one another that border on bullying." She tipped back in her chair and gave Linny a challenging look. "So there you have it."

Linny jumped in, the caffeine in the Revving Zinger starting to course through her veins. "That's not at all unusual with people in IT. All are smart and talented technically but many aren't so great with customer relations. Conflict throws them. When challenged, some try to duck it like your women hiding out in the bathroom, and others act like know-it-all experts, both of which just escalates things with upset customers."

Chanel nodded vigorously and gave her a relieved smile. "I was worried we were the only ones who stink at customer relations."

Linny shook her head. "Oh, no. It's as common as corn bread." She felt the blood rush to her face. One of her mama's favorite expressions had just rolled out of her mouth. Minnie Pearl shows up at the business meeting with this savvy, accomplished young woman.

But instead of shooing her out of the office and back to hillbillyland, the corner of Chanel's lips turned up. "Can you fix us?"

"I can help." Linny paused and thought about it. "I'd like to interview some of your employees and a few of your clients to find out more about the problems. Then we can set up training and let them practice with case studies based on real-life Green Sage client situations."

"Sounds smart," Chanel said but drummed her fingers on the door desk and looked glum. "But problem two: My people don't get along. I'm afraid there's some sexism going on here and, because of it, the men and the women have formed separate camps. One of my best women tried to quit on me last week. I managed to talk her out of it, and when I found out the reason why she wanted to leave, it made me angry." She scowled. "The guys here withhold information from the women, and there's too much trash talk that's got a real edge to it. Double entendres, ditsy women comments, borderline inappropriate comments about women in general, that sort of thing."

Oooh boy. A flame of indignation ignited in Linny's stomach and she tried to quickly tamp it down. Sexism could be a problem in all fields but she'd seen quite a bit of it in IT and engineering. She'd had enough experience addressing sexism in companies over the years to know how demoralizing it could be, and terribly expensive if it escalated to a legal matter.

"Now the female employees are ticked at the men and getting hostile with them." Chanel scrubbed her face with her hands and looked chagrined. "I grew up with three brothers and did an internship at a gaming company so I've got a thick skin. But I detest sexism," she said, her voice vehement. Chanel looked away for a moment. "And I've been so busy growing the business that I haven't noticed all this." She waved a hand vaguely in the direction of the offices and cubicles outside her office. "I'm mad at myself that this has happened in a workplace I created."

"You need a comfortable work environment free of harassment of any kind." Linny thought about it, remembering her work with other high-tech start-ups. Keeping her tone even, she added, "My hunch is that a lot of your employees don't even realize what they're doing and how damaging their interactions can be. Maybe it's their first job out of school, or maybe they've worked at companies where this kind of conduct was acceptable."

Chanel nodded vigorously, her intelligent eyes flashing that Linny was correct.

Linny went on. "So you've got to help them identify sexism and harassment—however subtle—and make it clear it won't be tolerated at Green Sage. You can present a code of conduct. You need to tell them your expectations that they work as a team and what happens if they don't." Linny gazed at her directly. "I can help you fix this."

On Chanel's face the sun burst from behind the clouds. "Thank goodness!"

"Let's talk about a plan," Linny said and pulled out her iPad.

As Chanel walked her out after their meeting, Linny's step was light. The Green Sage project was a solid piece of work and she was elated at being able to help this young woman and her team address a problem Linny herself felt so strongly about. As they walked by the work area, a male employee with an afro beard nudged the slouching fellow at the desk beside him, and they both smirked. A young woman watched her, looking sullen. Hoo boy. Linny tried to keep a bland, pleasant expression on her face, knowing she represented corporate and authority to them. What if they hated her? What if she was too old to relate to them and they yawned in boredom during her meetings with them and clammed up, viewing her with disdain? Linny stood up straighter and made herself smile coolly in their general direction. Wincing inwardly, Linny thought about how confident she'd sounded when she'd assured Chanel of her ability to help her get employees on track. From the looks of things it was going to take a lot of work—and maybe a small miracle—to help this group start to grow up and work together.

* * *

On the way home Linny had arranged to swing by to visit her sister and other best friend, Kate. She'd missed her while she'd been away on her honeymoon, even though they'd texted every day. Kate kept sending her darling pictures of her new baby, Ivy: asleep with her little fist curled up beside her rosebud mouth, Ivy and one of the family dogs having a stare-off, the infant in a sweet seersucker onesie and bucket hat that Linny had bought for her. After she and her husband, Jerry, had tried for so many years to have a baby, Kate was finally a new mother at aged forty. Though fatuously, over the moon in love with her baby, little Ivy was a screamer and, apparently, an insomniac. Though Kate was the sunniest, most optimistic person Linny knew, her usually mellow, meditation-practicing sister's texts had a baffled, tired tone to them.

Can't get Ivy to stop crying. Colicky?? Calling Dr. Grace as soon as office opens.

Breastfeeding not the blissful love fest the lactation consultant described. Small sharp-toothed animal gnawing at personal bits.

Kate opened the door to her charming Arts and Crafts bungalow. Instead of the welcoming smell of freshly baked bread, chicken potpie, or lemons she'd squeezed for homemade lemonade, the house smelled . . . well . . . of old coffee grounds and a hint of dirty diapers. Jiggling a wailing baby in her arms, Kate's skin was sallow, and she had Lyle Lovett hair and a desperate look in her eyes. No trace of her usual pixie, Audrey Hepburn-gone-country chic, Kate wore a gray T-shirt with stains on it that looked vaguely like continents: there was Asia, Australia. . . . Linny made herself look away, giving Kate an awkward sideways hug, her niece's cry volume up so high now that she wished she had on her noise-canceling headphones. "Rough day, sweets?" she said sympathetically.

"You don't even know," Kate said, closing her eyes for a moment and shaking her head. "I haven't bathed in two days and neither Jerry nor I have slept in three nights."

"Poor you," Linny said sympathetically.

Her sister thrust the baby at her. "Take her, please, and just let me get a shower. Just a quick shower." She scurried down the hall with a quick, furtive glance over her shoulder, as if she was afraid Linny might chase her to give the baby back.

Linny watched her retreating form and thought about it. Kate needed help: practical, hands-on help. Having a baby was hard enough, she'd heard. But having an insomniac crier of a baby after age forty had to leave a woman wrung out.

Clutching Ivy, Linny dropped her purse and sat on the sofa, repositioning her niece and talking in that singsong voice she used with the dogs. "Hello, Miss Ivy. Oh my. You are such a good crier. You really are." Remembering the trick she'd seen Kate's husband, Jerry, use, Linny fished in her purse and dangled her car keys in front of the baby. Ivy's big blue eyes focused on the shiny keys and she grasped at them, her grizzling subsiding.

Feeling proud of herself, Linny leaned in and inhaled her niece's scent: some mix of milk, baby powder, and the organic almond diaper cream Kate used. Ah, that lovely smell. Linny was hit with a wave of longing so strong she had to blink back tears. She *wanted* one of these....

But Linny thought about the fraught look in Kate's bloodshot eyes. She remembered how buoyant she'd just felt walking out of that good meeting at Green Sage, about the sad, hopeless air Neal had after he came home from his mom and stepdad's house, the grateful look in Jack's eyes when he walked in the door and she actually had dinner going, her upcoming SWAT Team trip to see the US of A; well, some of the US of A. She had so much going on in her life with still getting to know Neal and blending households. How in the world could she fit in a baby? They'd talked about it, and Jack had said if she wanted a baby, he'd be game for trying, and if she didn't, that suited him fine, too. But she was thirty-nine, and by the time the baby was in college . . . Linny's brain hurt when she thought about this baby business.

Ivy snatched the keys and began to gnaw at them. Linny tried to pry them from the iron grip of her fingers and anxiously looked around for a sanitizing wipe. She'd dropped those keys on the cement at the Shell Station when she was filling up that morning. Linny took a bottle of sanitizer from her purse and hurriedly wiped off the keys, gently swatting away Ivy's grasping miniature fingers, then worried that the gel would hurt Ivy's liver if she ingested it. Awkwardly clutching the baby to her, she edged over to the kitchen sink and washed the keys in hot water and organic soap.

Blowing out a sigh of relief, the two of them sat back down on the sofa. Linny dangled the keys again, but Ivy batted them away and, screwing up her face, wound up for another wailing jag. Her cries were piercing. Linny took a tissue from her purse, balled it up into two puffs, and stuck them in her ears to muffle the sound. Glancing down the hall, she willed Kate to hurry up with her shower.

If they could do some genetic twirling in an autoclave for gender selection of a baby, surely some geneticist in Switzerland was working feverishly over a Petri dish or trying to come up with an algorithm for a docile, quiet baby who kept banker's hours. Linny flushed with guilt at her thoughts and held her niece closer despite the increase in decibels. Maybe she'd put those motherhood dreams on the old back burner.

Kate strolled into the room, toweling off her wet hair and looking as relaxed as if she'd just spent a weekend at the Golden Door Spa. "I can't tell you how good that felt." She fluffed her wet hair with her fingers and eyed the baby warily. Sighing, she reached for Ivy.

Linny pulled the tissue from her ears and held up a hand. "No, Mama. Take a break." She jiggled Ivy on her shoulder and strangely, magically, the baby's writhing, tense body started to soften. Linny held her breath,

And Kate looked at her wide-eyed and hopeful as Ivy dozed off. Her sister touched her hands together in a silent prayer, grinning, and whispered, "You're amazing. A miracle worker."

Linny shook her head and gave a dismissive wave with her free hand. Kate motioned to the playpen and Linny gently eased Ivy onto the padded pink mat floor. "Sleep tight, baby," she said softly, gently brushing back her wispy curls. Ivy slept.

She and Kate tiptoed out of the room and back into the kitchen.

"You need help, Sister," Linny said firmly as she swung into a kitchen chair.

"I'm fine," Kate said with a dismissive wave, slipping into a chair beside her. "You just caught me at a bad time."

Linny raised a brow, not believing her. "Have you ever noticed how hard it is for Taylor women to ask for help?"

Kate looked chagrined. "I know. Why do you think that is?"

Linny glanced out the window. She and Kate had thought her parents had been happy until Dottie told them the truth last year. Her mama's transformation from dour woman to one who was living life to the fullest had been remarkable. "Probably got that from Mama. With Daddy away so much, she had to learn to do a lot of things on her own." Linny shook her head, remembering her mother fixing a flat tire, changing out storm windows, and putting up the Christmas tree, with just her and Kate as helpers. "She was probably too proud—and too stubborn—to let her guard down and tell Daddy how much she needed him."

Kate nodded thoughtfully. "She only changed when she let us—and her friends—help her."

"You need help," Linny said again, more firmly this time. "Let me check the calendar and clear things with Jack and Neal, but I want to take some shifts with the baby. You need to nap or go to a yoga class. Meet one of your friends for lunch or go out to supper with your husband."

Kate opened her mouth, looking like she was going to object, but closed it again. Quietly she said, "Thanks, girl."

"You're welcome."

"So you had a grand trip? How is that darling man and his darling son?" Kate asked.

Linny told her the details of the honeymoon she'd not already texted her, remembering bits and pieces of the relaxation and elation she'd felt just hanging out with Jack.

"You've got that look of a woman in love. I'm so glad." Kate gazed at her, smiling sweetly. "I remember our honeymoon. I just loved it. Loved our wedding, too. I can understand why people want to renew vows. That was the most perfect day." Looking dreamy, she clasped her hands together.

Linny nodded, remembering Jerry's nephew drinking too much beer and driving an ATV into the porta-potty the minister's wife was using, and Jerry's uncle from Possum Trot, North Carolina, eating his first shrimp ever and going into anaphylactic shock. But she just smiled at her sister.

Kate returned from her reverie. "So what else have I missed since we talked last?"

Linny filled Kate in on everything, and her perfect sister gasped, frowned, and looked delighted at all the right places. Winding down from her story telling, Linny cocked her head. "What's new with you, besides sleep deprivation?"

Her sister's eyes widened. "Have you seen the papers?"

Linny shook her head no and watched her sister rise, push aside a pizza box, and sort through an untidy stack of mail, coupon flyers, and newspapers on the usually spotless counter. Usually an immaculate housekeeper, Kate had to be stressed.

Kate held up a paper looking triumphant. "You will not believe this! Jerry is a celebrity." She handed Linny the paper and pointed to a feature article in the *Southern Style* section.

The headlines blared: Local Builder Hailed as a Visionary for Gracious Senior Living. In the photo her brother-in-law stood beside an older couple who were wearing hard hats, brandishing oversize ribbon-cutting scissors, and gazing up at him admiringly.

Linny whistled. "Whoa. Tell me about this."

Kate settled deeper into the couch. "Remember I told you Jerry found this old house in the Grandview neighborhood that he bought from a trust to fix up and sell? Well, the termite damage was worse than he thought, and the structural engineer said it was a teardown." She shook her head sympathetically. "He was worried he'd made a huge financial mistake."

Linny listened, rapt, but also wondering how she had missed such a big story in Kate and Jerry's lives. She'd been Miss Me-Me-Me ever since she got going with the wedding and she was going to be a better sister from now on.

Kate pulled one of her legs up on the chair and went on. "Anyhow, turns out it was zoned for more than one house. He'd been reading about the lack of housing options for older people who want to downsize and he's building these small-spec homes: really pretty, low-maintenance, clapboard-sided cottages. They're just one story, but they're laid out so they feel bigger. They have small yards, courtyards with fountains, small trees inside, and walking paths." She clapped her hands excitedly. "So the design is a big hit with people who don't want to live in senior condos or places with shared walls. He had a bidding war on the first one he put on the market and has already presold the rest. The best thing is, he's really happy." She gave Linny a meaningful look. "He loves working with older people. Don't ever tell him I told you this, but he says he's found his *calling*."

"Gosh," Linny said, touched at hearing Jerry had said that. "Very big news. Exciting."

"It is," Kate said. "After barely hanging on through the recession and then scrambling all over the state to find work when things stated to come back, now this," she said wonderingly.

Linny nodded, getting it. Jerry's drive to do whatever it took to keep the business strong—and his workaholic tendencies—had caused trouble in the past between him and Kate. "He can build what he likes and he can stay closer to home."

"That thrills me, especially with Ivy's arrival," Kate said, smiling. "He's only looking for projects in this area. He even claims he'll be home for lunch some days."

"That's big, Kate. Tell him I'm proud of him." She glanced at the time on her phone. "I need to run. I'm trying to do regular meals each night at six. Figure Neal probably needs a routine, and to enjoy a quiet supper with nobody yelling."

"Of course he does," her sister said indignantly. "Vera and Chaz ought to have a bucket of cold water thrown on them, just like you do when you break up a dogfight."

Linny gathered her purse, enjoying the mental picture. "Or we could put them on a permanent perch on a dunking bench over a vat of ice water, and I could have a remote-control-release switch at the ready. Any time they started acting up, I'd push that button."

Kate giggled, a happy sound coming from a woman who'd looked so close to the end of her tether just forty-five minutes earlier. "Keep me posted on every little thing."

Linny hugged her sister, who now smelled like lilies of the valley. She pulled the overflowing plastic bag from the trash can and snagged the pizza box to drop them at the big rolling cans outside.

Her sister sent her a grateful look. "Love you, girl," she called quietly.

"Love you back," Linny said.

After a small culinary victory at supper—a dump-the-bag-in-the-skillet type chicken and vegetables dish that both men liked—Linny glanced at the weather app on her phone and at the open door of her closet, stumped and obsessing as she tried to pick clothes for the trip that was just days away now. She never got packing right. She always seemed to bring shorts for the snowstorm or kicky heels for the spelunking trip.

Her shoulders slumped as she glanced back and forth from her hanging rows of clothes to the extended forecasts and projected temperatures for North Carolina and Tennessee. Though she hadn't put one item in her rolling bag, she was already overwhelmed. When the phone rang, Linny glanced at it, hoping for a reprieve. She smiled as she saw Diamond's name: her friend, the whip-smart, rich girl attorney who'd helped Linny track down the money Buck had stolen and hidden from her. "Hello, Diamond," she said warmly. "Help. Distract me. I'm packing."

"Hello, my little poodle," Diamond trilled. "I called to whisk you away for lunch. Late wedding present, etcetera, etcetera. Are you free Friday at eleven?"

"I am." Linny grinned, looking forward to hearing about her over-the-top friend's latest adventures.

"Mary Catherine's coming. I'll pick you two up at your place," Diamond said breezily, then hesitated. "I need some girlfriend-type advice, too."

Linny's antennae went up. Diamond rarely sounded so earnest. "We can do that," she said, wondering if Diamond's boyfriend Butch had proposed. She and Mary Catherine had been matchmakers for the unlikely pair: Diamond and the rugged, still-waters-run-deep big guy who owned Tucker Farms Sporting Clay Course. "Can you give me a hint? Should I be saving a date?"

"All will be revealed," Diamond promised, sounding mysterious. In a cheeky tone, she added, "I've been dreaming of fresh shrimp. Ta-ta, sweetcakes."

Linny ended the call and shook her head, smiling. No matter what she did with Diamond, she always enjoyed herself. Diamond was fun. Too prone to being dutiful, Linny could take a lesson from her friend: lessons on grabbing gusto, on doing just what she wanted and not caring so much about what other people thought, on not being so compelled to be productive and check items off her to-do list. She put her phone on the dresser and firmly closed the door of her closet. Forget the packing. She'd get to it. Right now what she wanted was to round up Jack, Neal, and the dogs and take a long walk down a few country roads in the sunlit evening.

CHAPTER 4

Making Adjustments

The next morning Linny dropped Neal off to visit Vera for the day. Chaz was working out of town so Neal's day should be a calm one. Afterward, as she tooled on over to her mother's house, Linny turned on the classical station in the car, trying to calm herself, but her hands stayed cold and clammy on the wheel of her Volvo. She was more than a little nervous about her upcoming driving lesson in the big tank of an RV.

After the hellos and cheek kisses, all four women sat in Dottie's living room chattering nervously as they waited for Mack to show up with a friend's RV so they could practice before the big trip.

"Did everybody do their homework and go to the rental company's website to watch the RV orientation videos?" Dessie asked, and everyone nodded.

Linny had bookmarked the website and watched the videos five or six times.

"Mack should be here any minute," Dottie assured them, standing to give a quick glance in the hall mirror. She rubbed lipstick off her teeth and gave her hairdo a few quick pats.

"Wait, Mama." Linny rose and zipped her three-quarters-of-the-way zipped dress all the way to the top. Her mother smelled faintly of roses. A new scent, Linny decided. "You smell good, Mama."

"Thank you, shug." Dottie gazed at Linny and turned her head slowly from side to side. "Notice my cheeks? I bought a contouring cream that defines and sculpts cheekbones."

"They do look defined and sculpted." Linny patted her mother's shoulder. It wasn't just Mack—her purportedly easy-breezy, nonromantic friend—who caused the uptick in primping. Willa, the personal shopper at Belk's who'd apparently turned into Dottie's close friend had convinced her to subscribe to a new fashion magazine called *Glam Golden Girls* and Mama had updated her wardrobe and makeup with only the first issue under her belt.

Mama turned to the others. "I don't know why you all won't let me take my turn behind the wheel. I'm a fine driver. Those dents in the back of my car are from shopping carts that got loose in the parking lot of Food Lion"

"How about those new dings in the side you got last week?" Dessie asked, looking up from the iPad and gazing at Dottie over the top of her reading glasses.

"I was just minding my own business driving along and a roadside work crew threw up rocks with their mowers." Her mother shook her head, presumably thinking dark thoughts about those careless mowers.

Dessie shot Linny a quick eye roll and glanced back down at her screen.

Ruby smiled brightly. "Well, I think you've contributed more than your fair share by paying for the rental of the RV. You need to just sit back and leave the driving to us."

Mama's winning $250,000 at the nickel slots on the cruise the three of them had taken together—and her subsequent promise to treat her girlfriends to this trip—was a once-in-a-lifetime thrill for all of the women. They didn't need any more thrills from Dottie driving. Linny breathed a quiet sigh of relief that Mama wasn't insisting.

Ruby flipped through *People* magazine and said in a chipper tone, "The instructional video says it's just like driving a car or van, only the camper is twelve feet tall and ten feet wide. It has automatic transmission and lots of mirrors."

Linny looked at her, not entirely sure she trusted a chirpy woman behind the wheel of the RV, even though Ruby claimed she'd driven school buses for three years. She looked distractible, like someone who could spot a red-tailed hawk or an Amish person and drive down an embankment while pointing it out to the others.

Dessie turned the iPad to show them the screen she'd been studying. "This is the trip-planning page of the RV rental company's website. I already made reservations at a lot of campgrounds but left a few days open where we'll wing it. I only picked places where the campsites were big. Never could stand it when Del and I found we'd picked a campsite so small you'd sneeze and your neighbors would say *bless you*." She shook her head. "So the first day we take it nice and slow. We're confirmed at the campground outside of Pigeon Forge for two nights, just fifteen minutes' drive to Dollywood. Then . . ." She muttered to herself as she peered back at the website, scratching her forehead with her pen and leaving a blue scribble mark on the skin beneath her bangs.

Linny eyed her. Again, not totally reassuring. This woman would take her turn behind the wheel of their twelve-thousand-pound, twenty-five-foot long home away from home, and Linny would be riding along in the back.

Mack rapped on the screen door and stuck in his head. "Hello, lovely ladies," he called out, grinning and sounding a little like the disembodied voice of Charlie talking to his Angels.

"Hey, Mack," they called out.

He gave Dottie a quick kiss on her cheek and, his eyes twinkling, turned to the group. "Let's go out and take her for a spin."

They all rose and followed him into the yard. Dottie pulled Linny aside and murmured, "I just love it when he wears that wedge-shaped driving cap. Doesn't he look just adorable in it?"

"Adorable," Linny agreed, meaning it. She'd initially been worried Mack was a gold digger. He'd been a dance instructor on the ship on which Mama had won all that money. But Mack had turned out to be a decent guy with a big heart—and money of his own. Linny watched as he teased them, cautioning, "No lead feet and no drag racing allowed." He smiled especially warmly at Dottie. Any man who treated Mama as well as Mack did made him a prize in her book, especially after the crumbs of attention her mother had settled for with Daddy.

Linny cringed inwardly as she remembered the way she and Kate had grilled Mack about his intentions, his finances, and the particulars of his late wife's death. Understandable, Linny reasoned, given she herself had just been bilked by her late hound dog of a husband and had been watching a tad too much *20/20*. Mack had stayed affable and unflappable throughout their not-so-subtle interrogation.

Mack eased into the driver's seat of the RV and Linny patted his arm as she walked by him and took a seat beside the other women on the sofa. She really liked Mack.

Ruby looked around at the dining room/kitchen combination, beaming. "If this isn't the cutest little thing..."

Linny examined the tidy compartments and comfortable-looking furniture of the camper and had to agree.

In the wide-open asphalt parking lot of Willow Hill High School, Mack gave them a few more pointers before the women took their practice spins. "The model you're renting has backup cameras and cameras on the sides, but you'll still need to get comfortable with the mirrors, ladies. They are your friends, especially in backing up the length and width of this vehicle. Whenever you switch drivers, take the time to readjust the mirrors to suit you, and remember you can fold them in when you're in a tight spot." He reached out the open window and demonstrated, pulling the mirror close to the RV. "When you're parking, one of you needs to be outside the RV, helping to direct the driver. If you're directing, you need to use clear hand signals and stay out of the driver's blind spot."

He looked at the women. "What other important safety measures do you remember from the safety videos?"

Linny raised a hand. "The co-driver sits up front and helps the driver. The rest of us need to sit in the back here with our seat belts on."

Dessie added, "Turn off all propane tanks when you're getting gas at the gas station."

Ruby chimed in. "Drive defensively, watch out for trucks and other RVs, and look out for tree branches and low bridges."

Dottie nodded. "Be careful changing lanes and turning because you're a lot wider than you think."

Mack looked impressed. "Well done, ladies. You've been studying hard. Now let's move from book learning to real life. Who wants to go first?"

"I'll go. My husband and I had a camper for years, but we pulled that behind our truck. This rig is different so let's hope I can drive it," Dessie said and stepped nimbly up to the driver's seat Mack had relinquished. She moved the seat forward, took her time getting the mirrors just right, and slipped on driving glasses as she cranked it up.

"I'll be your co-driver." Mack buckled his seat belt. "You can ask me anything." But Dessie looked like a pro, Linny decided, and blew out a breath. Until today she hadn't known how nervous she was about the others' driving.

Dessie accelerated gradually, carefully circled around trees, and braked slowly. She shot a grin over her shoulder at the girls as she put it in park. "Just like riding a bike," she said.

"I'm going to set up orange cones so you can practice parking. Ruby, how about you assist Dessie from outside?" Mack stepped down the stairs behind Ruby, helped her set up the traffic cones, and swung back inside to the co-driver seat.

Linny glanced out the back window, smiling as she watched Ruby make exaggerated waving signs, do some leaping that looked like old cheerleader moves, and belt out encouraging instructions as she directed Dessie through the cones. "Doing great. To the left a few more inches. A skooch more. Perfecto!"

When Dessie finished expertly parking, she grinned as she relinquished the driver's seat and strode to the back of the RV. The others cheered and patted her on the back like she was the quarterback getting back on the bus after winning the big away game.

Ruby was next. After adjusting the outside mirrors Ruby glanced in the rearview mirror and spent a long moment fluffing her bangs. Linny shot a worried glance at Dottie, whose eyes were wide. Good grief. Linny pulled her seat belt tighter.

Ruby was a chatty driver. "Oooh, it's so easy to put this in gear and the ride is smooth as pudding." She practiced using the turn signal and maneuvered the RV into a graceful arc past the "Go Willow Hill Wildcats" sign with the sculpture of the snarling wildcat mascot. "You know, when I drove those school buses, they were clunky old things. Nothing like this sweet ride."

Dottie spoke from the corner of her mouth. "Ruby talks when she's excited."

But while she talked, Ruby looked as relaxed as if she were driving her Chevy Malibu to a BOGO sale at Shoes, Shoes, Shoes. She let down the window and rested her arm on the door and called back to the others. "I've always wanted to put my arm out while driving some big rig with the wind blowing my hair. Maybe it's a *Thelma and Louise* kind of thing," she said and giggled.

Linny chuckled, too, until she pictured that T Bird flying over the cliff and sobered up.

For Ruby's orange cone–backing exercise, Linny scampered here and there, offering waving directions, but couldn't seem to get in the right place at the right time. Ruby called out the window to her, "You're in my blind spot" and "Still in my blind spot."

Despite Linny's inept signaling, Ruby nailed it every time she backed up.

Feeling chagrined, Linny climbed back on the RV. She needed to work on her waving technique.

Mack said to Ruby, "My dear, you are an excellent driver."

Pink cheeked with pleasure, Ruby made a little curtsy and slid into her seat.

"Show-off," Dottie called out.

Now it was Linny's turn. How hard could this be? She'd driven the truck on her parents' farm since she was twelve and had been a confident driver her whole life. She was good at driving Jack's big Ford F-350. Jack was also giving her lessons on backing a horse trailer. Once she realized she had to turn the wheel the opposite of the way she wanted the trailer to go, she stopped her zig-zagging and was getting to be a strong beginner backer.

In the driver's seat, though, Linny adjusted her mirrors and gave a shaky sigh as she grasped the enormity of the RV she was driving. It was like driving a house down the road.

Mack seemed to sense her unease and said quietly, "Relax, honey. You just take your time and put her in drive whenever you're ready. Get used to moving and to braking."

After an inner pep talk and sucking in a few deep breaths that were supposed to calm her but left her feeling slightly dizzy, Linny nodded grimly, released the brake, and shifted into drive. She drove a foot, stomped on the brake, drove another foot or two, and hit the brake again. In the rearview mirror she saw the other women's heads snap back and forth and, in between snapping, her mother smiling encouragingly. Finally, she gripped the wheel and inched around the perimeter of the parking lot. When she swung a little too close to the snarling wildcat, she heard a collective intake of breath. Overcorrecting, Linny grazed an overgrown azalea bush, but it sprang back, looking none the worse for wear.

"I never liked azaleas," Dessie sniffed.

Mack reached over and patted her shoulder and said calmly, "You're doing fine. Just remember, you have a big rear end."

"Nice thing to say to my daughter," Dottie said, pretending to huff.

Linny smiled, and began to enjoy driving. She slowly cruised around the lot, her hands relaxing their steely grip on the wheel. "I like how high up we sit," she called to the others and lined the RV up for backing.

But her mother offered wildly conflicting hand signals about which way to back. Linny heard the crunching sound and stared in horror at the mirror, praying she'd hit cones and not Dottie. But Mama appeared in her mirror, calling, "You almost missed them, sugar," and started again with her graceful but open-to-interpretation directing moves that looked like the ones Linny had seen at a performance at the American Dance Festival last fall.

The next round Linny nudged cones instead of running them over and Mack declared it a victory. "Let's call it a day, ladies. You've all done real well." His eyes sparkled as he looked at each woman, lingering when he came to Dottie. "Now I'd like to get home so I can take the lovely Miss Dottie out to supper before the big trip."

Dottie twinkled at him.

Linny watched the chemistry. Just friends my behind. But Linny had her own good-byes to say. On the short drive back to her mother's house she fought a wave of lonesomeness. Though she'd only be gone seven days, this was the longest she'd ever been away from Jack since they'd started dating. And even though Neal was in his slouch-and-sulk mode, she pictured that sweet, open smile of his. Linny missed both her men already.

That evening Linny stood in her kitchen, frowning in concentration as she read the recipe for Simple Chicken Potpie. Before she'd left for Mama's this morning, she'd marinated the chicken breasts in buttermilk, salt, and pepper and stuck them in the fridge. Birdie, the cooking instructor from the *A Fun Mom's Guide to Fast, Frugal Weeknight Cooking* class she'd taken last fall, always trilled about the marvels of buttermilk: *Buttermilk is your friend, my petunias!*

Linny grimaced as she picked up the slippery chicken breasts and arranged them in a Pyrex dish. She popped them in the oven at 450 degrees. They'd cook for six minutes on each side, then she'd add chicken broth and lower the heat. She'd cover the chicken in aluminum foil pup tents and let them cook for about twenty minutes more.

Linny carefully set the timer, chopped fresh vegetables and steamed them, and reread her directions. She wasn't a natural chef. Every good meal she prepared came from scrupulously following a recipe. She'd burned up a very expensive roast sirloin when she got sidetracked figuring out how to operate the food processor. Then there was the small fire she'd started—no fire extinguisher necessary—in the brand-new microwave because she accidentally set the timer to twenty minutes instead of two. She'd been humming and shucking corn when she saw the little flames and smelled that awful smell.

Linny shook her head, remembering, as she carefully checked the oven temperature. Jack had been so understanding about that mishap. Thank goodness he wasn't the type of man to give her a lecture. No *You could have burned down the house* or *We just threw away three hundred dollars*. Jack just patted her on the shoulder and said, "Glad you weren't hurt." He and Neal had just hopped in the truck, gone to Lowe's, and brought home a replacement microwave.

Linny's heart squeezed as she remembered how carefully Neal had watched his dad's reaction to that microwave incident. He'd looked like a deer who'd picked up a scent of danger and was about to bolt into the woods. Chaz and Vera's fighting spooked him. It had been good for the boy to see his dad's calm reaction to the problem.

But now Neal clomped into the kitchen, his eyes hooded.

"Hey, Neal," she said pleasantly, trying to read his mood. Was he just partly cloudy or was a squall approaching?

Grunting a greeting, Neal swung open the refrigerator and examined the contents as carefully as if he was studying for a big final exam.

Linny had a mental image of an arrow spinning crazily around the glass globe of their power meter like she'd seen in the old movies she loved but fought the urge to ask him to hurry up and close the door. She was also stung by the grunt. Didn't she even warrant a muttered *hey*? Trying to lighten his mood, Linny found herself prattling. "So this is one of your favorites, chicken potpie. And Dad's bringing home watermelon. He's stopping at that stand out on Pine Ridge Farm—the place where you all got the really sweet one last summer. Remember, the one we put on the bathroom scale and it weighed twenty-five pounds?" She glanced over at him, but he didn't answer.

Neal sat slumped in the kitchen chair, gnawing on a piece of leftover pizza and playing a game on his phone.

Okay. So she'd spent an hour preparing this meal and he was reaching for his second slice of pizza and eyeing the third in the box in front of him. What were the odds that he'd announce he wasn't hungry just as she dipped a spoon in the flaky golden crust of the pie? Pretty good, she'd bet. This was one of his favorite push-the-stepmother-away tactics, especially when she'd cooked a meal she'd heard was one of his favorites.

Linny washed the buttermilk bowl, propped it in the dish drying rack and faced him. Quietly, she asked, "May I speak to you just one minute?"

He heaved a sigh. Putting the phone down, he slid his eyes over to her, looking bored. "Okay."

Linny took a steadying breath, but her mind raced around, throwing its hands in the air. She couldn't say what she felt: *I'm sorry your mama and Chaz are acting so childish and pigheaded. I'm sorry you've had to witness all this drama that doesn't have anything to do with you.* She wouldn't overstep her bounds, and she and Jack had a pact to try to never talk badly about the boy's mother and stepfather. But her heart ached for the bright, sensitive young man, and she knew Jack wasn't that great at initiating conversation about emotions. She had to at least try to acknowledge what was going on. She tilted her head. "I'm sorry things have been tense at home, Neal. We hope things are going to get better. We love you a lot."

Not meeting her eyes, Neal gave a quick jerk of a nod, picked up his phone, and stomped out of the kitchen.

Linny put her hand to her forehead and shook her head. That was the best she could come up with? Carol Brady would have known exactly what to say and turned that conversation into a healing, breakthrough moment. Neal's eyes would have widened and he would have looked at her gratefully and said, "I get it. Mom and Chaz's problems are their own. I am still well-loved and needn't let their behavior impact my self-esteem." He'd have given her a grateful hug before he put the pizza away, sponged off the kitchen table, and walked off to double-check his homework before supper.

She thrust the hand mixer in the bowl of hot potatoes and thought of what one of the stepmothers had recently posted on the *Bodacious Bonus Moms* blog. Corrie from Charleston, South Carolina, had written about distant or surly teenaged stepchildren: *Talking to a stepchild who is a teen is like talking to a loved one in a coma. There's no sign they can hear you, but they do. Even though you think you're going nowhere, all the love you offer does sink in. You just won't know it until later.* Feeling vaguely reassured, she sloshed half-and-half in the potatoes and began whipping.

Jack ambled in from the barn and gave her that slow, meant-only-for-her smile that made her melt a little. "Hey you," he said and pulled her into his arms.

"Hey, there," she murmured, her face pressed into his chest, breathing him in. She hugged him tightly and just wished she could stay in this safe, protected place forever. The timer for the oven dinged and, reluctantly, she let him go. "Supper's ready, but I want to hear all about your day after we eat." With Neal staying with them more, she missed the intimate catch-up conversations they'd had when it was just two of them at supper.

"How was work?" she asked.

"Wanted to run something by you." Jack gave her an apologetic look. "Remember this winter I told the director of the Animal Guardians group that I'd volunteer for eight weeks at their low-cost spay and neuter clinic? Well, they sent me an email and have me on the schedule starting next week." He rubbed his chin with his hand, looking troubled. "The timing's not great, but I'd given them my word."

Linny nodded. The state she loved still had such a problem with overcrowded shelters and high numbers of unwanted animals being euthanized each year. Part of the problem was that the legislature wouldn't do enough to regulate puppy mills—a source of many of the abandoned, neglected and abused dogs in North Carolina.

Linny thought about it. That would be such an important and meaningful thing for Jack to do, but she'd be in charge of Neal one more night a week. If she only had some litmus paper she could press to the boy's forehead to tell her whether she'd get the boy who was practically bubbling as he showed her how to use his telescope and point out stars or the boy radiating baleful you've-ruined-my-life looks before slamming the door so hard the house seemed to shudder. Linny pushed her shoulders back. She could take him. "You need to go help at the clinic," she said simply.

"Thanks, Lin." Jack shot her a grateful look. "It's every Tuesday night from four to nine." Neal wandered back into the kitchen and Jack gazed at his son. "Hey, buddy. Can I count on you to help Linny around here every Tuesday night, and to behave well?"

Neal nodded his assent and leaned his shoulder into his dad's for a brief moment, a teenaged version of *Hello, Dad. Hope you had a good day.*

At the supper table Linny watched Neal push the potpie around his plate, cutting the golden crust into mush and hiding the chicken and vegetables under the leafy greens of the salad he hadn't touched.

This nutty supper routine happened almost every other meal. Because Jack had been scrawny up until he was a senior in high school and didn't want Neal to be picked on the way he had been, he tried to coerce the boy into eating instead of picking at his food. Linny would feel hurt and take it personally that Neal turned his nose up at a dish she'd prepared especially for him. Then, later on, the boy would sneak back into the kitchen, eat all the leftovers, rinse his plate, and slip it in the dishwasher to get rid of the evidence.

She and Jack had talked about this. If Neal got no reaction to picking at his food, maybe he'd stop. She tried to mentally telegraph Jack not to ask the boy about his appetite.

"Not hungry, Son?" Jack asked, pointing his fork at Neal's full but rearranged plate. "That's an awfully nice meal Linny has cooked for us."

Linny tried to send him signals, but her narrowed eyes and foot nudge under the table didn't hit the mark.

Jack just gave her a confused smile and looked at Neal. "If you want ice cream for dessert, you need to eat more than that. . . ."

As he went on talking about the vitamins and minerals needed to grow into a strong and healthy man, Linny steamed, forking her own chicken potpie. She ate fast and rose, speed walking to the stove to dish up seconds. She scooped out the rest of the mashed potatoes and a hungry-truck-driver-sized portion of the chicken potpie that remained. She saw Neal watching her, his eyes widening. "Adding half-and-half to those potatoes made them extra smooth," she announced to no one, went back to the table, and dove in.

Before the wedding she'd lost a stubborn ten pounds by drinking green protein shakes for breakfast and ordering salads when they ate out. But as she shoveled in the last bite of pot pie, Linny tried to look like the ecstatic foodie judge tasting the winning dish on a cooking competition on TV. Swallowing ice water to wash down the last bite, Linny felt bloated and regretful already.

Jack watched her, looking bemused.

"That was dee-licious," she said brightly and flushed. She'd never said *dee-licious* before in her whole life. Patting her mouth with her napkin, she shot a quick glance at Neal. He looked indignant, like someone had snatched a forkful of food away from his mouth. Hah. Mission accomplished. No leftovers for young Mr. Avery.

After the men started their kitchen cleanup, Linny rounded up Roy—who stopped mooning over Jack long enough to trot after her—and went to their bedroom to read. But her distended belly pooched above the waistband of her shorts and her stomach gurgled. She groaned and looked at Roy, who had curled up at her feet. "I need to rethink this eating-all-the-leftovers plan."

A soft knock sounded and Jack appeared in the doorway. Giving her a slow, sweet smile, he toed off his shoes, eased his long frame onto the bed beside her, and put his arms around her. "Good supper, Linny." He added mildly, "You were hungry."

Nestling into him, she blew out a breath and admitted, "I was being childish. I'm sick of trying really hard to cook what Neal likes and have him pick at it and then sneak back and eat it later." She gave him a reproachful gaze. "We were supposed to not comment on his lack of appetite, remember?"

He grimaced. "Sorry, Lin. I'll remember next time."

"You need to or I'm going to get really big, fast," she said.

"More to love, darling," he said, gathering her into his arms and breathing out a deep sigh.

Gazing at him, she heaved a happy sigh. "I miss talking to you alone over supper."

"I know, honey. We're just doing what needs to be done, and you're being flexible. You don't know how much I appreciate it," Jack said.

Linny *did* know, but it felt good to hear him say it.

"So tell me more about today. So Kate looked bushed?" Jack asked.

From her spot in the crook of his shoulder, Linny filled him in. She stopped when she heard Neal's phone ring from the other room—the distinctive Carolina Hurricanes fight song, "Roll with It"—from the other room. After a beat, an insistent rap sounded at their door.

"Dad. Dad!" Neal's muffled voice held a note of alarm.

Linny sprang up and Jack rolled out of the bed and opened the door. "What is it, Son?"

White-faced, Neal thrust the phone at him. "You talk to her."

A cold feeling of dread crept over her. The call had to be from Vera, and Linny instinctively knew it would mean trouble.

Jack took the phone and listened, raking a hand through his hair. He leaned into the doorframe and spoke in a tone he used with scared dogs at the clinic. "Okay. Okay. Slow down. So Chaz has left for a few days."

Vera's volume went up and Linny could hear her crying through the phone. She gave a worried glance at Neal, whose face looked etched in granite as he stood there listening, arms crossed.

Jack glanced at Neal, too, shot Linny an apologetic look, and walked toward the living room to continue the call. "Well, time apart might help," he murmured into the phone.

Linny felt like groaning, falling back onto the bed and putting a pillow over her mouth to yell her frustration. The man she had been seeing as delectable just a few moments ago sounded like one of those new-style Ken-doll-looking preachers Mama liked to watch on TV: the ones who talked earnestly about overcoming challenges in *their own marriages* and *their own lives* but probably flew around in *their own private jets*. Through the thin walls of the house, Linny grimaced as she heard him encourage Vera to *see the positive* and *give things time*. She fought the urge to march in, snatch the phone from him, and end the counseling session with his ex.

But as she stewed and tried to slow her breathing, Linny saw Neal. His eyes were stormy and his shoulders sagged. Her heart squeezed. Poor guy. He'd been through enough churn and didn't need to listen to this.

Linny pushed her hair back from her face and arranged her features in what she hoped was a calm expression. She touched his shoulder, half-expecting him to shake her off, but he didn't. "Come on, buddy. I just had a craving for a Heath bar double-dip cone. Let's hit the Dixie Pixie Ice Creamery." Linny waved to Jack, then pointed to Neal and to the door. He nodded. Steering Neal out of the room and out of earshot of the call, Linny grabbed her purse and paused, picking up the keys to Jack's prize vintage muscle car: the one he didn't like to let her drive. The Camaro had been part of the load of debt Buck had left her, but it turned out Jack had been ecstatic about the muscle car. When Linny finally cleared the debt, she'd given Jack the car. The Camaro was his pampered baby.

As Neal trudged toward her Volvo, Linny held up the keys to the Camaro, shook them, and gave him a devilish smile. "Feel like riding in a convertible tonight?"

Neal nodded, a spark coming into his dark eyes. "Yeah."

The two walked toward the barn, where Jack kept the fiery red rocket of a car protected in a converted stall. After they lowered the top Linny turned the key and felt a thrill as the powerful engine rumbled. She glanced over at Neal, who was trying not to smile, and she knew she'd done the right thing. She'd talk later to her preacher-man husband about getting sucked into Vera's latest drama. But for now Neal needed to be distracted by the cool air rushing through his hair, the starry sky, and pretty high-school-aged waitresses in short, pink-striped skirts serving him up as much ice cream as he wanted to eat.

CHAPTER 5

In the Sky with Diamond

On Friday morning Linny and Mary Catherine sat on the wooden swing on the porch and grinned as they watched Diamond's white Range Rover motor speedily toward the house and pull up with a dust-raising flourish.

Diamond hopped down in her stilettos and a very short red linen sundress, her bleached blond hair in a haystack of a hairdo. Her eyeliner was as swoopy as usual. This was Diamond's typical workday attire, which raised brows among the bar association crowd.

Diamond gave them both extravagant hugs. "Hello, darlings. So glad you could play hooky with me for a while."

Mary Catherine pointed to the car tires, her mouth twitching. Though the SUV was stopped, the whirling rims on the wheels made it look like it was still moving. "Nice spinners."

Diamond clasped her hands together delightedly. "Don't you love them? My masseur has them on his car and they just look so festive. So I had those put on. They're fun, aren't they?"

"They are," Linny marveled, picturing that ride pulling up at the Oakwood Hills Country Club, where Diamond's mama and daddy were charter members.

Despite her heels, Diamond strode confidently around the car and hopped up into the driver's seat. Mary Catherine and Linny climbed in, exchanging isn't-Diamond-a-kick grins. The blonde switched on the engine with long French-tipped fingernails and sped off.

Linny tightened her seat belt and swayed left, then right, then left again. Diamond wasn't big on braking at stop signs or slowing for curves.

Despite it being just the three of them in the SUV, Diamond called to them in a confidential tone, "I'm saving my big WRAL News–type headline for the restaurant."

"Okay," Mary Catherine said and then tilted her head. "Been on any exotic trips? I vicariously enjoy hearing about them."

Though she claimed she worked her fingers to the bone *lawyer-in'*, Diamond spent a good bit of time jetting off to one hot spot or another.

"I did a spa weekend at Jekyll Island Club last month, strictly because my skin looked tired and needed detoxification." Diamond scowled. "You really should be able to write those trips off as medical expenses."

Mary Catherine nodded solemnly. "What is wrong with our tax system in this country?"

"Exactly." Diamond gave a world-weary sigh.

Linny glanced at the directional road signs, puzzled. They were headed west, away from Willow Hill and from Raleigh.

After a while Diamond turned down a county road lined with green soybean fields and drew up at a tarmac dotted with tied-down aircrafts. They drove down beside a row of metal hangars and she wheeled in beside an elegant small plane.

Linny gaped. "Where are we, and what exactly are our lunch plans?"

"We're at Worth County Regional Airport and we're going to the coast for lunch," Diamond said gaily and stepped out of the car. She beamed at a man in a crisp white shirt who walked toward them and gave him a finger wave. "Hey there, Jim. Glad you could make it on such short notice."

"Always a pleasure, Ms. Diamond," the man said and held out a steadying hand for each of them as they climbed the stairs into the plane. He settled in the cockpit.

Diamond led the way into the handsome cabin. She plucked three Diet Pepsis from a refrigerated cabinet, handed one to each of her friends, and slid into a leather seat.

"I love having rich friends." Mary Catherine tried out the recline feature and took a pull of her soft drink.

"What kind of plane is this?" Linny asked as she sank into the buttery leather seat. Glancing around, she tried to memorize every detail so she could tell Jack about it, if she ever decided to talk to him again.

"It's a King Air: a twin-engine turboprop. It cruises along at two-hundred-seventy miles per hour." Diamond patted the burled wood on the side of the seat. "We don't use it much anymore. My parents are flying commercial these days. Coach." She wrinkled her nose. She sipped her cola, and gave them each a level look. "We need to enjoy it while we can. The plane's for sale. So is the big house. I'll fill you in at lunch."

Shooting Mary Catherine an uneasy glance, Linny fastened her seat belt, and instead of enjoying the glamour of flying to the beach for lunch in a private plane, she worried about Diamond's family. Her parents were wildly wealthy, something about venture capital and oil. Maybe they were in financial trouble. Linny's stomach flipped. Though Diamond was successful in her own right, family money accounted for the "cottage" at Holden Beach, her frequent jaunts to Cabo, the Homestead Resort, and shopping in New York. Linny shivered. The idea of Diamond running out of money didn't compute, and it scared her, too.

But as they taxied down the runway and picked up speed, Linny felt herself relax. She loved how she got pushed back in her seat on takeoff and marveled at how quiet it was in the cabin. Looking out the window, she searched for her and Jack's farm, the aqua blue trailer, and Mama's house.

Diamond offered them packages of Pepperidge Farm Goldfish. "So give me the skinny on each of your love lives and your work," she said. "Linny Lou, you start. How is married life?"

Mary Catherine was busy tearing the snack bag open with her teeth.

"Mostly lovely." Linny talked about some of the good parts and the troublesome ones, determined not to be one of those married women who acted like it was endless love all the time when she talked to her single friends.

After she and Mary Catherine finished giving Diamond their CliffsNotes, both women looked at Diamond. "How are things with Butch?" Linny tried to sound nonchalant.

"We're at an impasse. Stuck like rats in a trap," Diamond said, her features clouding. Her brow furrowed as she crunched a few Goldfish. "We're crazy about each other, and I was hoping it was ring time, but instead we have a *talk*." She gazed at them, not masking the disappointment on her face. "He says he'll never make enough money to give me the lifestyle I've been used to." She waved dismissively. "Money is no worry. I have piles of it."

"Some traditional Southern men have trouble with a woman who makes a lot more money than they do," Mary Catherine mumbled. She'd popped in a few too many fish.

Diamond nodded her agreement. "The bigger sticky wicket is how we're going to live. I told him I had no intention of trying to drag him into my world, but he says he can't see me living at the farm. He doesn't think I'd be happy without shopping and travel and . . . frippery."

"Would you?" Mary Catherine asked.

"I would," Diamond said with an emphatic nod.

"You've put effort into being the whimsical gadabout. You're really good at it," Mary Catherine pointed out.

"I know," Diamond said, smiling modestly.

"I'd miss it if you started acting normal," Linny said.

"I'm ready for big changes. I'll tell you more at lunch," Diamond promised as she reclined her seat, leaned her head back, and closed her eyes.

Soon the women sat on the pier at the Big Kahuna Restaurant, looking out at the glittering, azure-blue Atlantic Ocean. After placing their orders, Linny closed her eyes for a moment, sighing contentedly as the ocean breeze lifted the hair from her neck. Heavenly.

"What's your breaking news flash?" Mary Catherine asked Diamond and slipped on her sunglasses.

Diamond looked at them, all playfulness gone from her pretty features. "I hate being an attorney. I'm burned out."

Linny shuddered inwardly, remembering how stressed out she'd been at her old job, working with employees who'd just been laid off.

"People burn out, especially attorneys," Mary Catherine said in a matter-of-fact tone.

Diamond squeezed the lemon slice into her glass of ice water. "I went into law because Daddy wanted me to, and because I like challenges. I've had a good run with it."

This was an understatement, Linny knew. Diamond had a huge and thriving practice.

Diamond rested her chin in her hands and gazed at them. "Am I too old for a do-over?"

Linny shook her head vehemently. "Never. Look at me. The queen of the do-overs."

"Look at my husband. He went from laid-off engineer to schoolteacher and he's so happy it's sickening. Practically skips around like a girl," Mary Catherine said, glowering.

Linny hid a smile. Her friend pinched Mike when he got too happy. Got on her nerves.

A complimentary appetizer arrived and Diamond popped a shrimp into her mouth. "So here's my plan. Total do-over. I'm selling the practice. I'll quit being a career woman and become a housewife and a mother."

Trying to look like she was tracking with her, Linny asked, "Does Butch know this?"

"Not yet. The plan will unfold. First I'll prove to him I can live like a simple country girl," she said, wiping cocktail sauce off her elegant talons.

Linny nodded, having trouble picturing it. Diamond stayed in a wing of her parents' mansion and had her own three-car garage and a chef's kitchen equipped with an actual chef.

"You know, Mama and Daddy are taking more and more ecotourism trips. They stay in grass huts, dig wells, and hand out mosquito nets." Diamond shuddered prettily. "Ever since Daddy's cancer scare they're over the whole money thing and have practically taken vows of poverty. They're selling the big house, and the King Air. They're deeding me the guest cottage and the two acres it sits on." She lifted her chin. "That's where I'll live simply. I'm joining the tiny house movement."

"Is the guest cottage that tiny?" Linny asked, trying to be tactful. She'd driven by it a few times and remembered thinking that she and Jack could fit two houses the size of theirs inside it.

"It's just twenty-eight-hundred square feet," Diamond said, looking indignant. "I'll grow organic vegetables and lavender...." She waved airily, signaling that she'd make crop decisions later.

"And you're doing this to prove something to Butch?" Mary Catherine looked skeptical.

"Mainly I want a different life," Diamond said stubbornly. "But if Butch sees I can live a simpler life he might pop the question. If he doesn't, I'll find another man to marry," Diamond added, a determined look in her eye. "I *will* be a homemaker. The little woman.

The missus." A smile played at the corner of her mouth as she tried on names for her new avocation.

"Domestic goddess," Linny added, warming to the idea.

Mary Catherine looked intrigued. "You're like those building demolition guys who use dynamite. You blow up everything in your life to start fresh. I like the plan."

Linny gave Diamond's shoulder a pat. "I hope you get exactly what you want."

Back home, she finally got traction with her packing. Roy stood beside her, ears and tail drooping as he looked at the suitcase.

"Don't worry, buddy." Linny embraced him, giving his ears a scratch. "Promise I won't be gone long."

Hands on her hips, Linny stared at the open suitcase and the shorts, jeans, and T-shirts she'd put in neat stacks surrounding it. Dessie, the only seasoned camper of the bunch, had cautioned them to pack light. But how light? And they'd be in the mountains, so it would get chilly at night. She put another fleece in the bag, saw how much room it took up, and pulled it back out.

Padding into the kitchen, she went to the computer for advice on what to pack for a seven-day-long RV trip. She printed a list written by a traveler named Camping Cassandra and scanned it as she walked back to their room, hoping the snake bite kit, small hatchet, and emergency beacon on the list were overkill. Linny stopped in the doorway, startled. Roy had curled up in a perfect ball in her suitcase and gazed at her with soulful chocolate eyes.

"Oh, baby boy." Extricating his warm, soft body, Linny lay down beside him on the bed to give him a good long snuggle. She'd miss all her boys.

She heard Jack and Neal blow into the kitchen. Giving Roy a last few scratches, she rose smiling and marveling at how noisy men could be. She listened. The keys clattered on the counter. The two were debating college football lineups. The refrigerator door opened, closed, and opened again. A loud, long burp sounded: Neal's latest gross-out trick. Jack chided Neal.

Jack called, "Lin? Where are you?"

"Back here," she called. "I'm packing."

Jack appeared, gave her a cautious smile, and kissed her cheek. "How was your day?"

"Fine," she said, not even mentioning she'd flown to the coast for lunch in a private plane.

"You still mad at me?" Jack shoved his hands in his jeans pockets.

"Some," she admitted, noticing a scruffy spot he'd missed when he'd shaved that morning and the purplish circles under his eyes. Good. He'd had a rough night's sleep, too. "What's the latest with Vera?" she asked, busying herself refolding a shirt that was already perfectly folded.

"Fine, I guess. I haven't talked to her today." He shrugged, looking helpless. "I got off the phone as soon as I could last night, but she was crying and going on and on." He turned his hands palms up.

"Maybe she needs a therapist," Linny said crisply. "One she pays and wasn't married to." With more gusto than was called for, she balled up and stuffed clean white ankle socks into the toes of her tennis shoes the way Camping Cassandra had suggested.

Jack nodded and rubbed his chin. "Linny, I just wanted to try to settle things down for Neal's sake."

Linny looked at him, trying to keep her voice calm. "Vera told Neal that I was trailer trash. She told Neal's teacher that you and I were the cause of his sliding grades. She's tried to drive a wedge between me and your family. She's tried to bully you for money." Linny twirled back around to her suitcase and smoothed an imaginary wrinkle out of a shirt, blood pounding in her ears. The Bodacious Bonus Moms all recommended compromise and negotiation, but she just couldn't muster an ounce of either.

"You're right." He groaned, clasping his hands behind his neck. "But her not doing well means Neal suffers."

Linny thought about it and nodded grudgingly. But he seemed to be trying to appease Vera, not fix things.

"You tell me what to do," he said, searching her face.

Linny blew out a sigh and sank onto the bed. She didn't want to leave him for seven days with so much unresolved. She had to tell him how she felt. "I wish you would tell Vera to get her house in order, straighten things out with Chaz, or get out of the marriage. Let her know how concerned you are that she's creating such a tension-filled household for Neal. Ask her to put Neal first for once, stop the drama, and stop calling you to cry on your shoulder." Her eyes fixed on his as she tried to gauge his reaction.

He just shook his head, looking frustrated. "All you're saying is true, but you don't know Vera like I do. You can't tell that woman what to do. If I'm that direct with her, she'll take it as a challenge to her image as the perfect mother and start World War III."

"How much trouble could she start?" Linny asked, giving him a skeptical look.

Jack rolled his eyes. "Under that fragile exterior, she's a street fighter, especially if she doesn't get her way. She'll insist on keeping him even though there's mayhem in her house. We'll get dragged in to court. If you think Neal is in a bind now, wait until I try to tell her she's messing up with her parenting." He touched her arm and gave her a steady look. "Lin, I can't put Neal through that. He's endured enough and he doesn't deserve more."

Linny gazed at him for a moment, then nodded grudgingly as she saw how troubled he was. Maybe this was one of those situations you had to be a biological parent to understand. Maybe she was right, but Jack was going to have to figure it out in his own time. Either way she'd said her piece and she needed to let it go. Jack was struggling to do the best for his son. She stepped toward him and slid her arm around his waist. "Let's leave it all for now. You'll make the right call."

Linny stepped away from Jack as she heard a knock on the doorframe.

"Hey, lovebirds," Neal said, rolling his eyes and shaking his head but hiding a smile.

"Hey, yourself," Linny called, hoping the young man had come down the hall just that very moment and not overhead their conversation. She stuck her hands in the back pockets of her jeans.

"What's up, buddy?" Jack asked.

"Are you almost finished packing, Linny?" the boy asked, his eyes wandering to her suitcase.

"Almost," Linny said.

The boy shifted his weight from one sneakered foot to the other. "If you're out in the woods and a raccoon or fox wanders into your campsite acting friendly, don't touch it or try to feed it. The South has had an unusual number of rabies reports this year," he said, pushing back a shock of his hair. "Even if it's something as cute as a rabbit, although I never heard of a rabid rabbit." He looked at his father. "Dad, can rabbits get rabies?"

Jack stroked his chin, looking thoughtful. "Well, technically, rabbits are warm-blooded mammals so they could possibly get infected with the rabies virus if, say, another rabid animal bit them. Statistically, though, it happens very infrequently."

Neal nodded, looking relieved. "Good. Because you could see a soft little rabbit and think he was cute and he chomps you and you're dead—or at least foaming at the mouth."

Linny just nodded at this odd turn of conversation. Mama was worried about rabid beavers drowning her in a lake and Neal was concerned about Linny picking up wild forest animal and getting rabies.

Jack put a hand on Neal's shoulder. "Son, Linny's got a good head on her shoulders and will stay away from any odd-acting animals."

"I will, but I appreciate the reminder," Linny said. "Let's go feed the horses, buddy."

CHAPTER 6

Campfire Girls

The next day it was Neal's idea to give them a festive send-off as they left on their trip. Neal, Jack, and Mack whistled, waved enthusiastically, and threw handfuls of improvised confetti—thistle they usually put in the birdfeeder and ryegrass seed Jack used for bald spots in the lawn—as the RV slowly pulled away from Dottie's brick ranch. Linny grinned and blew kisses to the boys as she heard them call "bon voyage," "safe travels," and "remember to charge your phones." The women waved out the windows and Linny blinked back tears, feeling a wave of homesickness even though they weren't a quarter mile into their trip.

"We're off to see the US of A," Ruby called gleefully as the motor home glided down Mama's driveway, hardly registering the potholes in the long gravel road.

Dessie had volunteered for the first shift driving. Behind the wheel, she had an erect bearing and a calm demeanor, her steely-eyed gaze fixed on the road in front of them. Linny glanced at her admiringly. She was like a younger Queen Elizabeth behind the wheel of the Class C as it headed toward 1-40 West. Soon Dessie confirmed Linny's observation about her queenly manner by waving at a passing motor home in a decidedly screw-in-the-light-bulb manner.

"So should we wave at other campers on the road?" asked Ruby, the co-driver for the morning. She held a pen poised over paper, ready to take notes. Ruby took her co-driver role very seriously.

Dessie shrugged. "We always did when we camped. And sometimes we'd run into the same people we saw on the road at the campgrounds where we ended up staying."

"Oh, like a roving brotherhood of adventurers," Ruby said, clasping her hands at the romance of it all.

"Or sisterhood," Dessie clarified. "We made a lot of nice friends camping," she said, sounding wistful. Regally, she flipped on the turn signal and merged the RV onto the interstate.

Linny tried to read the novel she'd brought along but kept reading the same line over and over again. She was jangled about leaving Jack and keyed up about being a passenger in the house on wheels. From her perch on the dashboard, the Waze lady spoke a clear and melodious voice. Linny liked her directions, but also her alerts: *Debris ahead in the road* or *Car stopped on the shoulder ahead*. The Waze woman was on top of things.

Mack—aka Mr. Technology—had set up the Waze navigation system and backup GPS apps on all the women's phones. He'd also mapped out the route on a set of paper maps from Triple A in the unlikely event that they ran into a geomagnetic Bermuda Triangle situation that took out all their electronics.

As the miles went by, Linny felt her shoulders drop and the tension she'd been carrying start to ease. Dessie knew what she was doing and the Waze lady was reassuring, too. Traffic was light, the road stretched out in front of them, and as they cruised through the gentle roll of the North Carolina piedmont, Linny nodded off.

When Linny blinked open her eyes, several hours must have passed because they were making their winding ascent up to the mountains. "Holy moly," she breathed as she looked out the window and saw that a fragile-looking guardrail was the only protection against a steep drop over the side.

Linny swallowed hard. What if they hit an oil slick or a patch of gravel? Her eyes darted around, trying to measure the fear level of the others. Beside her, Dottie busily polished her sunglasses on the hem of her shirt. At the wheel, Dessie looked as relaxed as if she was out on a Sunday drive. Co-driver Ruby murmured to Dessie, "You're taking these hills like a champ. Very impressive." Popping in one of the CD's Perry had burned for their trip, Ruby started singing along with Willie to "On the Road Again." Dessie chuckled.

"What are those?" Ruby asked, pointing to the opposite side of the road.

Linny looked, her eyes widening as she saw what looked like a giant sandbox sloping upward on the side of the road, gouged with truck-sized tire tracks.

"Runaway truck ramps," Dessie replied in a matter-of-fact tone. "If you lose your brakes coming down the hill—which we won't—you can just steer your truck or RV into that sand and it'll slow you down."

Linny shot a quick glance at Dessie to make sure she still looked calm, and she did. Her hands relaxed on the wheel, she hummed along with Willie. Dottie slipped on a pair of extradark wraparound senior-citizen sunglasses. Maybe Mama had bought these from a special store for women intent on looking way older than their years.

"Be best if you didn't look, shug." Her mother reached out to pat her arm. "And try to keep breathing," she suggested, pulling an oversize pair of knitting needles out of her purse and looping on some wool.

Linny forced herself to stop searching for other sandboxes that might contain wrecked semis. Pulling her iPod from her purse, she slipped in earbuds. Leaning back, she closed her eyes, made herself breathe slowly, and listened to the mellow mindfulness meditation CD Kate had made her for the trip.

Finally, they arrived on the outskirts of Pigeon Forge, Tennessee. The woman behind the desk of the visitors' check-in center at the campground wore a name tag that said "Mrs. Don Boyer—Owner." "Evening, ladies," she said, speaking through shiny fuchsia lips that were so overly plumped that Linny had to fight the urge to lean over the desk and examine them more closely. "My husband and I hope you enjoy your stay. Here at Breathtaking Vista RV Resort, we run a quiet family campground. As our name says, we do indeed have breathtaking views of the mountains and a little lake for paddling, fishing, and walking or biking around," Mrs. Don Boyer added pleasantly, but then looked at them sternly over the top of her half glasses. "But we don't tolerate loud music, partying, whoopin' it up, or foolishness. No tuning up your motorcycles for hours. We will kick you out if need be."

Linny found herself trying to look innocent and made herself stop, feeling a flush of annoyance. She glanced at the others. Ruby's sweatshirt had kittens on it playing with a ball of yarn. Dessie's T-shirt identified her as World's Best Grammy and Dottie's shirt was emblazoned with praying hands.

Dottie gave the woman a level look and said in a plummy tone, "We appreciate the high standards you set here at your resort. We would hate to have our visit marred by riffraff."

Linny bit her lip to keep from smiling.

"Well, we're mighty glad to have you." Mrs. Don flushed, looking apologetic. "My husband makes me give that speech to every guest checking in, and maybe because of it, we've never had a lick of trouble at this resort."

As they piled back in the RV, Linny patted her mother's arm. "Mama, you sounded a little like that lady on *Downton Abbey*."

Dessie grinned mischievously. "There go our plans for an all-night keg party."

Dottie started to chuckle and Linny burst into laughter. The others joined in, with Ruby's giggles fueling the hilarity.

Grinning, Linny glanced at Dottie. "I'll bet this is the first time in your life you've been viewed as a potential roughneck."

Dottie folded her hands on her purse and smiled. "I liked it."

As Dessie cruised slowly down the lanes, they saw the wide pull-through camping areas, and other guests offered them friendly waves and nods. Ruby pointed out the window at the sparkling blue lake, the pin-perfect landscaping, and the grass as manicured as a golf green. "This is such a pretty spot."

Linny whistled, glancing out the windows on the other side of the road. "Check out that view." She pointed to the green lawn that sloped toward a backdrop of green-gray mountains. Cotton ball clouds floated by in a clear blue sky.

Dottie nodded emphatically. "We are going to have a grand time."

Parking was surprisingly easy. With Ruby outside springing around and doing her enthusiastic two-armed signals that just lacked pom-poms to be a full cheer, Dessie expertly eased the RV into their designated campsite.

Ruby bounced back into the RV, all smiles at her successful signaling.

The three of them stood together in the middle of the living room like sardines in a can, waiting for Dessie to push the button to open the slide outs and give them the extra six to eight feet of space that made it possible for them to fold out their beds and get settled into their quarters. Dessie pushed the button, scowled, and pushed it several more times. "Nothing is happening," she muttered and ducked to look underneath the dash for the source of the problem.

Dottie and Ruby sat in the cushioned seats of the U-shaped dinette while Linny went forward to see if she could help. "Is something broken?" she asked.

Dessie pulled off her visor and scratched her head. "This worked fine in the practice area at the RV place. Let me call the roadside assistance number."

While Dessie punched in numbers on her cell, a knock sounded at the open door.

A couple stood outside, smiling. With clavicle bones that protruded under a velour track suit that swam on her, the woman held a turkey-size platter wrapped in tinfoil. The man had short white hair and showed dimples when he smiled. Wearing boating moccasins and a white polo shirt, he had a round stomach protruding over the waistband of his blue-and-white-plaid shorts. "Howdy, neighbors. We're Hal and Letty and we're at the campsite right next door. Thought we'd stop by and say hello, see if there's anything we could do to help you get settled."

Linny stepped forward and shook Hal's hand and smiled at Letty. "I'm Linny, and this is Ruby and my mama, Dottie. That's Dessie in the driver's seat."

Letty held out the tray she carried. "I was making chocolate chip cookies and got carried away and ended up baking one-hundred forty-four. We brought you four dozen."

Linny gazed at her uncomprehendingly. She'd accidentally made twelve dozen cookies?

"Come right in," Dottie boomed with a graceful arm sweep of a welcoming gesture. "Let me help you with that heavy platter."

Dessie spoke up. "Hal, I'm having trouble getting the slide outs to open. If we have to stay the night on top of one another like this, there will likely be bloodshed. Can you come take a look?"

Looking thrilled to be asked for help, Hal strode toward the driver's seat, but his step faltered when he walked past Ruby, who was looking particularly fetching in dangly earrings and a purple flowing sundress with flip-flops printed on it. He stared at her for a moment, gave her a red-faced nod, and quick-stepped to the driver's seat. "So, Miss Dessie, tell me what you've done so far," he said in a kindly tone.

"I put it in park and put down the stabilizing jacks. When I pushed the button for the slides, nothing happened. Did I break the gear somehow?" she asked, looking stricken.

He paused and looked thoughtful. "Have you set the brake yet?"

Dessie groaned, pulled on the brake, and tried again. As the slides eased out smooth as butter, she smiled up at him gratefully. "Bless your heart. You're a genius."

"Many a seasoned RVer has made that mistake before," Hal said reassuringly.

Pushing aside her embarrassment, Linny held up a finger. "While we have you here, Hal, we have a few delicate questions about the whole black water, gray water, and bathroom cleaning-out procedure...."

Once Hal had finished his quick tutorials and show and tell, the women thanked him profusely and Hal and Letty headed back to their campsite. After hooking up to power, they unpacked. Linny refereed a mild skirmish between her mother and Ruby over who got to sleep first in the cute bedroom over the cab. After a lively debate, a four-day rotation schedule was agreed upon with Dottie getting first crack at it. The idea for a complicated lottery system for first dibs on the bathroom in the morning went by the wayside and they all agreed that the early bird caught the worm.

Dessie smiled wryly as she pulled from her suitcase a cookie jar in the shape of a cat, its head being the lid. "I made this in my unsuccessful stint in a ceramics class but thought we could use it as a kitty. We can all throw cash in and use it as need be." She placed it on the dinette with a clink. "I always hate it when my women friends eat out, ask the waiter for separate checks, and reach in their change purses to contribute their part down to the cent. Makes us women look petty."

"I agree. Good idea," Linny said and pulled bills from her wallet. "How about if we start with a hundred each?"

The others agreed and added their bills.

After an alfresco supper of hot dogs grilled over an open fire, plump juicy tomatoes from Dottie's garden, and Ruby's famous red-skinned potato salad with eggs, sweet pickle, and scallions, Linny slipped around to a picnic table near the back of the RV and called Jack. "Hey," she said softly.

"Hey, Lin," Jack said warmly. "I miss you already."

"And I miss you and Neal. A bunch. And I miss Roy like crazy, and the rest of the dogs." Linny felt a wave of yearning, picturing Jack's handsome, open face. How was she going to sleep without his comforting bulk by her side for six whole nights? She swallowed noisily, realizing she was close to tears.

"Tell me about your day," Jack said. "Neal's down at the barn. He'll be sorry he missed your call."

Linny pictured Jack in his khaki shorts and his Wolfpack T-shirt, stretched out on the living room couch flanked by dogs. She guessed he'd toed off his sneakers and had an open bag of chips next to him on the cushion. Feeling reassured by the homey mental picture, Linny filled him in on the details of the trip so far.

"You're off to a good start," he said after a few minutes. "I know your mama is glad you're there."

"She is," Linny said, knowing she'd made the right decision in coming. Gazing up at the quarter moon, she pictured Neal's skinny shoulders hunched over his telescope gazing at Orion from that crest beside the barn, the best spot on the farm for views of the sky. "Is Neal excited about your trip?" she asked.

"Beyond that." Jack chuckled. "He's wired. He's been packed for two days and probably won't be able to sleep tonight. He made us set not one but two alarms to make sure we leave the house by five a.m. to get to the airport in plenty of time."

"Yikes, early flight." Linny pictured the two of them hurriedly eating peanut butter and bananas on toast—their favorite weekday breakfast—and hefting their packs into the truck just as a tangerine sun rose over the farm.

"He's been watching and rewatching a National Geographic show on stars and meteors." Jack paused. "Hold on a sec, Lin. Neal just walked in and wants to say hello."

Her stepson came on the line.

"Hey, Linny. Bear attacks occur in the mountains of North Carolina and Tennessee. You need to put all your food away and take your trash out every night. Some attacks would have been preventable if people had taken better precautions," Neal said solemnly.

Bears had crossed her mind, too, but Linny grinned. "Thank you, Neal," she said but spoke to air. Having finished delivering his public service announcement, Neal must have handed the phone back to his father.

"Well, there you go," Jack said, back on the line with a smile in his voice. "Sorry, Linny. He had that bear issue on his mind all day. Between that and rabid rabbits, I think it's his way of saying be careful because he wants you to stay safe and come home in one piece."

"Well," Linny said, thrilled that Neal was conveying his caring, "tell him I love him."

"I will," Jack said gruffly. "And Lin, I love you."

"Love you, too." Linny swallowed hard, warmed by his words. "You men travel safely."

Ending the call, she rejoined the others as they sat around their crackling campfire, chatting softly. She sighed appreciatively as she took her seat in one of the canvas chairs Dessie had brought along for them.

"I love this chair." Linny stretched out her legs in front of her. She admired the handy drink holder where she'd slipped her paper cup of wine and the canvas panel you could pull over your head to get shade while reading on sunny days.

"You need to try this one," Dessie said from her extracomfy-looking zero-gravity lounge chair.

"I will," Linny promised. Though the campground was full, she only heard the wind rustling in the leaves and the soft murmuring of her friends' voices. It was a lovely night. Leaning back, she stared up at the darkening sky that was now dotted by the glitter of what looked like a thousand bright stars. Maybe she needed to take a lesson from stargazer Neal and remember to look up at the sky more. She exhaled slowly, remembering the dreamy-voiced fellow on her mellow mindfulness meditation CD. He talked about not thinking so much and enjoying the moment. So many days she scurried right past the beauty of the natural world because she was focused on getting things done. She needed to linger more in the present, she decided, and took a contemplative sip of chardonnay.

Her eyes shadowed by the dark, Ruby took a swallow of her margarita wine cooler and gazed at each of them, one at a time. "I have an announcement to make. I loved my husband, Pete. We had twenty-nine blissfully happy years together. He was everything a woman could want: romantic, caring, and as good-looking as George Clooney."

Linny intercepted her mother and Dessie exchanging quick eyebrow raises. From what Linny remembered, Pete had been a good man, but he was a regular-looking guy and had his faults like everyone did. He talked too much, wore a toupee that rose and fell in the wind, and often rolled his eyes when Ruby spoke.

Ruby gazed into the flames. "I like my life. I really do. I have Bunco every Tuesday. I go with girlfriends to matinee movies. I walk every morning with my neighbor, Sylvie. My kids call me twice a week and visit when they can. But I see each of you strolling off to make your calls to men who love you...." She trailed off, shaking her head sadly.

"But Mack and I are just friendly dating, not..." Dottie interjected but stopped when Ruby held up a hand.

"Dot, whether you admit it or not, you are on the road to romance," Ruby said firmly. "But back to me. I'm tired of being on my own. I'm going to find a future husband on this trip and I'm going to use the internet to do it."

Everyone was silent for a moment, taking in her announcement.

Dottie pursed her lips. "Can't you just meet a nice man at church, Ruby?"

Ruby gave her a knowing look. "Have you ever met a nice single man at church?"

"Well, no. But I wasn't really trying," Dottie admitted.

Ruby held up her hands in an I-told-you-so gesture. "And next y'all are going to start telling me that when you aren't looking, the right one will turn up. But I've been not looking for many years and the right one hasn't popped up." Her chin was set stubbornly. "I thought Captain Sven from the cruise ship was my Prince Charming, but his love and his lady were the sea." She shook her head sorrowfully.

Linny didn't want to look at her mother, whom she knew would be sending her significant looks and mouthing the letters *G-A-Y*.

"How about the grocery store?" Dessie asked.

"Twice I've tried talking to men when I was at the produce section of Lowes Foods, and each time a wife steamed up, mad as a wet hen. Why don't men wear wedding rings if they're married?" She gave them a school teacher-ish gaze, as if they'd personally told married men not to wear rings if they didn't feel like it. "Y'all just happened upon such catches! Jack is such a baby doll, and his son, too. Then Dessie lucks up at prayer group on the cruise and meets Perry, who looks just like the hunk driving the Mustang convertible in the Cialis commercials."

Linny blinked.

But Ruby wasn't finished detailing the great luck of her girlfriends. "Then Dottie stumbles upon—truly stumbles upon—dreamy Mack during a rumba lesson and he turns out to be a keeper." She shook her head. "I just want it to be my time to find love again."

First Diamond and then Ruby. All these women were all of a sudden determined to find husbands. But Linny couldn't fault them. She remembered how abjectly lonely she'd been after her beloved first husband Andy had died suddenly. One day she was happy and the next, her world had turned into Armageddon. Moved, Linny touched her foot to Ruby's. "I'll help you. We'll sort through those men together."

Ruby sent her a grateful smile.

"I'm in too," Dessie said, trying to bump her foot on Ruby's but accidentally kicking her. "I can help out if you run into any shady characters, especially with all my experience doing PIing."

Linny had to hide a smile. For the past few months Dessie *had* been helping Mary Catherine by secretly taking pictures of a photographer who had been hired by two dirty lawyers to try to bias judges in custody cases. Dessie liked to use *PI* as a verb.

Dottie gave a resigned sigh. "Well, the dating-by-computer idea worries me some, but a friend from church met her husband online, and in those Christian romances I read, women fall in love in all sorts of ways. Last one, a woman on the way to a church homecoming crashed her car into a fellow's car, and after he came out of the coma, she ended up marrying him. And turns out he was an earl, and a millionaire." She shook her head, impressed by the coincidences. "Anyway, count on me to help. We're the SWAT Team, after all." She bumped her foot on Ruby's foot, too.

Eyes glittering with unshed tears, Ruby gave her friends a tremulous smile. "Thank you."

"I'll get the iPad and bring it out. We can get this manhunt underway." Dessie swung up smoothly from her chair and strode into the RV.

"We need pictures, too, don't we?" Dottie asked. "Flattering and friendly-looking. No ex-husbands or boyfriends cut out."

Linny grinned. "I'm impressed, Mama. How did you know that?"

"Oh, I'm very with it on all these new things," she said airily, but then admitted, "AARP had a big article on dating on the internet. If you hadn't met Jack, I thought I might persuade you to sign up."

Linny just shook her head. She was only thirty-nine.

Dessie was back with the iPad. "We need to come up with a description of you, who you are and what you're looking for," she read from the screen.

"You want to be honest but use language that's evocative." Dottie nodded for emphasis.

"Evocative, huh?" Linny gave her a knowing glance. "Mama, you *studied* that article."

Dottie tossed a log on the fire and goosed it with a stick, pretending not to hear her.

"I have to describe myself?" Ruby asked, her eyes wide.

"Yup," Dessie said. "We need to start with a physical description."

Ruby looked away for a moment. "Well, I'm overweight by forty pounds. . . ."

"You're curvy," Dottie suggested and took a swallow of her iced tea. "You're a smart, curvy blonde with a bubbly laugh and big blue eyes."

"Oh my. I like how I'm sounding," Ruby said, her eyes dancing.

"Keep it coming, ladies." Dessie's fingers flew. "What do you do for fun? What are your hobbies and interests?"

"Don't say long walks on the beach and moonlight. They all say that," Dottie advised.

Dessie piped up, "How about *enjoys trying new things, spending time at home, weekend getaways, and family get-togethers*?"

"Good, good." Ruby bobbed her head so hard her camp chair wobbled.

"We should put some man bait in there, too," Dottie said, raising both eyebrows. "How about *Enjoys boat rides, makes excellent fried chicken and mashed potatoes, and reads James Patterson and David Baldacci.*" Looking thoughtful, she put a finger to her cheek and added, *"Looking for marriage-minded man to spend the best years of our lives."*

Linny whistled. "Mama, that's great man bait!"

Dessie tapped away, then explained to Linny, "It's mostly true about Ruby, too. I'd say she *endured* boat rides more than enjoyed them, but that's close enough."

"I know what men like," her mother said with a slightly superior smile. "It's all right there in those God's Blessing Inspirational Romances."

Later that night the four women got cozy in their respective beds. "I brought *9 to 5*. I just loved Dolly in that movie," said Ruby as she turned on her iPad.

Linny also had a movie going but had pulled out the earbuds and eavesdropped, enjoying listening to the friends talk. She liked her sleeping nook, which was underneath and off to the side of the spacious over-the-cab bedroom that the girls had already dubbed the Penthouse.

From the coveted perch, Dottie called, "I've got *Cedar Cove*, some Hallmark movies, and both seasons of *Southern Living and Loving* if anyone wants to see them." She paused a moment and marveled, "I still can't believe there's a dating site for RVers. That is just so handy."

Mama had quickly warmed to the whole internet dating idea once Dessie showed her the statistics on how many people met their spouses online.

From the dining room table that had been converted into her bunk with the push of a button, Dessie glanced up from her screen and called, "Between the RV site, Matching Destinies, Nifty over Fifty, and Christian Single No More, we ought to get some nibbles on the line." She chortled. "We'll reel them in and look for a keeper."

"I'm tickled to death," Ruby said, sounding sleepy. "Do you think I should join the dating site for farmers?"

Linny eyed her. Ruby wore some sort of lacy peignoir to bed and had hogged the bathroom with an elaborate skin routine before bed. She just couldn't picture Ruby riding beside a farmer on his tractor.

"I'm not sure that's you, Ruby," Dessie said, ever the diplomat.

"You may be right," Ruby said, stifling a yawn. "We need to get some better pictures of me tomorrow, though. Those artsy ones Linny took by the campfire just made me look sunburned."

Just then, Mama sat up straighter in the Penthouse, frowned and waved her arms to get Linny's attention. Startled, Linny pulled her earbuds all the way out and stared. Her mother had slipped on one of those protect-your-hairdo sleep bonnets like the Wolf wore when he was trying to convince Red Riding Hood that he was her grandmother. Must have ordered them from the same store where she'd gotten her sunglasses: the one that catered to women trying to dress like their grandmothers. But Linny just smiled. "Yes? May I help you?"

Her mother pointed at Linny's iPad screen as Tom Cruise flew a helicopter under a bridge and leaned out to fire a machine gun at a bad guy. "You don't like those kinds of movies."

Linny paused the movie, feeling sheepish. "I know, but Jack and Neal do, so I thought I'd try to like them. Give us more choices if we go out to a movie."

"Those movies give me knots in my stomach. Maybe you shouldn't watch something like that before bed. Might give you bad dreams. Can't you find something happy and Christian?" Having dispensed her advice, Dottie swung her head back up into better real estate.

Linny stared at the screen. Tom was hanging on the landing skids of the helicopter now, and another bad guy was piloting the copter and trying to shake him off. Linny paused the movie, her stomach grabbing. Why was she trying to make herself like an action movie? She liked romantic comedies, classic movies, and happy endings. Giving her head a little shake, she ended the Tom Cruise thriller and glanced through the ones she'd brought along—*Chef, Best Exotic Marigold Hotel, The Proposal, Roman Holiday,* and other similar films. Trying to talk herself into movies just to be a good sport for her two men wasn't going to happen. With a sigh of contentment, she slid in *Moonrise Kingdom* and settled in for the night.

Early the next morning, after folding the convertible bed back, Dessie, Dottie, and Linny sat around the U-shaped dinette, sipping coffee, eating cereal, and examining the tickets and brochures spread out on the table.

Dessie stuck a finger in the venetian blinds and peeked out. "Ruby should be back any minute. She calls this her morning power walk, but she's been gone twenty minutes and I can see she's only made it fifty yards from our RV. I'll bet she's stopped and chatted with people at every campsite between here and the bend in the road."

Linny was considering a second cup of coffee when Ruby popped in the door wearing shiny jogging shorts, a tank top, and yellow terry-cloth sweatbands on her head and wrists. With her hair frizzing in the humidity, she looked like a pretty, well-endowed Richard Simmons. "Whew." She dabbed at her face with a wrist sweatband.

"Tough workout?" Dottie asked drily.

"Mainly working my mouth, but it's hot already." She poured a glass of ice water and gulped it down. "The little lake is just right there and it has paths all around it. I met such nice people. Linda and Beau are the ones next door cooking bacon outside on their little grill. They're from Myrtle Beach and like to shag dance." She pointed to the other side of their site. "Hal and Letty are two sites down and they're from Panama City, Florida. They're going out west. He's a sweetie pie, but she's a little . . . energetic." Ruby thought about it. "She kept sweeping the cement patio outside their camper when it was perfectly clean already. Anyhow, I met a bunch more. Four neighbors invited me to have cups of coffee with them, so I'm a little jumped up," she admitted and slid into the booth beside Dottie. "Other camping facts I learned: People tow golf carts or cars behind their RVs so they can get around. One of the fellows has an electric tricycle. He just whizzes along so quietly."

Linny cocked a brow. Chitty-chatty Ruby was more than a little caffeinated.

But she wasn't done yet. "People string LED lights on their awnings and it looks so festive at night. Like Cinco de Mayo! And I met a man named Fitch who owns three Biscuitville Restaurants and his wife just passed." She tapped a finger on her mouth. "I wonder if I have time to make him brownies?" Before anyone could answer, she went on. "You would not believe how many are headed to Graceland and Branson, too. So we'll have RV friends on the road with us."

Linny was comforted by the idea. If they had a flat tire or tore off the top of the RV going under a too-short bridge, they could just pull over, keep the air conditioning cranked, and wait for one of Ruby's friends to pull over and help.

"We're getting our day organized." Linny pushed a bowl and a box of cereal toward Ruby. Maybe it'd sop up some of the caffeine. "We're staying here tonight, too?" she asked Dessie.

"Yup. We need two days to see Dollywood, and then we're off to Nashville and then Memphis." Dessie put her empty cereal bowl on the counter and studied her iPad and the brochures. "Now, it'll take us half an hour to get to the park. Some campgrounds are closer, but they were booked up by the time we made our plans. So the resort runs a courtesy shuttle twice a day. We'll take that and then ride trams to get around. We'll still walk a lot, so wear good shoes. What are our final decisions on what we want to do once we get to Dollywood?" she asked, pushing the brochures toward the others for a final look.

Ruby put down her spoon and gazed at them earnestly. "Let's spread our wings and fly. Let's say *yes* to things we'd usually say *no* to, and do new things. This is an *adventure* trip."

"What did you have in mind?" Dottie eyeballed her warily.

"I'm scared of roller coasters so I'm trying one," Ruby said, lifting her chin. "Closed spaces make me a bundle of nerves so I'll go on the ride through the abandoned coal mine."

"I'm not spreading wings and flying." Dottie patted her curls. "I just fixed my hair."

"I'll tag along with you, Mama," Linny said, trying to size up her mother's demeanor to see how much of her fearfulness about the trip lingered.

"Well, I'd be happy for the company," Dottie said and dabbed her mouth with a napkin. "This morning I'd like to spend a few hours at the Southern Gospel Museum and Hall of Fame."

Linny tried not to cringe. The twanging and refrains about going on to their home in the sky would be torture. "Great," she said gaily. "That would be fun."

Dottie eyed her. "You sure you aren't doing this just for me, are you?"

"I'm sure," Linny lied. The park was big. Mama would need her company.

Mama nodded, looking satisfied. "I also want to go see the blacksmith and the crafts. I hear they do amazing things with gourds."

"Gourds. Huh." Linny tried hard to muster some enthusiasm but failed. She glanced down at a train on the cover of a brochure and examined it. Now here was something that appealed to her. "Afterward, maybe we could ride the steam locomotive around the park."

"I didn't bring any Dramamine and trains can make my stomach flip," Dottie announced and made a delicate hand movement to convey upchucking.

"We all ought to do whatever suits our fancy," Dessie said firmly. "You girls start out at the museum, then Linny can go off on her own and Dottie can catch up with us. We'll call each other." She held up her phone. "Who wants to come with me to the candy store and the Sweet Shoppe later on? Their cinnamon buns are famous."

Dottie's eyes lit up. "I would."

"Me too," Ruby chimed in, smiling as she rose and stretched. "I'd like to ride the train with you, Linny." The blonde bounced on her toes a little, looking raring to go.

"So, that's our plan." Dessie rested her hands flat on the table for emphasis and turned to Linny. "After the museum you're off duty for the rest of the day. You do what you want and don't need to worry so much about your mama."

Linny sighed inwardly. The girls did not know Mama had almost chickened out of the trip.

"People pleasing is a bad habit." Dottie pursed her lips, looking virtuous. "I hope I raised a daughter who pays attention to what she wants."

Linny looked away. Neglecting her own needs was exactly what Mama had done for as long as Linny could remember. Dottie had tried to understand Daddy, turned the other cheek, and not raised Cain with him when she should have. He'd treated her shabbily and she'd just kept trying to be a better wife. Finally, she'd given up and gotten bitter, pouring all her energy into her daughters—and church.

Tidying up the breakfast dishes, Linny thought about it. Maybe she was being a people pleaser: trying to like action movies because the boys did, striving to be the perfect stepmother—except for the chicken potpie incident. She flushed, realizing she'd studied the Bodacious Bonus Moms blog on a daily basis like it was the Bible. Linny needed to just be herself and pay more attention to what she wanted. She'd practice on this trip.

After visiting the gospel music museum with Mama, Linny would try to be a carefree woman—a feather floating in the breeze. The whole idea made her jumpy, but she'd figure it out.

CHAPTER 7

The Delights of Dollywood

At the museum, Linny shifted her weight from one foot to another and tried to resist the impulse to check her phone while Dottie hummed along and sometimes broke into song while they listened to recordings of the gospel greats. Her mother leaned toward her and whispered reverently, "I can't believe we saw the Blackwood Brothers' bus."

After two and a half hours of hearing songs from the pioneers of gospel music, seeing the suits and dresses of the greats, watching interactive DVDs and animatronics of various performing artists, Dottie was finally ready to go. "That was the best museum I've ever visited." She gave Linny a knowing look. "You tried to hide it, but you were bored."

"A little," Linny admitted. "I like country music, but gospel's not my thing."

Her mother pressed her lips together. "Well, you go on. Skedaddle." She waved her away. "I'll catch up with the girls." Pulling her cell from her purse, she dismissed Linny.

Feeling a swell of freedom, Linny tried not to skip away. She had the whole day to herself. No family to feed, no snappy stepson, no laundry to do, no worries about work. Linny was footloose and fancy free. She'd not make a mental to-do list. She'd drift around, feather like.

After a busy day, their home sweet home on wheels had never looked so good. Linny fed twigs to tiny flames and started a crackling fire while the others pulled together supper. Munching hastily made sandwiches, they sat around the flickering fire and talked about their day.

Ruby crunched a potato chip and said, "The glassworks and the crafts were my favorites, except for the train ride with you, Linny."

Dessie took a long swallow of iced tea. "I liked the gristmill and the blacksmith."

"The Sweet Shoppe was very nice," Dottie said primly.

"We each ate two slices of apple pie with extra ice cream on top to fortify ourselves. We worked up appetites walking," Dessie explained, finishing the last bite of sandwich and patting her mouth with a napkin.

Dottie gazed at Linny suspiciously. "Did you get your hair wet today? It looks . . . disorganized."

"I got hot and walked through the spray grounds," Linny admitted, grinning sheepishly. "I was one of the only adults there. And earlier, I went on the tame kiddie rides like the Ferris wheel and the Lemon Twist. Again, one of the only adults there without a kid."

Dessie gazed at her admiringly. "Good for you, shug. What else did you do?"

"I visited the Wings of America Birds of Prey exhibit. They had amazing owls and two dozen bald eagles living in the eagle sanctuary," Linny said, still feeling thrilled at seeing them.

"What else did you do?" Ruby asked, grinning like she was proud of Linny.

Linny felt a wave of embarrassment for having done even more kid stuff but shook it off. Being a drifting feather was *fun*. "I saw the bubble show and rode the train for a second time." Linny grinned at them. "I had a really good time."

The next day the women stayed busy catching exhibits and sites they'd missed and attending the musicals. As the women wound their way back to the courtesy shuttle pickup spot, Dessie hummed one of the fifties songs from the show they'd just seen, Dreamland Drive-In.

"The roller coaster yesterday made me want to kiss the ground so I went on another one today," Ruby said, looking pleased with herself. "I also got to look inside Dolly's retired touring bus and saw a bunch of her actual makeup, a fabulous wig she wore, and her very own pink potpourri in the bathroom. That was so exciting!" Ruby said with feeling. "I could just imagine her walking in, tired after a show, and pulling off her sparkly boots."

The four of them found spots on benches and waited for the van that would ferry them back to the campground for their last night there.

Her phone sounded and Linny read the text, grinning. Jack had liked her messages and the photos she'd sent. He'd written: *U r having fun. Good! Will share pics with Neal. Miss u. XO*

"I looked at every big-haired blond lady in the place but never saw Dolly. I know she visits often." Ruby gave a wistful sigh and glanced around, taking one more visual sweep for her idol. Gasping, she stood and pointed a shaking finger at a small group just a stone's throw away.

Linny and the others rose excitedly and, shielding their eyes from the sun, gazed where Ruby was pointing and now waving madly.

A petite woman with blond hair piled high on her head walked by in sky-high heels, flanked by three men in suits who were bending toward her to hear every word she said. The blonde must have spotted Ruby's frantic waving and turned toward them. Spotting the women, she gave a dazzling smile and a friendly wave with bejeweled fingers.

"Oh my stars," Ruby gasped out, hand to her throat. "She was looking directly at me! I think she was wishing me good luck and telling me to shoot for the moon about this husband-finding project."

Linny wasn't sure about the telepathic eye message, but she'd just bet Dolly Parton would be encouraging. "She would wish you well."

"She'd tell you to go for it," Dessie said with a little fist pump.

Mama harrumphed and sat back down. "That probably wasn't Dolly Parton. Lots of women wear outfits like that and have that hairdo."

Ruby's mouth drooped.

Linny cut her eyes at her mother, trying to telegraph a stop-being-such-a-killjoy look.

Dottie caught the look and said in a conciliatory tone, "But then again, lots of women don't have that figure. I believe that was Dolly."

Linny smiled at Dottie gratefully, but her mother pretended not to see it.

Back at the Breathtaking Vista they all freshened up and put on more casual clothes for the evening. Sweatpants were de rigueur for campfire sitting, and Linny loved it. No confining waistbands, no pulling in her stomach to slide up a zipper. She threw on a sweatshirt and trotted down the stairs of the RV that was feeling more like home every day.

Ruby had laid the fire and lit the kindling and the crumpled newspaper underneath the wood. Linny pulled her canvas chair up next to Ruby's and they both watched the fire catch. Breathing in the smell of the woodsmoke, Linny felt a pang of sweet nostalgia, remembering fall days when she was a girl. She and Kate would rake leaves with their dad and he'd let them jump in the piles several times before he called them off, grinning as he raked the leaves back together and held a match to them. Despite his gradual disappearing act, Linny did have happy memories of her father.

Ruby sat and picked up her iPad, just as Dessie descended from the RV in her comfy clothes, rubbing her hands together gleefully. "I checked Ruby's accounts a minute ago and we have seventeen fish on the line."

"This is so much fun!" Ruby bounced up and down in her chair in excitement as she pulled up the websites. "Oooh. This fellow says I am 'the prettiest woman he's ever seen.' That is so sweet!"

Dessie skooched in and peered at the screen. "He claims he's fifty-five, but he looks like he shaved fifteen years off. And he smokes. You don't want that, do you?"

"Oh snap." Ruby's face fell and she hit Delete.

Carrying a canvas tote, Dottie slipped into her camp chair, bright-eyed at the prospect of sorting through more men. "Slow down, now. I don't want to miss out on anything." She reached in the tote and handed each of them a turkey wrap, bagel chips, paper plates, and bottles of water.

Linny took a too-large bite and chewed happily. Their meals so far had been simple but so good. Food always tasted better if someone else prepared it, she decided.

"How about this man? His headline says 'Roses and Romance.' That sounds lovely." Ruby took another bite of her wrap and kept reading. She scowled. "But just wait a dang minute. Underneath it says he 'wants a free-spirited and adventuresome woman who craves intimacy.' Does that mean what I think it means?" She glanced at the girls, her eyes narrowed.

Dessie hooked a thumb over her shoulder like an umpire. "He's out."

Ruby shook her head and hit Delete. "Oh my. This next fellow is from the single RVer site. He's cute and he's from North Carolina. He's a retired hospital administrator, sixty-two years old, and he's going to be camping at Branson right around the same time we are. Maybe I could meet him for a cup of coffee." She thrust the iPad at Dessie. "Here, read this to make sure I didn't miss any red flags."

Dessie daintily nabbed a second turkey wrap and skimmed the note. "Nope. The man looks pretty normal."

Ruby read the next profile and cocked a head at the girls. "A naturist is someone who likes flora and fauna, right?"

Linny tried to hide her smile. "A naturalist is into nature; a naturist is a nudist."

Ruby hit the Delete button so hard she had to examine her fingernail afterward. Luckily, nothing was broken.

After they winnowed the list down to six men and ate the brownies Dottie had pulled from her canvas bag, the three of them helped Ruby compose replies to her notes.

The moon rose and they all stared dreamily into the crackling fire.

Linny glanced at Dessie. "What was your husband like, Dess?"

"Husbands," she corrected with a smile. She smoothed back her wavy salt-and-pepper bob. "Well, my first husband and I only stayed married ten months. We just wanted different things." She shrugged.

"As in he wanted a man instead of a woman," Dottie clarified helpfully.

"That's true," Dessie said, not looking at all insulted. Her eyes danced. "Now my second husband, Del, was a different story. He was funny as could be, but he had an artistic side. He was a big ole softie. On one of our dates he saw a box turtle in the middle of a highway and stopped the car to move him so he wouldn't get run over. I decided to marry him right then."

"He was a photographer and you ended up working with him, right?" Linny asked, remembering.

"I did the advertising, the scheduling, and helped him with the shoots," Dessie said, nodding. "We did a lot of wedding and family photographs, but his bread-and-butter work was taking photos for senior pictures and high school yearbooks."

"Nowadays people take pictures digitally of every little thing, but back then having your picture taken by a professional was a big deal." Ruby nodded, getting a faraway look in her eye. "Girls would practice smiling in the bathroom mirror for weeks before the photographer came. They would roll their hair in giant hot rollers or iron it out with their mamas' irons. It was a big to-do."

Linny glanced at Dottie. "Mama, did you practice smiling?" she asked in a teasing tone.

"I didn't have time for such foolishness," Dottie said tartly.

But Dessie whooped with laughter. "She was a hot-roller girl. She had the prettiest hair, all long and golden. And she was so cheerful, her nickname was sunny. The boys in the senior class were all in love with her."

Linny had to work to keep her mouth from dropping open. "Hunh." With her ashy blond hair and her even features, her mother was an attractive woman, but she'd seemed so serious for much of Linny's life. She couldn't picture her as sunny whom the boys all loved.

Her mother caught her gaze. "Good marriages make you happy. Bad ones wring the joy right out of you," she said with a trace of sadness in her eyes.

"But even in good marriages you have times when you want to wring his neck," Ruby reminded them.

"God's own truth," Dessie agreed. "Women don't talk about the times you look at your own husband and just want to pinch him."

Dottie weighed in. "Boyd could snore loud as a freight train, act like I was a silly woman, and you didn't want to see him eat a barbecue sandwich." She shuddered.

Linny listened, rapt. Mama and her girlfriends were just getting more and more interesting.

"One time I wished Pete would drown," Ruby said blithely. "When we had our little boat he would turn into Captain Bligh, yelling at me and telling me what to do even though I knew what to do. One time I couldn't stand it anymore and just dove off the boat and swam all the way to shore. It was a good little ways, too. He putt-putted along behind me, begging me to get back on board but trying to keep his voice down so the other men in boats wouldn't hear him. The thought of drowning *him* crossed my mind." She chuckled, looking like she was recalling a fond memory. "You don't read about that in Oprah's magazine," she said with a wry grin.

"You sure you want a new husband?" Dottie asked.

"I do," said Ruby with a dreamy look.

"Well, we're going to find you one, shug." Dessie patted her on the arm.

"What's Perry like, Dess?" Linny asked. Del would be a tough act to follow.

"He's awfully good to me," she said, shaking her head in wonder at her good luck. "I said the RV didn't have a television and that we'd be mostly watching movies on our iPads or reading. So he ordered me a whole box of movies and books I'd said I might like. He remembered that from when we were on the cruise and had one of those first-date conversations, when you talk about what kinds of books and movies you like. Thoughtful." She pushed back her bangs. "He cares what happens in my life. He's gruff, he's a churchgoer but not a holier-than-thou type. But there is one problem. . . ." She drew in a breath and blew it out slowly.

Ruby jumped in. "Perry was married to a Miss New Hanover County for thirty years," she said to Linny, looking solemn. "She left him, but still . . ."

Mama and her friends exchanged worried glances.

Not sure what that meant, Linny must have looked baffled.

Ruby explained. "They grow a lot of pretty women in the Wilmington area. All peaches-and-cream type beauty queens headed to medical school with talents like opera singing."

"Exactly." Dessie's face fell. "I've seen pictures. She was one of those very pretty, perfectly put-together wives. And look at me." She turned up her hands and shook her head. "I hardly wear makeup. I play tennis and my hair stays a little green from my water aerobics classes. I do my PIing when Mary Catherine calls on me. I'm more of a plain Jane, wash-and-wear lady. When is he going to wake up and decide he needs more color and grace in his life?"

"You're perfect just the way you are," Ruby said staunchly. "He sees that."

Linny gazed at her. Dessie was a wholesome kind of pretty. With her smattering of freckles, expressive brown eyes, and trim figure, she looked approachable, competent, kind. She added her two cents. "Jack's ex-wife is a size two, white-blond beauty with one of those raspy, baby-girl voices that make men drool." Editing out *who is currently crying on my husband's shoulder and may be trying to worm her way back closer to him*, she blew out a breath.

Ruby looked thoughtful. "Maybe some men want women who are kind and companionable instead of extra young and glamorous."

Dottie snorted. "They do not. They still want glamour." She smoothed the poufy curls on the side of her head. "I try my best to be alluring for Mack, with the new clothes and the cheek-contouring and such."

Linny had to work to keep from rolling her eyes.

Dottie examined Dessie. "Next time we get to a store, let's buy you some new clothes and gussy you up. Let's give Miss New Hanover County a run for her money."

The beauty queen had divorced Perry, so technically she wasn't interested in a run for the money, but Linny decided not to quibble.

But Ruby looked delighted at the prospect of helping with Dessie's makeover. "Leopard print. Men love leopard print. And you need high heels and to start wearing more color."

Dessie nodded uncertainly. "Well, if you think it would help."

"It would," Dottie said with all the authority of a woman who claimed she wasn't dating.

Linny crossed her arms and gave Dottie an appraising look. "How about you, Mama? You seem to be palling around an awful lot with Mack if he's just a friend."

Her mother gave an exaggerated yawn. "I'm getting sleepy. I need to call Mack before it gets too late." Phone in hand, she walked away from the others for some privacy.

Linny strolled to the vacant campsite beside theirs and made a FaceTime call to Jack, her heart beating double-time in anticipation of seeing his sweet face. The men had just arrived in Arizona. With their plans to camp in the hills to get the highest altitude and least light pollution for their stargazing, who knew when they'd get cell signal again. "Hey, sweets," she said as he picked up. His face came into view and the background blurred, as if he was ducking into a quiet corner.

Linny could hear airport noises of flights being called and travelers talking.

"Hey, Lin," he said with that long, slow smile. "How are you, honey?"

"I'm good." She smiled. "How was your flight?"

"Long, but we're finally in Tucson," he said with a tired smile. "We're at baggage claim and then we'll pick up the rental car." Jack paused and seemed to be listening to a murmuring. His mouth quirked in a smile and looked at Linny. "Neal wants to say hello."

Neal's face came into view. Looking like a little professor in his horn-rimmed glasses, he spoke in a serious tone. "Hey. Snakes are out this time of year. Watch out for copperheads and the rattlers. Stay away from rotted stumps. Everybody says suck the venom out, but that's just not true. Take a Benadryl and go to the emergency room if you get bitten."

Before she could thank him for the info, he swam out of view and Jack was back, his eyes twinkling. "You got another public service announcement. That was guy code for *be careful, because I like you and might even love you.*" Jack's eyes twinkled.

"I'm starting to get that," she said, laughing softly, touched by Neal's concern. Linny heard a beep and then another. "Do you need to take that call?"

His brows furrowed. "Nah. That'll be Vera double-checking that we got here in one piece. She can call back."

The beeping started again. His ex-wife was simply redialing when Jack didn't pick up. "Pretty anxious to talk to you all," Linny observed.

A look of annoyance flashed across Jack's face. "She already called once as the plane taxied in. She's nervous about Neal's being so far away from home, and also about the rough camping."

Linny thought about it, feeling the prickle of irritation grow. "But Neal's been away from home before. He flew to Florida to see his grandparents and he skied in Aspen. You two rough camped this spring."

Jack shook his head. "I know, I know, but . . ." He stopped as the phone beeped yet again.

Unblinking, Linny just gazed at his image, not saying a word.

"I probably need to take this, Lin," Jack apologized. "Can I call you back in a minute?"

"That's okay," Linny said with a cool nod. She wasn't going to throw a hissy fit while she was almost two thousand miles away and they were about to be out of cell range for several days. "I probably need to get back."

Jack's face fell. "I'm sorry, Lin. I don't know why . . ."

The phone beep interrupted them again and Linny made herself smile. "Call me when things settle down and you get a signal. You two have a great time."

Jack looked crestfallen as she ended the call.

Good, Linny thought meanly. Let him have a long gabfest with his difficult ex-wife.

The mosquitoes descended in squadrons and Linny, Dessie and Ruby retreated inside to the living room. Linny slid into her folddown bed, feeling sorry for herself, when Dottie stalked into the RV after making her call to Mack. Her hands were bunched into fists at her side.

"What's going on, Mama?" Linny asked, sitting up straight in her alarm and bumping her head on the counter.

"You won't believe this. Mack has gotten casseroles from two different women since I've been away. Trina Baldwin sent him over that awful tuna fish, noodle, and potato chip dish she brought to Richmond Jenkins's funeral. Martine Galax brought him that beef tostado and tomato deal that she brings to potlucks at the church. It is somewhat tasty but will cause his reflux to flame right up." She flexed her fingers in the air to demonstrate the shooting flames, then shook her head, looking grim. "I just can't believe the tackiness. I am out of state, not dead." Dottie glared at each of the others, as though daring them to challenge her.

"Maybe they thought they were doing you all a favor and making sure Mack didn't starve while you were gone," Linny said hurriedly, hoping her mother wasn't reverting back into her old, grumpy church lady ways.

"But they're not really her friends, Linny. They're more acquaintances," Ruby explained. "And they're widows, and you all know how widows can be."

All four had been widowed and *not* been man-chasing opportunists but nodded solemnly at the wisdom of that statement.

Dessie leaned forward and gave Dottie a comforting pat. "I do think it's tacky, but I'm sure you're comforted by the fact that Mack is really just a pal."

Dottie glared at her friend, but Dessie just looked at her innocently. "Tacky," she repeated and shook her head reprovingly.

With a haughty sniff, Dottie swept back out of the RV, cell phone clutched in her hand. Linny was brushing her teeth when Mama clumped back up the stairs, the pep back in her step.

Linny rinsed her mouth and looked at her inquiringly. "Anything new, Mama?"

"I called Mack back and dropped a hint that he needed to stop acting so grateful for the casseroles and just eat frozen dinners or pick up meals at the drive through at Chick-fil-A like a grown man." She nodded, looking proud of her tact.

"How did he take that?" Linny asked.

"Oh, he was grateful for the friendly suggestion," Dottie said, looking bland as she smoothed her hairdo.

The next morning the women had a leisurely breakfast, having decided there was no need to race to leave. After the blueberry pancakes were gone Dessie cocked her head and looked at the others, a glint in her eye. "With all this talk about spreading our wings and flying, I want to take a bike ride before we go. They rent them at the office. Haven't ridden one in years and I think it'd be fun to take a spin around the little lake." She moved to the sofa, slipped off her sandals, and pulled on running shoes.

Ruby smiled gamely. "I'll come. The paths are paved and the ground is level."

Linny glanced out at the lake, glittering blue in the morning sun. "I'm up for it, too."

"Come on, then." Dessie grinned and grabbed bottles of water from the fridge.

"Wait for me," Mama called, slipping on her fanny pack.

Linny tried not to look shocked as she smoothed on sunscreen and pulled on a ball cap. Mama on a bike was something she had to see.

After a few practice laps in a packed dirt driveway where the fall wouldn't be so hard if they tipped over, the women began their lakefront ride looking wobbly. They all gained confidence and began to ride more steadily.

"Whee," Ruby called, picking up some speed. "When I was a girl we rode bikes everywhere."

The women gave and got friendly waves as they cruised by the campers at the sites right on the lakefront.

The air smelled of cooking sausage and woodsmoke. Linny smiled at a couple sitting side by side in their camp chairs, sipping coffee and reading, their Chihuahua asleep at their feet. A young father helped his small son feed bread to a duck. A white-haired woman sat beside what could have been her gangly granddaughter and laughed as they pedaled a paddleboat around in a circle. A man as tall as a pro-basketball player walked a Pomeranian wearing a tiny plaid bow tie. Camping was peaceful, Linny decided. She liked it.

"I wish we could wake up to this view every morning." Dessie swept an arm toward the dancing waves and the cattails and the graceful grasses that rimmed the little lake.

Linny felt the breeze caress her skin and her hair blow back. She grinned, thrilled at how little effort she had to expend pedaling to get the bike just whizzing along.

Dottie rolled along as slowly, steadily, and grandly as a luxury liner leaving the New York docks for a transatlantic voyage.

The sun was climbing in the sky by the time they dropped the bikes back at the office. Linny glanced at the others. All were pink-cheeked, windblown, and looking very pleased with themselves. Ruby, Dessie, and Mama lingered in the office to look at postcards and T-shirts, but Linny hoofed it back to the RV. She wanted to check messages before they packed up and left the Wi-Fi at the Breathtaking Vista.

Pulling off the lanyard she'd looped around her neck, Linny held the door to insert the key in the lock, but the door just pushed open. She gasped. She could have sworn she locked it.

But after one step inside Linny's legs and arms turned to water. Drawers were pulled open halfway and clothes hung out the side of Ruby's suitcase, but Dessie's expensive camera was still on her bedside table. Linny's eyes flew right to where they kept their valuables. Their purses were still tucked in the cubby where the women stowed them. Linny grabbed hers and checked, her mouth dry and her heart banging, but her wallet, credit cards, and cash were exactly where they belonged. She looked in the other purses and gasped. No money or credit cards in any of the wallets. Her friends had been robbed.

Heart pounding, she looked around the room again. The dinette looked different. The smiling ceramic kitty that contained cash for their trip was missing.

Linny's head began to throb above her right temple. The sense of peace she'd come to feel in their little home was gone. She stalked around, her eyes sweeping the carpet and furnishings for clues. Their iPads and phones were lined up on the counter, charging.

By the time the others trailed back inside, Linny had already made calls. The police and Mrs. Don Boyer were on their way.

"Your money and credit cards are gone. The kitty's gone. I'm so sorry." Linny put her hands on her head. "I thought I locked the door, but the dead bolt must not have clicked."

"That just steams my grits that somebody just slipped in and helped himself to our kitty money." Dottie's mouth was a thin, straight line. "But honey, we didn't lose anything in our wallets."

Linny stared at her uncomprehendingly.

Dottie turned her fanny pack around front and patted it. "All my money and cards are in here."

Ruby reached down the front of her shirt, rummaged around, and pulled out a wad of cash and credit cards wrapped tidily in a rubber band. "My valuables stay in my bra for safekeeping."

Linny looked at Dessie, who lifted her shirt from her waistband and pointed to a tan money belt. "Old habits die hard. Had my purse stolen once and I decided never again."

Linny shook her head, her knees weak with relief. "So all we lost was what was in the kitty: a few hundred dollars." Linny gave them a crooked smile. "You all are wily foxes." But then her heart lurched. Her rings. She and Dessie had taken a late-night dip in the pool before bed last night. Afraid her rings might slip off her finger in the water, she'd removed them and put them in a glass dish on the kitchen counter. Scurrying over, her eyes darted around. The glass dish was empty. She moved the toaster, lifted the drain board, and reached down the sink. Nothing. Linny put her hands to her flaming cheeks. "They stole my rings!" she cried.

CHAPTER 8

Rolling on to Music City

Linny's wedding rings were made from the emeralds Jack and Neal had unearthed at a mine in Hiddenite, a small town in the North Carolina mountains. Linny thought about the hours the two of them had sifted through buckets of dirt, their thrill at finding the stones, and their excitement at working with the jeweler to fashion the rings. She remembered their barely concealed elation when she'd opened the box, and Jack's tender look when he'd slipped the rings on her finger. She put her hands over her face and burst into tears.

Dottie gathered her into a hug. "There, there, sugar. It's a hard thing, but it's not the end of the world."

The other women murmured consoling words, but Linny still felt bereft. How could she have been so careless as to not lock a door? With her rings gone and her sense of safety violated, how was she going to stay in this RV for the last few days of this trip? She wanted to go home. All she wanted to do was talk to Jack and let him comfort her. But he was clear across the United States and out of cell range.

With a tough-as-nails look in her eyes, Dessie threw back her shoulders, grabbed her phone, and announced, "I'm going to scout out this place for clues and suspects."

A scowling Ruby leaped to her feet. "I'm coming with you. We can talk to my friends at nearby campsites to see if they saw anything suspicious."

The two marched out.

"I need to call Kate," Linny said, brushing the streaming tears from her face with the back of her wrist.

"Of course you do," Mama said in a soothing tone and handed her a box of Kleenex. "Go on out to the picnic table where you can get you a little privacy and I'll bring you some iced tea."

She slumped onto the picnic table and dialed her sister. When Kate answered Linny spilled her story, brushing away the tears starting to trail down her cheek again. "Someone has my rings. I keep picturing some thug's teenaged girlfriend who'll wear them on her right hand while she's shoplifting makeup from the drugstore. They're *my* rings."

"I know, honey, I know," Kate said and took one of her Tai Chi–inspired deep breaths. "Would it help you to picture a desperate older man stealing it to pay for his poor wife's medication that they can't afford?"

Linny thought about it. "Not really."

Kate sighed. "Wouldn't help me either, but it was worth a try." She paused. "I've been reading the teachings of the Dalai Lama."

Linny sat up straighter and felt chagrined. Though typically a voracious reader, these days life was going too fast for her to concentrate enough to read a book, let alone a serious one. The last thing she'd read had been in a *Star* magazine Mary Catherine had passed on to her: an article about how starlets attained the Kim Kardashian rear end.

"You're probably having a she's-so-deep-and-I'm-not moment, but cut it out," Kate said firmly. "A new woman in our book club picked the book and we all grumbled about having to read it, but it's really good. Anyhow, the Dalai Lama says we need to become detached from worldly goods and treasure the jewels of inner peace and love."

Linny thought about it for a long moment, feeling some of her racing anxiety quiet.

"So he would say a ring is just a symbol of your love and that your love stays strong with or without the ring. He'd say let no one and nothing rob you of your peace." Kate sighed. "Now, having said that enlightened stuff, I need to go tidy up Miss Ivy and prepare to yell at Jerry. He high-tailed it out the door to Lowe's for a sudden and urgent errand because the baby pooed in her diaper and he didn't want to change her."

Linny burst out laughing. "Love you, Kate."

"Love you back."

Linny stood and rolled her shoulders to stretch them out. She felt a little better. As much sentimental attachment as she had to the rings, she could work on thinking about them as just things. She'd loved them while she had them. Her phone signaled and her mouth crooked up as she read the text from Kate: *One more thing. Go find a health food store, buy white sage, and smudge the heck out of that RV ASAP.*

By the time Dessie and Ruby got back, Officer Delmarco, a young policeman from the Pigeon Forge Police Department with an earnest air about him, had arrived. He asked the women questions and took careful notes. After searching the RV and the perimeter for clues, Officer Delmarco shook his head, handed them his card, and promised to be in touch.

Mrs. Don Boyer stopped by, wringing her hands, apologizing profusely, and begging them not to write bad reviews online about the Breathtaking Vista.

When they'd both left the four women sat around the dining room table looking dejected.

"When Mrs. Don said this had never happened before in the six years they've been owners, I believed her," Dessie said. "Her eyes weren't darting back and forth like liars' eyes do."

"Plus the hyperventilating," Ruby, the budding junior PI added. "Seems like liars wouldn't have to breathe into a paper bag."

"You two Jessica Fletchers come up with any clues outside?" Dottie asked.

"Not a one," Dessie said, her shoulders slumping. "No one has seen anyone or anything suspicious." She glanced at each of them darkly. "I just wonder if this deal was an inside job."

Glumly, the women finished packing up and got ready to leave. Usually when they set off for the day, their spirits were high. They giggled about something funny that had happened the night before and speculated wildly about upcoming adventures. But today they were subdued as they buttoned up the RV. The burglary had deflated their spirits.

Clinking a spoon on a saucepan to get their attention, Linny looked at the others. "I have a thought for the day. Kate says no matter what was stolen, no one can rob us of the most important thing we have: our inner peace and our love for one another." Nervously, she glanced at the others to gauge how her spiritual talk was being received. The others gaped at her.

Dessie cleared her throat. "Very deep for early in the day, but I agree. Let's leave all that mess behind us and enjoy every minute of this trip."

Her mother nodded and said staunchly, "That's what Jesus would say to do."

Ruby joined the pep talk. "We're on a grand adventure with amazing friends. It's going to be a beautiful day and we're headed to Music City!" She stood and put her hands on her hips. "Hey, let's all wear our SWAT Team T-shirts. We haven't all worn them on the same day and we could kind of make a statement about..." She paused and glanced at the ceiling.

"Solidarity," Dottie said firmly and nodded. "I'll get mine."

Linny breathed a sigh of relief as she pulled out of the Breathtaking Vista, now dubbed the Money and Ring Taking Vista by the women. Mama, her co-driver, slipped on her Ray Charles sunglasses, turned on Waze, and buckled in. She called back to Dessie, who was seated in the back. "So what's our plan, Dess?"

"Nashville is about four hours away. We'll take our time, not try to set any land speed records and get there around suppertime. Our campground is just fifteen minutes from downtown. We can Uber to the sites we want to see. Tomorrow we'll visit the Johnny Cash Museum, the Ryman Auditorium and ride out to the Grand Ole Opry." Dessie smiled like the cat who'd found the cream. "We splashed out and booked a backstage tour."

"Oh my!" Ruby sounded thrilled.

Before they knew it they were on the outskirts of Nashville. The women said they needed to stock up on food and a few supplies, so Linny wheeled into a Walmart Supercenter. Still nervous about trying to maneuver a twenty-five-foot RV in tight spaces, she came to a stop a safe half a football field away from the cars. She was happy to stay in the RV while the others shopped. Enjoying the time by herself, she phoned Officer Delmarco see if there'd been any developments in their case. He wasn't in, but she left him a voice mail.

She sank back in her seat and felt a sinking pang of homesickness. The Avery men would be out of touch for much of the next few days. She rubbed her face with her hands, a knot forming in her stomach as she thought about how she'd left things with Jack. Did Vera see Linny's being out of town as an opportunity? Was she using her confabs about Neal and their trip to insinuate herself more and more into Jack's life? Linny gave herself a mental shake. No sense getting all revved up about it, but still, she was feeling unsettled.

A bracing dose of Mary Catherine's bright self would be a tonic. Linny picked up the phone and dialed.

A woman with an upbeat voice identified herself as Shania, the new office manager, and asked her to hold for Mary Catherine.

Her friend came on the line and without a hello said, "I've missed you. Just had a client cancel. Talk to me."

Linny exhaled, smiling. "I've missed you, too." She stretched out her legs and leaned back, ready for a chat. "How is Shania working out for you? Are you being nice?"

"Shania is both chirpy and bossy," Mary Catherine pretended to grouse.

"So she's working out great," Linny said knowingly.

"Yeah," Mary Catherine admitted.

"What's been going on with you all?" Linny crossed her legs.

"Work is way too busy. Mike's painting some fancy coating on the floor of the garage. Dare brought his new girlfriend Breeze home for supper. He didn't bother to tell me she was vegan." Mary Catherine blew out a frustrated sigh. "Mike had grilled steaks and I'd whipped up au gratin potatoes and even made a cheesecake. All she ate was some green beans and a few pine nuts I'd used in a recipe last year. No wonder she's skinny as a twig."

"Do you like her?" Linny asked.

"I do," Mary Catherine said. "She's the smart, quiet type and she gives Dare a hard time. Always a good trait in a woman. Give me the lowdown on the trip. Are you and Dottie getting along? Is it peaceful, bucolic? Maybe a little dull?"

"Hardly," Linny said ruefully. "This morning someone stole my wedding band and engagement ring." She filled her friend in.

"Sorry about your rings. I really am. But you can't let the trashy people get you down. I work with them every day so I know. You *cannot* let them get you down," Mary Catherine said firmly. "Other than that, how is the trip going?"

Linny smiled, reassured. "Everybody's getting along pretty well.

Mama's still claiming she and Mack are just old-shoe kinds of pals, never mind that they've been madly dating for months." Linny paused. "Ruby is on a manhunt for a new husband and has been hitting the internet hard and filling up her shopping cart with husband prospects. We're helping screen the men. Dessie has decided she's going to start being more of a femme fatale because her new beau Perry the junk man's ex-wife was a Miss New Hanover County."

"Good grief." Mary Catherine burst out laughing. "There goes my pretty picture of a peaceful, pajama-party-and-girl-talk trip. I'm around men so much, I guess I'd kind of dressed up a girls' trip in my mind."

Linny grinned. "On another note, did you know that if you can't find a campsite, you can park your RV overnight in most Walmart parking lots?" Linny watched the shoppers pulling in and out of the parking lot, a safe distance away from where she'd parked.

"Fascinating," Mary Catherine said drily. "You're turning into a real camping girl. You'll have to fill me in on everything when you get back."

"I will," Linny promised and saw Mama and her friends walking toward the RV, their arms laden with grocery bags and laughing about something. "Oops, the women are back. I need to run." Promising to call Mary Catherine when she got home, Linny ended the call.

The women clomped into the RV.

"The SWAT Team T-shirts were a hit. Some man insisted we go in front of him at the checkout. I didn't have the heart to tell him we weren't officers of the law," Ruby said, easing her handful of grocery bags onto the table.

"Show me what you bought." Linny grinned at the three shoppers.

"We stuck to our lists and tried to stay within a budget," Dessie said, unpacking. "Milk, cheese, bread, tuna, lunch meat, push-up bra, lip plumper..." She shot a sheepish glance at Linny. "The girls made me buy those last two items."

"I only got necessities," Mama said, looking self-righteous as she pulled out toilet tissue, marshmallows, two half gallons of ice cream, caramel popcorn, a bag of pork rinds, and a big box of Luzianne tea. "We were dangerously low on tea bags," she explained.

"I mainly focused on Dessie. I always try to help others," Ruby said virtuously. Her purchases included avocados, a bag of tortilla chips, a box of false eyelashes, a leopard print skirt, and a red silky shirt with a plunging neckline.

Linny shook her head and grinned as she sat back down in the driver's seat. "We have one more stop. Kate says we need to hit a health food store to find sage to burn and get the thief's bad energy out of the RV."

"Sounds like Episcopalian claptrap, but if it makes you feel better, okay," Dottie said, sighing like a martyr as she opened the pork rinds and popped one in her mouth.

"I'll find a store." Dessie grabbed her phone and started tapping. "There's a Healthy World just eight miles away in the next town," she announced.

They set off. Linny clutched the wheel and fought heart palpitations as she navigated alarmingly narrow streets and squeaked under one low-clearance bridge with no height restriction sign. She blew out a breath when they finally wheeled into the parking lot of the shopping center. Dessie jumped out to buy the sage.

"We're supposed to open all the windows and doors," Linny said, and the other two women hopped to.

When Dessie got back, bag in hand, Linny dropped the bundle in a bowl and tried to remember what Kate had said when she'd smudged her aqua trailer the year before. The pressure was on with the three women lined up beside one another on the couch, looking nervous and watching as she lit the small bundle. Linny paused. Seemed like a pretty personal thing to do with her mama and her friends, but burning sage would make her feel like she was reclaiming control. Glancing at her bare left hand, she pushed her shoulders back and started smudging. Waving the earthy tang of smoke into every space, Linny said, "We call upon God, the angels, and the universe to clear out negative energies and purify our home. We invite in positive energy, light, peace, and calm."

"And keep the creeps out of our RV," Dessie added.

"Amen," Mama said loudly.

Soon they were on the road again. Linny adjusted the big sun visor and Dessie, her second-shift co-driver, checked the Waze map route against the Triple A route and nodded approvingly.

Ruby called to them from the sofa. "I saved up all my new responses from the love websites on my desktop. I've got enough battery to read them to you and you can tell me what you think."

"Good. Let's hear some," Dottie said, as she knitted away, her needles making quiet clicking sounds that Linny heard from up-front and somehow found comforting.

Ruby clapped, sounding excited as she began. "This fellow is named Charles and he's from... Bangor, Maine. Hmmm. Must be freezing up there." She leaned in to look more closely at the screen. "It looks like he wrote this at two in the morning. He says he loves the institution of marriage. Hmmm. He must love it. He's been married four times and has eleven grandchildren. LOL." She frowned, looking baffled. "What's the LOL for? Is what he said funny?"

"Delete," Dottie said firmly.

Ruby got rid of him with an emphatic click of a keystroke. "Now this fellow says he's an incredibly successful businessman who wants a confident and fun woman to travel with him to Italy, Greece, Bora Bora, and other dream destinations." She sighed, and said, "I've always wanted to go to those places. I think I should write him."

"He's throwing out a lot of bait there," Dottie said. "Did he say anything about what you wrote about yourself or your interests? Did he say why he liked your write-up?"

"Go, Mama," Linny called over her shoulder.

"Maybe because I look confident and fun," Ruby said, sounding a little miffed.

"Well, it can't hurt to drop him a note," Dessie said. "But ask him why he liked your profile. Let's make sure he's not a Casanova doing some cutting and pasting."

They ruled out a man who had been separated for three years and the man who was looking for a lady to change my mind about all women being evil.

"This gentleman is not into head games," Ruby read and giggled as she hit Delete. "Darn. I just love head games."

Dottie weighed in. "Mack's dance instructor buddies from the cruise ships say it's just as rough out there in the dating world for middle-aged men. He says the women have gotten into money messes and need to be bailed out or have sons who just got out of rehab or bankruptcy who are living with them or want a man to slip right into the old shoes of their late husbands." She heaved a dramatic sigh. "Thank goodness I'm not in the dating world."

The silence spun out until Dessie finally spoke. "Then what exactly are you and Mack doing, Dottie? Seems like you're eating out at fun restaurants, seeing shows, playing pickle ball, and going to church. These days, is that not called dating?"

Dottie's needles clicked away faster. "I'm not sure what we're doing," she admitted. "We're keeping each other company is all I know."

"Well, there's not a thing in the world wrong with that," Ruby said. "Just because I'm getting married doesn't mean the rest of you need to get married. You all can just let the wind blow you wherever you want to go."

Dessie looked over her shoulder and said firmly, "Nobody on this bus is blowing in the wind, Ruby. Dottie and I are just taking our time and getting to know these fellows. Getting married isn't the hard part. Mr. Bangor Cabin would probably marry you next week. Finding a man who'll make you happy: now that's the hard part."

Her mouth in a thin line, Ruby rose and flounced off, which was hard to do because the RV was so short. From a seat in the sofa that converted to her bed, she clicked on her seat belt, pulled out a copy of *Good Housekeeping*, and rustled the pages of the magazine as she aggressively flipped through it.

Thursday morning Ruby had recovered from her snit and Dessie was at the wheel as they motored away from the Nashville skyline toward Memphis. Though Linny and the others were all tired, they chatted animatedly, rehashing the highlights of their visit to Music City.

Ruby lay stretched out on the couch of the RV with a seat belt fastened cattywampus around her waist. She sighed happily. "The Opry was amazing. Can you believe we saw Blake Shelton, Larry Gatlin, and that darling Scotty McCreery?"

"All fine examples of American manhood," Dottie said staunchly, as if she was admiring the patriotism of the group of singers instead of their collective hunkiness.

Linny shook her head from her co-driver's seat. "I always liked Johnny Cash, but now that we went to that museum, I'm deeply in like with him. Deeply," she said reverently.

"Listening to those recordings and reading old letters he wrote to June. So soulful," Ruby said wistfully and put a hand to her heart. "That was a big love."

"No man ever wrote me letters like that," her mother said quietly.

"Maybe Mack will," Linny said.

"Mack is just a friend," her mother reminded her.

"A friend who calls or FaceTimes you once or twice a day," Dessie said drily. She glanced at the now wrinkled-looking itinerary in her hand and sounded bemused. "On to Elvis and Graceland. I hadn't planned it this way, but this is the hunky male singer leg of our trip."

"It is." Linny smiled. "What were you all's favorite Elvis songs?"

Dessie spoke with no hesitation, "Mine was 'That's All Right.' Oh my goodness, he was something." She pretended to fan herself with her hand.

"'Love Me Tender.'" Ruby gave a swoony sigh. "That one just melted me."

"Mine was 'How Great Thou Art.' That man had a fine gospel voice," Dottie said firmly. Pausing for a moment, she admitted, "I also loved 'Can't Help Falling in Love.' It just got me the way he couldn't help himself."

Linny glanced back at her, understanding her desire for that intensity. "I love that song, too, Mama."

"I heard Elvis bought Graceland when he was young, just after he started to make it big," Ruby said.

"That's true." Dessie nodded. "I read it online. He bought the mansion and the thirteen acres of grounds in 1957 for about one hundred thousand dollars."

Linny thought about it. "So why was Graceland on y'alls bucket list? Is it because you loved the music and Elvis was such a heartthrob?"

The three women were quiet for a moment.

"He was a good bit older than the three of us," Dessie said slowly. "But his voice was amazing and he was pure breath taking with those heavy-lidded eyes and that curled lip. I could see why the girls screamed and fainted when they saw him perform."

"He was a good-lookin' man," Dottie admitted. "But I also liked that he was Southern and he was good to his mama and daddy. He got mixed up with that fast crowd, but he was a Christian man at heart, and his roots were in gospel music." She gave a swooning sigh. "He was a real original."

Ruby weighed in. "I loved his romance with Priscilla. Imagine, him falling in love with her when she was so young and then waiting to marry her. It was the romance of a lifetime."

Until they divorced, Linny thought but didn't say. She was determined to keep the mood happy.

After the tour of Graceland, the four women wearily climbed back on the RV.

"I can't believe I'm saying this, but I'm officially Elvised out." Dessie collapsed on the sofa in the back.

"That was so much fun, but my dogs are barking." Ruby sat, slipped off her tennis shoes, and rubbed her feet. "Can you believe we lucked out and met those men who were going to compete in the Elvis Tribute Artist Contest this year? They looked so much like the King, it was like seeing his ghost."

Dessie nabbed a drink from the refrigerator, sat down heavily, and took a long swallow. "I just loved that place. Wore me plumb out, but going through the house and the museum and seeing his car and his planes—we were just walking through history."

Linny lay down on the carpeted floor and groaned. "My back hurts, but I've seen the Jungle Room."

As dusk gathered, the four of them sat in their camp chairs watching the flames of their campfire, finishing off the last of what they referred to as the *Last Supper*. Linny was flying home in the morning. The grilled chicken, baked potatoes, green bean casserole, and pecan pie topped with vanilla ice cream had been delicious. They all were subdued: tired from the day and aware that this was Linny's last night of the trip with them.

"That was a fine meal, Ruby," Linny said, wishing she hadn't eaten seconds on the pie. "With our busy schedule I can't believe you pulled that meal off. You went to an awful lot of trouble."

"Don't be silly," Ruby said with a little wave. "We couldn't let you go without a special send-off supper."

Dottie gave Linny a brave smile. "I can't believe you're leaving us tomorrow. It just won't seem right without you."

"You've been good company," Dessie said.

Linny glanced fondly at the now familiar faces, all looking relaxed and flushed by the heat of the fire. She'd gotten to know each woman better—including her mother—and grown to like them more and more. She'd enjoyed Ruby's bubbling personality and bright optimism, Dessie's quiet calm and keen observations about people, and Mama's dry wit and sense of adventure. As excited as she was about getting home and seeing Jack and Neal, Linny felt sad, too. "I had a great time. Thank you for letting me tag along." She raised her glass of wine. "A toast?"

The other women smiled and raised their glasses.

Linny said, "To the SWAT Team having even more wonderful adventures on the rest of the trip, and to having fun with the men who will be joining you. Send pictures, FaceTime me, and we'll leave the front-porch light on for you back in Willow Hill."

They touched glasses and drank.

Determined to lighten the mood, Linny looked at Ruby. "How's your fishing coming? What kind of nibbles are you getting from the notes you answered?"

"Lots of nibbles and bites," she said brightly. "Mr. Successful Businessman—who is named Byron, by the way—has written me twice. He's on his way to Dubai for a business meeting. He's going to call me as soon as he gets back to the States. Those were his words: back to the States. He sounds so international."

Dottie gave her a sideways glance. "What does he do for a living?" she asked.

Ruby looked away for a moment. "I can't remember. I'm getting them all mixed up."

Dottie popped the last of her sandwich in her mouth. "Could be all hat and no cattle."

"You don't know that, Dottie. Just because of your experience with men doesn't mean that..." Ruby's eyes widened and she sat up straight in her chair and pointed excitedly at a couple approaching. "That's that Hal and Letty. He told me they were headed to Graceland today, too." She stood and waved madly. "Hey, Letty! Hey, Hal!"

Hal gave a friendly wave and walked over, but his wife hung back.

Ruby's face flushed and she smiled brightly.

"Hey there, Miss Ruby." Hal gave her a boyish grin and quickly turned to the others. "Evening, ladies."

As Hal chatted with the women about their Graceland tour, Linny watched Letty from behind her sunglasses. The woman seemed to be chewing double-time on the piece of gum in her mouth. Despite today's ninety-four-degree heat, she wore a long-sleeved cotton dress that looked too big on her, and her hand gripped the purse she wore strapped diagonally across her chest. Maybe she was afraid she'd get her purse stolen because the four of them had been burgled, but still . . . There was something off about the woman.

"Your cookies were delicious," Dottie called to the skinny woman. "The girls and I really enjoyed them."

Linny arched a brow at her mother, but Dottie ignored her. Technically, Mama had eaten every one of the cookies at some point in the middle of the night, but Linny wasn't one to split hairs.

"We heard you all were headed for Branson, too," Hal said.

"We are, right after we drop this one off at the airport tomorrow." Dessie pointed to Linny.

"It's been real nice meeting you," Hal said, smiling shyly at Linny.

"Nice meeting you, too," Linny said, liking the man.

Hal looked at the others, cocking his head. "How long are you staying and where are you camping?"

Probably doing math in her head about the drive time, Dessie thought a minute. "We'll be in Branson from late Friday through Monday and we're staying at Quiet Creekside RV Resort."

"Good," Hal said, looking pleased. "We're staying just down the road at Scenic Valley. We'll look out for you ladies on the road and catch up with you all there." He pulled a pen and a crumpled receipt from his shirt pocket, scribbled down a number, and handed it to Dessie. "Here's my cell in case you all need it. Have a good evening." With a tip of an imaginary hat, Hal ambled off.

"Such a sweet man," Ruby breathed. "Too bad the good ones are taken."

Linny smiled and then watched the friends talk and tease each other. Dottie pulled out her knitting but announced she was going to cut herself *a smidge more pie.* She glanced at Ruby as she threw back her head and laughed at an aside Dessie had made. With or without her, the adventures would continue for these three. Linny's job was done. Mama not only had her sea legs, she was having the time of her life.

CHAPTER 9

Homecoming

As she scrabbled in the bottom of her purse for stray bills to add to the cab driver's tip, Linny marveled again at her good luck. In these days of TSA lines and overbooked flights, she'd gotten lucky and managed to catch an earlier plane home. She'd tried to get hold of Jack to tell him not to pick her up at the airport but hadn't heard back from him. Even if he didn't check his phone, she was home at six p.m. instead of nine, so she had plenty of time to head Neal and him off before they made the trip to RDU.

Their dogs barked as they bounded out from behind the house. Linny called to them and grinned, showering pats on the yipping and swarming pack. They gave her doggie smiles when she rubbed them, and Linny paused to give extra love to her best man, Roy. Jack's truck wasn't in its usual parking space. Was he down at the barn or had he and Neal gone to run errands?

Linny took a deep breath, enjoying the familiar scents: faint whiffs of gardenias mixed with the earthier smells of horse manure and recently plowed field. So good to be home. She bumped her bag onto the front porch of Jack's—no, *their*—old farmhouse and felt a shiver of delicious anticipation. All the fretting about intrusive Vera had dissolved with the passing days and all Linny could think about now was stepping into Jack's arms. She couldn't wait to tell him about her trip and find out all about their adventures.

As she fit the key in the lock, the door swung open without her turning the key. Linny felt the hair on the back of her neck stand up. This was the second time this week a door that was supposed to be locked was open. Cautiously, she poked her head in the house and breathed in the delicious scent of warm corn bread. Linny paused for a moment, feeling almost teary with gratitude. Jack and Neal had guessed she'd be road weary and pulled out the cookbooks to make supper for her.

But from the direction of the kitchen, a woman's voice called out, "Yoo-hoo."

Linny froze, wondering wildly if the voice was Vera's. Had she just moved in like a carpetbagger as soon as Linny left North Carolina? Her heart thundered.

"Y'all go wash up. Supper is almost ready!" the woman called.

Linny heard the distinctive clicking of kitten heels and sighed inwardly. The drawling trill was her mother-in-law, Ceecee. The two of them had had a rocky start, with Ceecee still being brokenhearted about Jack's divorce from her best friend's daughter. But once Ceecee learned the truth about Vera's abandoning the marriage, and as she'd come to know Linny, the two women had begun forging a bond of respect and affection. Still, Linny felt slightly wary around Ceecee, as if she needed to be on her best behavior. All she wanted to do tonight was relax, not have to make conversation with anyone but Jack and Neal. Forcing a smile, Linny stepped into the kitchen.

Ceecee looked startled, but then her eyes lit up and she threw her arms around Linny in an extravagant hug. "I heard the dogs barking and thought you were the boys. Welcome home, you little traveler!"

"Thank you," Linny said, flushing and feeling inordinately pleased at her warm greeting. But Ceecee was wearing Linny's favorite apron: a vintage number with cabbage roses and ribbons on it that Jack had given her for Christmas that year. Fighting a hot crawl of possessiveness, she reminded herself that she wasn't three years old and that Ceecee was doing something nice for her family by cooking them a home-cooked meal.

"Well, when we all sit down for supper I want to hear all about your trip. You can tell us every little thing." Ceecee's low heels clicked as she bustled around the kitchen, pulling out silverware and glasses. "The boys are at the feedstore. They got home yesterday afternoon and were just starving to death, so I came over and cooked for them. Thought I'd cook again tonight because Jack told me that he and Neal planned on just ordering pizza or cooking one of those instant dump-the-bag-in-the-skillet-and-stir-it-around deals. Probably full of preservatives." She shook her head and peered inside the oven.

Linny gave Ceecee a wry grin and admitted, "One of the last suppers I cooked before the trip was a dump-it-in-the-skillet meal. The boys gave it five stars."

Ceecee's eyes widened but with a determinedly positive smile backtracked smoothly. "Well, I just can't imagine how clever you are to have your little business and still have time to get a meal on the table for two men." Clasping her hands in front of her waist, her charm bracelet tinkling, Ceecee got a fond look in her eye. "When Jack was Neal's age he could go through a gallon of milk and a loaf of bread in just two days. And bologna sandwiches; that young man loved bologna sandwiches. Neal is always hungry, too, isn't he?" she asked, bright-eyed as she cocked her head.

"He can be . . ." Linny started but stopped herself, remembering her new truth-telling policy. "Neal turns up his nose at a lot of my meals because his mama cooks it better," she admitted, crossing her arms and bracing herself, remembering how Ceecee used to wax rhapsodically about her ex-daughter-in-law's cooking.

But Ceecee just tutted and shot her a sympathetic look. "Try not to let that worry you. Boys that age can be contrary, and he's had a lot of changes lately. He'll come around." Ceecee slipped on oven mitts and pulled the steaming corn bread from the oven. Peeking into Linny's slow cooker, she gave a stir to the spicy-smelling contents. "Seafood gumbo."

Linny inhaled the mouthwateringly delicious aroma of garlic, tomato, and peppers and smiled. "It smells amazing."

She gave a satisfied little nod. "I hope you don't mind, but I was planning on staying for supper. Rush dropped me off here on the way to his Rotary Club's board of directors' meeting. That doesn't end until nine so I'm just as free as a bird." She made a fluttering movement with her fingers, a little free bird just flying away. "Maybe we could play Scrabble or Monopoly after supper."

"Good," Linny said, trying to muster up polite enthusiasm. But board games plain bored her and she was exhausted. All the sleeping on a too-thin mattress with no Jack beside her, the stress of driving the RV, the lack of privacy in the past week, and changing time zones was catching up with her. She pointed to the bedroom. "I'd like to go freshen up."

"Of course you would," Ceecee said with a firm nod. "I've got everything under control here. We'll just wait for our men to come home." Her charms jingled again as she gave the gumbo a stir. "You know, I've enjoyed spending time with young Neal. He's turning into such a darling young man. He and I have had some good long chats. I taught him to play gin rummy and he's teaching me to play poker," she said with a mischievous smile.

Linny trudged back to the bedroom, glad for the reprieve but picturing a chatty meal and a marathon game of Monopoly. All she wanted to do was go slip on shorts and a T-shirt, hug the boys tightly, snuggle with Roy, and make it an early night.

Her mother's words came back to her: *People pleasing is a bad habit* and *I hope I raised a daughter who pays attention to what she wants.*

Linny stopped abruptly, turned around, and walked back to the kitchen.

Ceecee's brows flew up. "Everything okay?" she asked solicitously.

Linny met her beautiful green eyes—the ones Jack had inherited. "Ceecee, I am just so tired. Will you please take charge tonight? You're doing a great job. I'm going to go get Roy to keep me company, make a peanut butter sandwich, grab a glass of wine, and go lie down."

Ceecee paused and broke into tentative smile. She reached out to pat Linny's arm, her eyes kind. "Of course you're tired, darling. You've been taking such good care of your mama. Now you go get yourself comfy. I'll fix you a little tray and bring it to you in your room." She twirled away, tiptoeing up to grab a loaf of bread from on top of the refrigerator. "Now do you want that sandwich on white or wheat, and would you like white or red wine?"

"White and white," Linny croaked, her mouth suddenly dry. Standing stock-still, she felt a wave of giddy relief. Ceecee hadn't raised a brow at the odd meal request or Linny bailing on the family supper and games night. "Thank you," she said, flashing Ceecee a grateful smile, relieved to be able to just be herself.

"Of course." Ceecee gave a dismissive wave, but she bustled around with a pleased smile playing at the corners of her mouth.

"Let me go round up Roy," Linny said and walked outside to call the dog. She breezed back through the kitchen with Roy's claws skittering on the wood floors behind her, and paused to give Ceecee a peck on the cheek. Watching her mother-in-law color with pleasure, Linny smiled as she wheeled her suitcase toward her room.

In a clean cotton nightgown, Linny sighed deeply, wriggled her toes, and pulled up the chenille bedspread, deciding she was as thrilled to be in her own bed as the people were in the mattress commercials. With Roy snuggled in the crook of her arm and Alexander McCall Smith's *The Sunday Philosophy Club* open in her lap, Linny finished the delicious sandwich. She was having trouble keeping her eyes open but wanted to try to stay awake to say hello to Jack. A soft knock sounded at the door and she felt a flutter of happiness as a beaming Jack poked his head in. "Hey, there," she said softly and patted the bed beside her.

"Hey, you," he said as he slipped onto the bed and kissed her thoroughly. "Glad to have you home, peanut butter girl."

She grinned. "You can still taste it? I was too tired to even brush my teeth."

"I think it's peanut butter, but I need to double-check." He pulled her toward him and kissed her again. He picked up her left hand and examined it. "I'm sorry about the rings, sugar."

She blew out a sigh. "I worked hard on that spiritual talk, but I really miss them."

Jack took her hand and kissed her fingers. "Maybe Neal and I can go back to the gem mines, find new emeralds, and get them remade." He raised a brow at her. "Or maybe we can do something wild like go to the jewelry store and buy you new ones."

"No," Linny said and touched the empty spot on her finger with her thumb and remembering how hard a time she'd had accepting the rings from him in the first place, thanks to her late, untrustworthy husband. "Maybe the girls will find them," she said, glancing at him for reassurance.

"Maybe," he said neutrally.

"How's Neal?" Linny asked. "I'll get up to say hello to him."

"No need, Lin." He frowned, looking weary. "He's been in a bad mood all day. Just now he was snappy with Mama and I sent him to his room."

"Maybe he's overtired from the trip." With her finger, Linny smoothed the crease between his brows.

Jack shook his head, looking discouraged. "We had a great time in Arizona, but as soon as we got back home, he got moody again."

"He probably missed his mama, and Chaz," Linny said mildly. "Anything new on that front?"

"Let's see. Chaz moved back home with Vera again. They had a happy day or two, but now they're fighting again." He raised his eyes heavenward. "I'll get my daily blow-by-blow later when Vera calls."

Daily? Linny pulled herself up and leaned on her elbow, staring at him. "Don't you think your ex-wife calling you every day is odd? What do you talk about—gas prices, the stock market?"

He put a steadying hand on her arm and said quietly, "We talk about Neal."

But Linny wasn't having it. "Jack, it's too much. You have got to set clearer boundaries with her." With a gusty exhale, she flopped back down on her pillow. Her heart ached for Neal. At twelve he had already been through one divorce and was probably imagining another looming on the horizon, just as he'd gotten attached to his stepfather. But a small flicker of anger in her stomach began to burn hotter. "Does Vera know the harm she's causing Neal by exposing him to their fighting?"

Jack shook his head, looking disgusted. "I've talked to her about it and she talks about how hard things are for her."

Because it's always all about Vera, Linny thought, trying to unclench her teeth.

"She says things are improving, but until things settle down Neal's staying here," Jack said firmly.

"I agree." But Linny's indignation was replaced by a sinking feeling. She pictured herself stooped and gray-haired, stirring a pot of pinto beans as a balding Neal skulked through the kitchen in his sweat suit, sucking down a soft drink, and grunting a greeting. It could happen.

He brushed her forehead with a kiss. "Let me help Mama finish cleaning up and see her out. I'll be back in just a few minutes. I've missed you, darlin' girl," Jack said.

"Missed you, too." She shivered deliciously at the thought of being close to him again.

Monday afternoon Linny dropped Neal off at Jack's office and headed over to Green Sage for her meetings to get employee input about issues Chanel identified as being problematic. Linny would do six half-hour interviews today and the rest over the next two weeks.

In the waiting room she glanced down at her black creased trousers, shiny black Oxfords, and geometric-print, possibly hip jacket. She hoped her outfit made her look relatable. Swarms of butterflies revved in her stomach. It was one thing to win the work and yet another to make good on her promise to help Chanel Green improve her company.

Glancing at her iPad, she took one last look at the proposal she'd sent the young business owner after their first meeting. She'd interview twenty-five employees and a few clients, give Chanel the results, and coach the woman on how to set the tone for the changes she wanted her employees to make. Then Linny would customize a training program to hit the problem areas hard. This approach had worked well for her in the past, she reminded herself, and took a few surreptitious deep breaths and glanced at her screen. The meeting was to start at two o'clock and it was ten after.

Chanel burst into the waiting room, red-faced and panting slightly. Wearing neon running shoes, short shorts, and a jogging bra, she smiled apologetically. "Sorry. I was running and time got away from me."

Your shirt got away from you, too, Linny thought. Was Chanel planning on staying dressed like that all day? Trying to keep her expression bland, Linny stuck out her hand. "Hey, Chanel."

"You don't want to shake my hand. I'm sweaty," Chanel said with a rueful laugh and wiped her brow with her arm. "You know where my office is. Let me catch a quick shower and I'll be right in." She gave her a parting grin. "Give Sage a scratch for me. He's in his usual spot."

Linny winced inwardly as Chanel walked right through the employee area in her skimpy outfit on her way to the locker room. Linny expected employees' heads to swivel as she walked by but none did. Maybe all the young employees ran and wore clothing like that and she was just being a prude. In Chanel's office she leaned down and gave the snoozing dog a scratch.

A young man with a bun walked by the glass wall close enough for Linny to see that the slogan on his shirt read *Drunk Girls Think I'm Hot.* Chanel needed a no-statement T-shirt policy. Another place to make changes. Trying to peer outside to check out other employees' attires without looking like a peeper, she groaned quietly. A young woman on the phone wore furry pink bedroom slippers, a skirt, and a sheer blouse with a black bra visible beneath it. Had these people never heard of professional work attire?

Chanel bounced into the room, finger combing her short, still damp hair. Wearing a pale blue linen shift, an oatmeal-colored cardigan, and sandals, she, at least, now looked appropriate. "So, let the games begin," she said, picking up a paper on her desk and handing it to Linny. "We've got you set up in a quiet private conference room. Here's the list of folks you're going to talk with this afternoon and those scheduled over the next two weeks. Any questions?"

Linny paused, deciding to save the talk about unprofessional attire for after she'd done the interviews. She had a feeling she was going to hear some doozy stories today. "No, all set."

In the conference room Rachel said she *loved* her job and *loved* her customers, but she'd had a brief thing with Raj and now they didn't speak. Her women friends at work *thought he was a love rat and froze him, too*. Linny wrote down *love rat* and *froze him*. This sounded like a reality show where young people lived in the same house and fought. How did you work with a teammate and not talk to him?

Vaya was the fellow with the Afro beard and was cooperative but noted, "The men and the chicks are like oil and water." As they talked, Linny made tiny hash marks every time he used the word *chicks* to describe his female co-workers. Six marks in thirty minutes.

Jax said employees joked around a lot, but that it was all in good fun. The female co-worker he sat beside kept wearing a ball cap that said *I'm with Stupid* and an arrow that pointed at him, so he'd bought the same hat with the arrow pointing the other way, toward her. Wow. That T-shirt policy needed to be expanded to include all articles of clothing.

Linny tilted her head. "Do customers ever come here to meet with you all?"

"Sure," he'd said, popping a Jolly Rancher candy in his mouth. "All the time."

Jarrett scratched his head and smiled vaguely, saying he thought the company culture was *on fleek*, which Linny guessed from his tone meant something good. He'd heard of a company that bought hammocks for employees to use in their cubicles and asked her *to run that suggestion up the flagpole*. Linny wrote down *hammock* and *flagpole*.

Tiny, quiet Ava said, "Everyone treats customers too casually. Raj calls the men *bro*." She wrinkled her nose. "And we're slack about calling people back right away. You can't wait a day or two to get back to already frustrated clients."

As Linny drove home, her brain raced. All of the employees she'd spoken with today had given her similar stories. She shook her head, chagrined. If the rest of her interviews went anything like today's, her follow-up meeting with Chanel Green was going to be a humdinger.

Back home Linny shucked her work clothes, threw on shorts and a T-shirt, and shot a glance at the clock on the stove, feeling harried. She'd gone flat-out all day. Blowing out a sigh, she scrabbled in the freezer. Pulling out the family-sized package of frozen chicken piccata, she tossed it into the microwave. These days she was getting help from the frozen foods aisle at Trader Joe's, but at least they hadn't resorted to a lot of takeout. On the Bodacious Bonus Moms' site, Angie from Atlanta suggested newly blended families eat supper together every night and take turns sharing about your days. She had a feeling the sharing would bomb, but she'd give it a whirl.

Filling a saucepan with a few inches of water, she clattered it onto a burner on the stove. Turning the heat up high, she tossed in the frozen vegetables. Roy sat in a safe spot in the corner and gazed at her unblinkingly as she scurried around the kitchen.

The dogs barked and Linny heard the doors to the truck thunk shut. Jack and Neal walked in. "Hey, men," she called. "How was work?"

"Awful. All I do is clean poop out of dog and cat cages," Neal said, his face mutinous. He stomped toward his room and slammed the door.

"That's all he did all afternoon?" Linny arched a brow. "You didn't let him do surgery?"

"I'm unreasonable." Jack broke into a smile and gave her a quick hug.

"Rough day?" Linny asked.

He grimaced as he stood at the counter and sorted through the mail. "He was only with me at the office about an hour. His mom came by and took him to lunch and a movie and dropped him back off. He liked that. But he came back in a bad mood."

"He misses her and he's probably mad at us for keeping him from her." Linny thought about it as she placed flatware on napkins. "He's been with us over two weeks, and besides your Tucson trip, we've both had to fit him in around our work schedules. He hasn't seen much of his friends and he misses home. I'd be cranky, too."

The muscle in Jack's jaw worked. "I know. This can't have been a great summer for him and school's going to be starting soon."

Linny felt a stab of guilt. Bad stepmother. "He needs meaningful activity, he needs his friends, and he needs more of our undivided attention." She made a decision. Wondering just how she was going to make it work, Linny said, "I'm going to clear my schedule tomorrow. If I can just get a little work done, he and I can spend the rest of the day doing something fun."

Jack nodded and gave her a grateful look. "Maybe we can get one or two of his buddies over to the house one weekend soon. The boys could ride the horses, maybe cook out."

"Great idea," Linny said and turned down the heat on the vegetables. "We've just been patching things together, but we need to make things more normal for him around here."

Jack gave a crooked grin. "How did you get so smart and how did I get so lucky?"

The next day Linny made good on her vow. The exhibit Neal had picked—*Is There Life on Other Planets? Star Trek, NASA, and Aliens*—had been a big hit. Linny smiled as she drove them home from the science museum.

Beside her, Neal looked positively sunny and chatted to her about a man in the Netherlands who had found a rare stamp and an astrological event that was coming up. He'd been pleasant all day long.

"Do you know why the moon is going broke?" Neal asked.

"No, tell me," Linny said, hiding a smile.

"It's down to its last quarter." He snorted with laughter.

She grinned. Bad science jokes were a new development, and she liked seeing him being silly.

Emboldened, Neal went on. "What does a subatomic duck say?"

"I don't know." Linny grinned, cocking her brow expectantly.

"Quark." He smacked his thigh, laughing hard.

She hadn't really *gotten* the joke, but she laughed anyway, enjoying him. Moments like these reminded her of what a bright sweetheart of a guy Neal was, despite their ups and downs.

As they drew closer to the farm, Linny knew she needed to talk with him about what she guessed he was feeling. "Can we talk for a minute, bud?" she asked, keeping her eyes on the road.

"Okay," he said warily.

She paused a beat. "You must miss your mama and Chaz, and I'm sure it's tough to be away from your home and your friends."

He nodded wordlessly and stared hard out the window.

"It might take a week or two, but your dad and I are going to figure out better schedules and find more fun things for you to do while you're here. We'll help you see your friends more."

Neal gave another nod, this one more vigorous.

"You've had a lot of changes lately, including your dad getting married again and you having to share him." Linny gave him a sideways glance. "How are you doing with that?"

"Okay," he said and shot her a quick glance. "Better."

"Good," Linny said, trying to sound matter-of-fact when inside she was cheering. "Even with me here, he's got plenty of love to go around."

He nodded, picked up his phone, and began to play a game.

Linny hid her smile. Progress.

That evening Linny examined the trip itinerary Dessie had printed for their families. Her mama and friends had been in Branson for three days and were heading out in the morning. She picked up the phone and FaceTimed Mama. "Hey there," she called as Dottie answered.

Mama and her friends crowded around the screen waving, their faces wreathed in smiles.

"Hey, honey bunch," her mother boomed out, still convinced that video over the airwaves meant she needed to talk loud.

"Inside voice," Ruby said softly, and Mama nodded.

"How was Branson?" Linny asked, resting her chin in her hand.

"Fabulous! The shows were just great. Such talented performers," Ruby enthused.

Dessie leaned her face in close to the screen, looking pensive. "Will you look at my eyebrows? These two are trying to beautify me, but I think they used too dark a pencil."

Dessie's eyebrows looked like two black pipe cleaners. Linny tried not to look startled and cleared her throat. "They're more . . . expressive. Might be a titch too dark?"

"I knew it." Dessie shot an I-told-you-so look at Dottie and Ruby and wiped at her brows with a piece of Kleenex.

"I FaceTimed Curtis over at Kate's house. That dog knew to look right in the middle of the screen," Mama said admiringly. "Kate said he was getting along fine with her dogs and that he'd learned to shake hands." She gave the modest but proud look worn by parents of prodigies.

Linny suppressed a grin. "Did you also get a chance to talk to your grandbaby?"

"Of course," her mother said with a sniff. "She's as precious as a lamb."

"We had to remind her. She got so wound up talking sugar to Curtis that she almost forgot to ask about her grandbaby," Dessie said with a grin.

"I miss that dog so much," Mama said. "Your sister looked tired. She's not working herself to the bone with that new baby, is she?"

"She's fine," Linny said, hedging, and felt a pang of guilt about not following through on her offer to babysit Ivy. She'd call soon. Linny looked at Ruby. "How's the manhunt going?"

"She's a husband-interviewing machine," Dessie said proudly. "She's had seven or eight fellows pursuing her hot and heavy online. We threw back a few . . ."

Ruby jumped in. ". . . like the one who asked snoopy questions about how much money I had in my retirement account, and the one who had five of his grown kids living with him." She shivered dramatically. "But I met a retired admiral and he's real distinguished-looking."

"Don't forget that military pension," Dottie added helpfully.

Ruby nodded. "And I'm meeting a man from the Single RVers for coffee when we get to Mount Rushmore. He's a younger fellow who teaches high school math and he's a cutie patootie."

"We forgot the main news. We might have a lead in the missing ring and kitty caper," Dessie announced, a decidedly Joe Friday–like cadence to her voice.

Linny felt her heart tick up a beat and leaned forward. "Tell me."

"Remember Mack got us all on new phones so we could FaceTime?" Dessie asked.

Linny nodded. Her mother's beau/friend/acquaintance kept up

with new technology and had gotten all of them on board with devices that would work best while traveling.

"The phone takes such good pictures that I went snap crazy for a few days," Dessie said.

Linny groaned. "You deleted those morning shots of me in my sleep mask, right?"

"Right," Dessie said evasively. "The day we got burgled, I took tons of pictures. Yesterday I cross-examined them." She separated her thumb from her middle finger.

Mama snorted.

Ignoring her, Dessie went on. "In a few shots Letty walked by real close to the RV."

"But she walked all over the campground," Ruby pointed out. "That's why she's so thin."

Mama nodded. "And our campsite was right on the road. Anyone walking passed close to our RV."

Dessie gave them both you-poor-naïve-Pollyannas looks and went on. "She's a suspect."

"Why would a man marry someone so keyed up? She walks like this." Ruby modeled the high, gyrating arms of a power walker, almost hitting the girls with her elbows.

With an exaggerated look of patience, Dessie waited until she'd finished. "In other shots I caught Hal lurking around the RV. Now why would he do that?"

Ruby rolled her eyes. "Because he was worried about us." She gave Linny a confidential look. "He fixed a problem we had with a valve getting stuck and us not being able to dump the gray or black water. Not a good situation," she said with a shudder.

"Let's not jump at straws," Dottie said and wrapped up the story. "So Dessie thinks she's got a perp and Ruby can't believe it's Hal because she's got a little crush on him."

"I do not," Ruby said hotly.

"What do you think, Mama?" Linny asked.

"It'll all come out in the wash. At Mount Rushmore we'll be staying at the same campground they are. We can do more investigating then," Dottie said with a knowing nod.

"Any other news?" Linny asked.

"Perry and Mack are flying up to tag along for a few days. They're going to camp in tents at the campgrounds where we're staying."

Dessie's eyes twinkled. "Neither have camped in twenty years, but they're gung ho about it. Wait until they sleep on those air mattresses."

Linny chuckled. Roy, Wilbur, and Orville slipped in the dog door one after the other and milled around her legs, ready to eat. "I need to get going. Y'all be safe now, and Jack and Neal send their love."

"Send them our love, and we'll call you soon." Dottie blew her a kiss.

Grinning, Linny blew one back.

Still smiling as she thought about their conversation, Linny scooped kibble into bowls, the dogs dancing around her feet. Her phone rang. "Hey, Kate."

Her sister sounded calm but strained, her voice one octave higher than usual. "I tripped on a dog toy and fell down a few steps. I believe I've broken some bones."

CHAPTER 10
Oh, Baby, Baby

Linny gasped into the phone as she hurried toward their bedroom to get Jack. "Are you okay? Is Ivy okay?"

"Ivy was down for a nap. I fell down three stairs. My arm is probably broken and my ankle hurts like a bear." Kate's voice faltered. "Jerry's in DC at a conference." She was crying now. "Can you and Jack come get the baby? I called 911 and the ambulance is on the way. I'll wait for you to get here."

The atmosphere inside the truck was tense and Jack, Neal, and Linny were quiet as they drove the ten minutes to Kate and Jerry's house. Linny squirmed in her seat, wishing Jack would step on it, but he drove the same way all the time: steadily and carefully. As they pulled up in front of the familiar Craftsman bungalow, Neal's hand snaked over the seat and patted her on the shoulder. "It'll be okay," he said softly.

Touched, Linny tried to pat his hand, but it was gone. As soon as Jack put the truck in park, Linny had her seat belt off and her door flung open. As she raced up the front walkway with the Avery men right at her heels, the boxy ambulance pulled up.

"Thank goodness," she murmured as she used her spare key to open Kate's door.

Her sister's dogs, Duke and Delilah, barked madly and Curtis joined in with his ferocious woof. But they recognized Linny and milled around her as she pushed open the door. "Hush, fellas." Linny gave them quick pats and brushed past them.

Her sister sat on a straight-backed chair in the kitchen, white-faced with pain. Tears leaked down her face. She cradled her right arm in her hand and her left leg was stretched out straight in front of her. Her right cheek was swollen.

"Hey, honey." Linny's heart lurched as she hurried over and kissed the top of her head. "The EMTs are right behind me."

"Can you put the dogs up and go check on the baby?" Kate asked, wincing as she tried to move her outstretched leg.

Linny nodded. Rounding up the dogs, she shut them in the spare bedroom. In the nursery Baby Ivy gurgled as she waved her arms around and batted at an airplane mobile. "Hey, Miss Ivy," Linny called softly and smiled as she scooped her up and rested the baby on her shoulder. Carrying her into the kitchen, she cradled her low in front of Kate. Jack and Neal hurried in, followed by the EMTs wheeling in the gurney.

Grimacing as she rested her hurt arm on her chest, Kate brushed away her tears and touched her baby's face with her good hand, love shining in her eyes. "Hey, baby girl! How was your nap?"

The baby's swimmy eyes focused on her mother's face and she cooed.

Kate spoke to Linny in an urgent tone. "I need y'all to keep Ivy until Jerry gets home." She groaned. "If my ankle and wrist are broken how am I going to manage this baby over the next few weeks?" She began to cry in earnest now.

Linny blinked back her own tears, and touched the top of Kate's head.

Drawing a deep breath, Kate brushed away tears with the back of her hand. "I don't want Mama to know this happened or she'll cut short her trip. Jerry and I can figure out a way to make this work until she comes home."

"We'll help," Linny said and glanced at Jack and Neal, both of whom nodded in confirmation.

Kate shook her head. "You can't. You have work and Neal and . . ."

"We're going to help," Linny said firmly.

"These might only be sprains," the pretty brunette EMT reminded Kate. But Kate yelped when the woman eased off her shoe. When the EMT gently touched the side of her foot, Kate blanched and tears trickled down her face.

As the EMTs sized up the injuries, Linny and Jack spoke in hushed tones and made plans. Linny would take Kate's car and follow the ambulance to the hospital. The men would take Ivy home and set up the den as a temporary baby's room. Linny would text updates to them and to Jerry.

Linny watched anxiously as the paramedics loaded Kate up for the ride to Raleigh Memorial Hospital. The three of them quickly kissed Kate.

Linny jiggled the mercifully quiet baby on her shoulder while Jack and Neal rummaged around the baby's room, trying to find the baby supplies they'd need. "Kate usually keeps an already packed diaper bag somewhere. It's pink and has ponies on it."

"Here." Looking triumphant, Neal held up the bag he'd found behind the door.

"Good job, bud." Jack rubbed his chin. "As I remember, we'll need a baby sling or a carrier, milk, the playpen, and a baby monitor. Neal, you and I need to go get the car seat out of Kate's car and put it in the truck."

As the men walked purposefully toward the door, Linny gave Jack an admiring look. "I'm impressed."

Jack gave her a crooked grin and put a hand on the back of Neal's neck. "Wasn't that long ago I was lugging this guy around in a carrier."

"Dad!" Neal said but didn't pull away.

As she hopped into Kate's Honda and started toward the hospital, Linny worried about her sister. A nurse friend had told her once that if a patient who has fallen says they think they've broken a bone, nine times out of ten the X-rays confirmed a break. If Kate had fractured her wrist—her right hand, of course—and her ankle, she probably was looking at a daunting recovery time. She'd not only need help with the baby, she'd need help with daily life: bathing, dressing, and cooking. Plus she'd need physical therapy. To calm herself, Linny began a mental to-do list.

But her mind still raced with worry. Work was busy. She had another meeting with Chanel at Green Sage. That project would take time. She'd heard from another old client the day before about doing more training for them and she had another customer service class for small businesses filling up fast at Earth and Sky. Realistically, Neal might become a more full-time member of their household, which would require much more of her time and attention, at least until school started up again. Linny felt a clutching anxiety in her stomach. How was she going to manage all that?

* * *

Four days later Jerry dropped a sleeping Ivy off after lunch, easing the baby over to Linny as carefully as if he were handing her a ticking time bomb. His hair was parted unevenly and he had a dab of toothpaste on his beard.

When she slipped the baby into the crib they'd set up in the den, Jerry breathed a sigh of pure relief.

They tiptoed into the kitchen. Linny gave him a sympathetic look. "How are you holding up?"

"Okay," he said, but his eyes were underslung with blue circles. "Ivy's a little pistol. She drifts off when we wake up and raises Cain when we sleep. She has a pair of lungs on her," he added.

"How's Kate today?" Linny asked, pressing a glass of fresh iced tea into his hand.

He gave her a grateful look and took a long swallow. "Shaky. She wants to shower, but she's too weak for that even with the shower chair and grab bars. The bathroom is hard for her. She's embarrassed." He shook his head sympathetically. "I told her it was nothing I hadn't seen before and she started crying," he said, shutting his eyes and rubbing them. "The wheelchair won't fit in the bathroom. All my houses from now on are going to have total wheelchair access and be disability friendly out the wazoo," he vowed.

Jerry was a nice man. Linny patted his shoulder. "You're a great husband and father."

"Timing is always off, isn't it? I'm worried about Kate and the baby. The mayor wants to see me and *Innovative Housing Design* magazine has given me an award and wants an interview. This new turn to the business is going to let me have more normal hours and spend time with my girls, but between now and when I get there, I've got a landslide of work." His face clouded. "Thanks for babysitting. Friends have offered to help, too, but everybody works or has small kids, and we don't want to overburden anyone." He tilted his head and met her eyes. "Are you sure this isn't too much?"

"We're happy to help. That's what family and friends are for," Linny said, pushing down the niggling worry about just how she and Jack were going to pull this off. She paused for a moment, hoping she wasn't bringing up a touchy subject. "Kate said you all decided not to call your folks for help."

He shook his head, a glint of humor in his eyes. "Let me refresh your memory about my Holy Roller parents. At the wedding Daddy gave the long blessing concentrating on the sin of fornication and Mama hollered about the evils of drink while trying to wrestle bottles of Kendall-Jackson from the poor college student bartender." He gave a lopsided grin. "We decided not to call on them."

Linny smiled but sobered, thinking about her one-armed, one-legged sister trying to care for a baby. "Are you managing?"

"We're bumping along." Jerry gave his beard a scratch.

"Good," Linny said. "Mama will be home from her trip soon and she'll be thrilled to help." She thought about it. "You sure I shouldn't call Mama and get her home sooner?"

"No, Kate wouldn't want that. I can hold it together for two more weeks," Jerry said as he rose to go. "Thanks again, Linny, and tell Jack how grateful we are."

"I'm glad we can help," Linny said but again thought about the mountain of work on her desk and her decision to change her schedule so she could create more of a routine for Neal. "Remember, the doctor said that every day Kate is getting stronger and stronger."

"Right," he said, nodding like he was trying to convince himself. "I need to head out. Thanks, Lin." He leaned down and kissed the top of her head, then slipped out the door. Though they'd spoken in voices softer than whispers and the house was still, Linny froze as Ivy started to wail. Wilbur, Orville, and Roy slunk out of the living room, tails between their legs, and scooted out the dog door, slick as grease. She didn't blame them.

Linny touched the spot on her temple that was beginning to throb, shot a hopeless glance at her desk, and walked to the other room with heavy steps to see what could be done to calm Miss Ivy.

Linny stared out the window at the bright green soybean fields and their crimson barn as she tried to settle her mind. She jotted down a to-do list for the day and sipped coffee with her feet resting on Roy, who was snoozing underneath the kitchen table. Ivy had kept her hopping yesterday. This morning she was stopping by to bring Kate a cup of coffee and to try to cheer her up. She'd swing by Jack's office to pick up Neal, take him to a dental appointment, and buy him a few new pairs of shorts. She'd drop him back at Jack's office, run over to Green Sage for her follow-up meeting with Chanel at two, and then go back by Jack's to get Neal again and take him to the driving range. She shot a guilty glance at the laundry room, where dirty clothes bulged over the sides of assorted laundry baskets. Housekeeping was getting sketchy at their house.

She rubbed her face with her hands. Meals were getting spotty, too. Most new wives and stepmothers were probably still preparing home-cooked meals and thoughtfully packing nutritious and tasty lunches, throwing in real pancakes for breakfast to sweeten the pot. They'd ordered pizza from Gino's Gas and Go for the past two nights. Linny pushed back her hair and frowned. Grooming was another thing that was slipping. She was pushing it on day four without a shampoo, saving time wherever she could.

Glancing at the calendar on the refrigerator, she realized it was Thursday. She'd not heard from Mama and the SWAT Team in a while. After she'd left them in Tennessee, Mama had called twice a day and sometimes FaceTimed her, too. But the more at ease Dottie felt on her road trip, the less she called. Still, Linny felt a flutter of worry. She picked up her phone, checked her emails, and blew out a sigh, relieved. Dottie had written. She opened the note and grinned. Her mother wrote long emails and formatted them like letters.

> *Dear Linny,*
> *We girls are still having a grand time. Ruby is still hogging the bathroom and the hot water in the mornings. We switched up the shower schedule and now she's last. Ha! We stopped at a flea market today and Dessie bought a talking bass that you hang on the wall. He sings, too. We just need new AA batteries.*
> *Were in Omaha yesterday. We wanted to drive by Warren Buffet's house but RV too big for neighborhood streets. Ruby was hoping he was single, but I read online that he has a nice lady friend.*
> *I'm in high cotton, sleeping back in the Penthouse again.*
> *We are traveling footloose and fancy free, going unscheduled for these next few days.*
> *It's our freestyling mode, just like Frank and Mike on that American Pickers television show but in an RV. We stopped at Custer State Park. That was real pretty and we saw bison.*
> *Ruby heard about some festival in a little town nearby so we're headed there tomorrow. Should be fun. She didn't get all the details but says it's an arts and crafts show at a place*

called Sturgis. Hope they have some of those gourds made into birdhouses. So precious.

Hugs from your lovin' Mama

PS – I miss Curtis something terrible, but we'll be home soon, right?

Linny shook her head and grinned as she closed the laptop. Typical of Mama to admit to missing a dog but not to missing her and Kate. The SWAT Team was hitting its stride, though, if they'd discussed tracking down Warren Buffett and trying to lasso him for Ruby.

Catching a glimpse of herself in the mirror in the hall, Linny grimaced. All right, she'd wash her hair. Swigging coffee from the mug she carried like a security blanket, Linny made herself hurry. She was due at Kate's in an hour and a half and she needed to stop by the grocery store on the way over to get supplies for her family. She wouldn't be home until supper so she'd stick a cooler with ice in her trunk for the refrigerated items. And she'd take her laptop. Maybe she could get some work done while Neal got his teeth cleaned. Blowing out a sigh, she padded to the shower. The faster she tried to go, the more behind she seemed to get.

Jack rang as she pulled up in front of Kate's house and she answered, trying to sound cheerful and energetic. "Hi, sweets. How's your morning going?" He'd told her last night he was worried she was pushing herself too hard and she'd told him she was *fine, just fine.*

"Dogs chasing cars and catching them, dogs swallowing knee-highs, cats getting into bees' nests. Add staff infighting and that's my morning," he said wryly. "Oh, and my ex-wife called to ask how to get a virus off her laptop. Told Ruthie it was an emergency so she'd put her through." He blew out an exasperated breath.

Linny exhaled, willing her blood pressure to go back down. She was too tired and too irritated to even comment on this last bit of news. But she had to know. "Did you stop to tell her?"

"No, I didn't. I told her I had to go and to call a computer place," Jack said, sounding reasonable.

"Good," she said, though she'd have liked it better if he'd just told Vera to buzz off and not call him at work instead of offering her the helpful tip about finding a computer professional, but she wasn't splitting hairs. Maybe he was coming along with not being at Vera's beck and call. "I'll be by the clinic to pick Neal up later this morning."

"Good. He's walking dogs for the techs and having a ball. Heard from your mama?" he asked. He knew she'd been concerned about the radio silence from the SWAT Team.

"Yes." Linny breathed out thankfully. "She and the girls are fine. They're going to a big crafts festival in a place called Sturgis," she said, glancing at her watch.

Jack paused a beat. "Lin, do they have their facts straight?"

"I guess." That third cup of coffee she shouldn't have had made her only half-listen to Jack. She needed to wash Kate's hair with the dry shampoo she'd picked up at the drug store and make sure she was doing her physical therapy exercises. As she unbuckled her seat belt and reached for her purse, she heard the last of what Jack was saying.

". . . and those boys can be, um . . . high spirited," he said.

She froze. "I didn't catch what you just said."

He spoke patiently. "Sturgis hosts the biggest motorcycle rally in the country this week. Five hundred thousand bikers were there last year. They're a nice bunch for the most part, but it will be loud and rowdy and there'll be some folks who are . . . high-spirited," Jack said.

Linny's legs and arms turned to water. "What do you mean by high-spirited? You mean like rowdiness?"

"Possibly, and possibly roaring bikes and women in skimpy biker gear. I think your mama and the girls will be fine," he said, but paused a beat. "But is there any way to head them off?"

Linny groaned. "Based on the time of her email, they're already there." She closed her eyes and rested her head on the steering wheel. "So my mama and her girlfriends are accidentally going to the motorcycle rally?"

"I think so, Lin," Jack said in his extracalm voice that he only used when there could be trouble. "They'll be fine. They can take care of themselves."

But Linny wasn't so sure. As soon as she ended the call, she hurriedly called her mother but got no answer. She tried twice more. Ruby and Dessie didn't pick up either. She blew out an exasperated sigh. So much for their tech savvy. They knew ten times more about devices than most people their age did but hadn't gotten the compulsion about needing cells on their person and switched on at all times. She sent texts to all three that read: *U R going to motorcycle rally. That is what Sturgis is!! Call me!!*

She stared at the screen, willing one of them to respond, but all she saw was the blue background of her message. Her mother had so little experience with people outside her friends, neighbors, and members of her church.

Her breathing grew shallow as she remembered a scene from a movie in which an elderly woman accidentally backed her Volkswagen bug into a motorcycle that crashed onto the one parked beside it and triggered a domino effect with a whole row of motorcycles. Angry motorcycle gang members chased her as she putt-putted off, unaware of the chaos she'd caused.

A cold knot formed in her stomach as she had another thought. Mama watched just enough Christian TV shows to think that justice prevailed and bad guys always got caught. She could picture Dottie going into full-bore church lady mode if she came across a group of rowdy partiers. Linny blinked to try to erase the mental picture of Dottie marching up and telling them to pipe down and be considerate of others.

She drew in a deep breath and tried to calm herself. Dessie was calm under pressure and Ruby was good with people. They could handle themselves, she decided, giving the phone one last glance and slipping it into her purse. Not a whole lot she could do when she was half the United States away. She sent up a little prayer: *God, please be on the lookout for my mama and her friends. Please protect nice little ladies from North Carolina.*

Linny got out of the car, found the spare key on her key ring, and walked up to Kate's front door. As she drew closer, she heard Baby Ivy squalling. She fought a smile, though.

Her news would be a good distraction for Kate. She couldn't wait to tell her sister that Mama was looking for gourd birdhouses at the motorcycle rally.

That afternoon, Linny took a seat in the reception room of Green Sage, folded her hands in her lap, and tried to look like a competent, unruffled professional. With the news she had to deliver to Chanel about her lack of leadership being a big part of her company's problems, today's meeting could go downhill fast.

"Hello, Linny." Chanel was poker-faced as she stuck out her hand.

"Hello, Chanel." Linny shook the young woman's hand. Chanel looked more nervous than Linny felt. Her shoulders were hunched up and she raked her hair back with her fingers, leaving a tuft in front that was standing on end.

"I didn't sleep last night," Chanel admitted as she walked Linny to her office. "I was dreading this meeting—worried you were going to tell me I didn't know how to run a business and that my employees are all knuckleheads."

"Not true," Linny assured her. Before she sat she rustled in her purse and pulled out two big dog cookies baked in the shape of squirrels. "I brought treats for Sage. These are organic and have limited ingredients. Are these okay to give to him?"

Chanel nodded, looking slightly less wary, and wheeled her chair away from her desk to make way for Linny. Sage was snoring and twitching this morning, but the old boy woke as she drew closer to him.

Kneeling, Linny proffered her gifts. Daintily, the big dog took them and crunched into them. Crumbs fell all around him. The good fellow must be missing a few teeth. Linny gave him a reverent pat and pushed herself up on creaky knees.

Now Chanel's smile was a few degrees warmer. "Thank you," she said.

Linny just nodded and pulled from her briefcase a two-page summary of her interviews. "Before I give these to you let me just give you the bottom line."

Chanel's skinny shoulders hunched up higher. "Go ahead and shoot."

Linny met her gaze, willing her to relax. If Chanel rejected what Linny told her, she'd never get the help she needed. "I worked with a company that operated in a big new building with fixed windows."

Chanel cocked her head, but a look of impatience flickered across her face.

Linny went on. "One day the AC went out in the whole building and it got hot as blazes. A supervisor walked past the cubicle of one of his fresh-from-college hires and his mouth dropped open because the young man was working diligently at his desk but was buck naked from the waist up." She grinned at Chanel. "He explained it to his supervisor. It was hot. He took his shirt off. That's what he did in the frat house when it got hot."

Chanel broke into a smile and shook her head. "Please tell me none of my employees are working with their shirts off."

"No, but remember in the beginning we talked about how most of your employees came to Green Sage straight out of college and that this was their first professional job? This group of employees has no knowledge about what is expected of them working in a professional work environment. They don't even know what they don't know. They're guessing how to dress and act with one another and with customers." Linny paused. "Initially, I thought we might be looking at sexism, bullying, or a hostile work environment: a lot more serious stuff to eradicate."

Chanel's face brightened and she breathed out a whooshing sigh of relief.

Linny held up a hand and cautioned her, "They need to work on some things in those areas, too, but I think the biggest problems are professionalism and customer service."

"Thank goodness," Chanel said, nodding slowly, but a moment later she crossed her arms and the wary look was back. "I like the environment like this, though. I worked hard to make it casual and fun. Despite some of the foolishness, we're a creative and hardworking group."

"The workplace can still be fun, but it needs to be respectful," Linny said. "Your team members need to demonstrate respect for one another and present a confident and competent impression to customers. They need to be aware of the appropriate behaviors they need to grow the business. They need to understand what customers want and deliver it. They need to graciously and expertly solve customer problems."

Chanel nodded slowly. She leaned back in her chair and steepled her fingers together. "They don't always show respect for me either. I don't like the way some of them talk to me," she admitted. "Just because I knew them from school doesn't mean I'm not their boss. Some make comments about my salary. You know, jokey stuff but with an edge to it. For example, one of the guys was lusting over a Ducati motorcycle, and this other guy says, *Get Chanel to buy it for you. She's loaded.*" Her eyes narrowed. "That really ticked me off. For one, I'm not loaded. We're getting stronger and stronger, but there've been a lot of months when I didn't draw a paycheck because the money wasn't there."

Linny nodded. "It's none of their business anyhow."

Chanel gave Linny a searching look and then her words came rushing out. "They don't understand sixty-hour weeks or how many times I've worked all night, or maxed out my credit cards to float us during lean times or . . . other sacrifices I've made."

Linny gazed at Chanel. "You've put your personal life on hold to build this business, haven't you?"

Chanel slumped, suddenly looking vulnerable. "Yeah."

"You need to look at that, too," Linny said quietly. "You can't grow a business without making sacrifices. I get that. But you can change how you lead. When you grow your business to a certain point—unless you want no life at all—you've got to start delegating more, cut back on doing the direct work yourself and focus more on your main job, which is leading. I've seen too many business owners who'd made no time for love or family or enjoying life end up deeply regretting it."

Chanel's eyes began to tear up and she grabbed a tissue to blot them. Taking a moment to collect herself, she straightened in her chair and gave Linny a cheeky smile. "We need you to help get us on track. If you're willing to work with our sorry butts, let's get this party started."

Linny grinned. "Let's do."

CHAPTER 11
Jailhouse Mama

On the way home Linny had just paid for her celebratory iced tea at the drive-through when the phone rang. Pulling over, she snatched the cell from her bag, saw the name, and broke into a smile. "Hey, Dessie," she caroled, relief making her practically sing.

"Hey there," Dessie said, her voice sounding reedy. "We've had a little misunderstanding. We're down at the police station talking to a gentleman named Sergeant Allen Bowman."

"Okay," Linny said, trying to still the quaver in her voice. "What kind of misunderstanding?"

"Well, turns out Sturgis isn't an arts and crafts festival and your mama accidentally got arrested," Dessie said evenly.

Her breathing grew shallow and Linny asked, "How do you accidentally get arrested?"

"It was a wrong place, wrong time, wrong person situation," Dessie said, sounding regretful. "Let me let Ruby talk to you. I'm going to try to get Mack on the phone."

Ruby came on, sounding subdued. "Hey there, Linny," she said cautiously.

"Details, please," Linny said grimly.

"Your mama's fine and no one got hurt badly, so everything is fine. Well, except for the charges. Your mama and the whole crowd of them got arrested. Let me just have you talk to Sergeant Bowman. He's with the Meade County Sheriff's Department and can explain everything."

After fumbling sounds, a man barked, "Bowman here,"

"Sergeant, this is Linny Taylor, Dorothy Taylor's daughter. Can you tell me what's going on?" Linny said, trying to stay calm but fighting panic.

"Your mother is under arrest. She's been charged with disturbing the peace, disorderly conduct, simple assault, and resisting arrest. She's in custody until the bail hearing tomorrow."

"Officer, my mama is a small-town church lady...." Linny trailed off, not quite grasping what he'd said. Her heart galloped as she pictured Dottie sharpening shivs with the whole cast of *Orange Is the New Black*.

"Ma'am, this town goes from a population of sixty-five hundred to five hundred thousand this week." He breathed a weary sigh. "We get a lot of small-town churchgoers who have a little too much fun during the bike rally. The magistrate is just getting in and we'll have a bail hearing for her and the sixteen others we arrested last night. She'll stay at the Meade County Jail until bond is posted."

"This has to be a mistake." Linny shuddered. Now the mental picture was of Mama in a jumpsuit doing crafts with hardened lady criminals.

"No mistake, I'm afraid. The jail is comfortable, and we'll keep her separate from the rowdies," he said, his voice softening. "I need to go now, ma'am."

Dessie came back on the line. "Mack's going to come out here," she said briskly.

"I'll be out as soon as I can. Have him call me and we can make a plan." Linny ended the call. She'd tried to sound confident to reassure Dessie, but she had no idea of a plan. Squeezing shut her eyes, she rubbed the bridge of her nose and tried to think.

Her thoughts darted around at lightning speed. Sitting up straighter, she felt a flutter of excitement in her chest. Jack often kidded her about having so many lawyers in her life. She'd get hold of them all: Mary Catherine, Diamond—if she'd not gone full housewife yet—and even Chaz, if need be. She'd put in a quick call to Jack to let him know the situation, but she wouldn't tell Kate. She had enough on her plate without worrying about a jailbird mother.

Ninety minutes later Linny wore her good black linen dress and pearls as she stood beside the sleek King Air at the Worth County Regional Airport and talked with the pilot, Jim, about the weather report for flying.

Diamond pulled up in her wheel-spinning Range Rover and gave a cheery little wave as she strode toward them, a decided pep to her step. She stuck out a hand to Jim and gave Linny's neck a quick hug. "I'm so excited. Being a housewife was getting on my nerves. Let's go spring your mama from jail."

Mack wheeled up his gray Jeep Grand Cherokee and stepped out. He looked calm but had a steely set to his jaw. He wore Ray-Ban Aviators, a blue blazer, and a button-down shirt in place of his usual retired gent outfit of a fleece, baggy khakis, and New Balance tennis shoes. He had a dignity and gravitas about him and looked every bit like the successful businessman who'd made a bundle selling his natural gas company.

Linny introduced him to Diamond and moments later the aircraft gathered power and winged toward South Dakota.

At the Meade County Courthouse, Diamond smiled confidently at the desk officer, introduced herself, and the three were ushered into a green cement-block room.

A female guard with a boxy build escorted Dottie in. Her mama beamed and waved at them but paused to say to the guard, "Now, Ginger, you need to get to the doctor about that congestion. After three weeks it's probably a sinus infection." The guard flashed her a look of gratitude, gave her arm a little pat, and left the room.

"Mama." Linny gave her mother a warm hug, then watched Mack embrace her. "This is Diamond, the lawyer friend we brought with us from home."

"My, my, my. All this fuss. I'm sure we could have gotten something worked out without disturbing all of y'all." Dottie led them over to a green pleather couch in a seating area and made a graceful, sweeping gesture for them all to sit, just like she was inviting in her bridge group and getting ready to serve them chicken salad sandwiches and lemon bars.

"So, Miss Dottie, can you tell us about your little scrape and how exactly you came to be a guest here at the Meade County Jail?" Diamond held a gold pen poised over a small notebook she'd pulled from her crocodile purse. When she crossed her legs a flirty ankle bracelet tinkled.

"Well, as I told that Sergeant Bowman, this was all a misunderstanding," Dottie began.

Mama's two girlfriends burst into the room, smiling with relief. Dessie said, "We just got coffee. The guard told us you were here and that we could talk to you and your mama. We're so happy you're here!" Dessie threw her arms around Linny, and Ruby joined in the hug.

Linny introduced Diamond to the two of them and they all took seats.

Ruby handed Dottie a Diet Pepsi and a box of Krispy Kremes.

"Oh, bless you. I've been parched and starving." Mama popped open the tab on the soft drink and took a long swallow.

"Well, the Sturgis festival turned out to be very... colorful," Ruby said, her voice bright and brittle.

"Can you cut to the chase, Ruby?" Dessie suggested.

Ruby looked hurt but soldiered on. "We were walking around downtown and Dessie and I stopped to use the ladies' room. Your mama stayed outside, saw this group of motorcycle riders standing around talking, and thought she smelled marijuana. One of the ladies in her prayer group has a son who got real messed up on pot, so she felt she just had to go talk to this man about the dangers of drug use. That's when we caught up with her. The man was big as a bear, with a bushy beard and a motorcycle helmet with two giant steer horns coming out the side. But she just marched up to him and began telling him how smoking marijuana could ruin his life."

Mama was nodding along with the story, her mouth full, but she interjected, mumbling, "They didn't have any of the Chocolate Iced Custard Filled?" She managed to look indignant with crumbs stuck to her mouth.

Mack patted her on the shoulder.

Dessie glanced at Linny and rolled her eyes.

Ruby went on. "Turns out the fellow was smoking a clove cigarette because he was trying to quit smoking tobacco. In fact, this whole little group ended up being a group of just-say-no-to-drugs-and-alcohol motorcycle riders called the Sober Sentinels, but your mama had clamped her hands to his wrists while he was trying to explain to her about the cloves. Then other folks walking by thought the big man was holding on to your mama, and they charged in trying to save her and a scuffle broke out...." Ruby trailed off, shaking her head.

Dessie explained, "One man thought he was breaking up a domestic dispute, then another fellow piled on. Dottie was wearing the

SWAT Team T-shirt and another man in law enforcement jumped in to give her a hand." She raised her eyes heavenward. "It was a big mess."

Dottie sighed. "The biggest problem was that there were just too many nice men trying to rescue me at Sturgis."

"A pile of nice men." Ruby shook her head, looking regretful. "And I missed out on most of it because I was in the ladies' room."

"How about resisting arrest and assault on an officer? The officers don't take kindly to those particular charges." Diamond leaned forward with her notebook, looking intrigued.

Ruby's eyes grew big as she recounted the end of the story. "Your mama didn't like the Sober Sentinel getting piled on, so she just took her purse and swung it, trying to dislodge the fellow on top by hitting him on the shoulders."

"But I missed and hit his head. He was an undercover policeman." Dottie shook her head, looking regretful. "Knocked him clean out."

"Your mama's purse is heavy." Dessie winced, remembering.

"Well, she does carry rocks," Ruby volunteered, looking philosophical. "She's been picking up a rock or two at each of her favorite places on this trip so she can bring them home to put in the front garden as souvenirs. She hadn't emptied her rocks out of her purse from the day before. So, technically, it was assault with a deadly weapon."

"Ah," Diamond said, and scribbled a note.

"The undercover policeman's name was Roddie, and he was fine once he came to. Just a little blue spot where the purse clasp hit him." Dottie pointed to a spot on her own head to show where he had been bruised. "I apologized over and over. Then we got to talking about yard sales. He's a big fan. We're going to Instagram each other pictures of our finds," she continued.

Mack gazed at her like she was the cleverest thing, and Dottie twinkled up at him.

Linny heaved a sigh, but the absurdity of the situation hit her and she began to laugh, slowly at first and then harder. Only her mama could make friends at a brawl. The others looked at her for a moment and, one by one, began laughing, too.

Her eyes shining with suppressed mirth, Diamond hushed them. But as she trotted off to talk to the powers that be, she whispered to Linny, "Your mama's a firecracker. I just love her to pieces."

While they waited for Diamond to come back, Linny walked her mother over to a corner, put a hand on her shoulder, and gazed at her steadily. "Are you really all right, Mama?"

"I am," Dottie said. "I was only in that cell for a couple of hours and that nice Sergeant Bowman put me in a jail room by myself. Luckily, I had some knitting in my bag and Lila, the guard, and I had some good long talks. She was raised Baptist, too. I told her all about the gospel music museum and she told me about problems she was having with her teenaged daughter." She sent Linny a pitying glance. "I'll keep those stories to myself, especially because you've just taken on Neal, who is about her daughter's age."

Linny flushed but was unwilling to get sidetracked. "Promise me you will never, ever, ever approach a man you do not know and try to talk to him about his lifestyle."

Her mother nodded, looking repentant. "I agree. Even Diesel told me it was wrong."

Linny pinched the spot between her brow. "Who is Diesel?"

"The fellow smoking the clove cigarettes." Her mother looked at Linny like she needed to pick up the pace conversationally. "We had a good talk on the ride down to the jail, and he's a nice man. But he said that what I did was dangerous. I promised him I'd never do it again." She bobbed her head, as if confirming her decision.

But Dottie made the vow with a lightness more suited to swearing off desserts for a week or trying to drink eight glasses of water a day. Linny stared at her and spoke slowly. "Mama, this is serious. If you had chastised a mean or angry man, you could have been seriously hurt."

"I know." Her mother shook her head, continuing to look repentant. "Luckily, it was Diesel."

Linny scrubbed her face with her hands. "So you and Diesel are chums now?"

Her mother nodded. "We're going to Facebook each other. I'm going to hitch him up with the lady in my prayer group whose pot-smoking son is giving her a fit. He said he used to be a druggie and might have some wisdom for her."

Linny cocked her head, still confused about why her mother looked so darned cheerful after her ordeal. "What's going on with you, Mama? A few weeks ago you were scared as a rabbit about being away from home and now you're bouncing back from a night in jail and making friends with a man named Diesel."

Her mother looked away for a moment, seemingly gathering her thoughts. "Living with your father all those years—especially toward the end, when he had that other woman and lost interest in me—I shrank inside myself," she said, her voice quavering slightly. Breathing a shuddery sigh, she went on. "My heart was hard as a walnut and I felt real bad about myself."

Linnny squeezed her shoulder. Mama never talked much about feelings and would roll her eyes when Oprah's guests used to talk about low self-esteem or being good to yourself.

"Underneath it all, I was mad. It probably came out as me being a bit judgmental," Dottie said.

Linny gave a restrained nod at that understatement. When Mama was in full-bore church lady mode, you'd confess to sins you didn't even commit.

"But I've been coming back to life ever since I told my friends and my prayer group about my bad marriage. I'm *feeling* more. I'm trying to be open to people and experiences I would have steered clear of in the past," her mother said.

Linny raised a brow. "Like this trip and your *friend* Mack?"

Dottie nodded, blushing. "I'm starting to care about people more; even ones that have hats on with steer horns coming out the side. Suspecting he was smoking dope got me all riled up. My friend's drugged-up son got two girls in the family way, ran up her credit cards, and even sold her family silver at the flea market." Her mother's eyes flashed at that last, most grievous offense, a sacrilege in the eyes of every good Southern woman.

Linny leaned over and gave her a brisk hug. "I'm proud of you, Mama."

"Thank you, honey," her mother said, almost shyly. "Isn't it wonderful?"

"It is, but no more accosting strange men," Linny said with a hand on her hip. She remembered what the bailiff had told her and winced. "Did you really threaten to make a citizen's arrest?"

"I got carried away," Dottie said sheepishly. "I promise, I'll just mind my own beeswax and enjoy my friends and the US of A."

After some negotiating by Diamond—who laughed gaily as she reminded people she had no business practicing law in South Dakota—charges against Dottie were dropped and she was released. Linny stood with her little pack outside the Meade County Courthouse, gave Diamond a grateful smile, and rolled her shoulders, trying to release the knots of tension. A breeze kicked up, blowing their hair this way and that, and the day was clear and sunny and full of promise.

"I wouldn't blame you girls if you wanted to pull the plug on this trip and come on home," Linny said but narrowed her eyes as she glanced at Mama and her friends. The women seemed brighter and more jovial since their foray into lawlessness and brawling.

"We're fine, honey. Appreciate you all coming all this way for us, but we had things under control," Dottie said to Linny and smoothed her hair to make sure all her curls were in place.

Linny widened her eyes at Diamond, who hid her smile.

"This is all part of the freewheeling RV experience, just like they said in the brochure," Ruby said with a carefree shrug.

"I'm not leaving. I'm having a ton of fun. Haven't had so much excitement since . . . well, ever," Dessie admitted, grinning. "Plus Perry's flying out this afternoon and the boys are going to rent a car and tag along with us."

Ruby raised a hand. "Before we leave Sturgis and hit the open road I have two requests. One: There's a policeman in Sturgis named Tony who dances when he directs traffic." Ruby rolled her hands Tina Turner–style to demonstrate. "And two: I heard Frank from *American Pickers* is here this week. He is just a cutie pie and I'm pretty sure he's single. I'd like to real casually run into him." She fished a tube of lipstick from her purse and expertly smoothed on a scarlet red coat without a mirror in sight.

Linny watched them and grinned. Hands over their mouths, Ruby and Dessie cackled over some joke while Dottie dimpled up at Mack, who was gallantly draping his blue blazer around her shoulders because she said she was chilly. No one seemed traumatized. In fact, she and Diamond were decidedly the fifth and sixth wheels.

After they dropped Mack and the women back at the campground and hugged and kissed them all good-bye, Linny and Diamond motored back to drop off the rental car and fly home.

As they strode across the tarmac toward a smiling Jim, Linny bumped shoulders with Diamond. "I don't know how I can thank you."

"Don't be silly," Diamond said with a flip of her hand. "I had a blast."

Soon they were settled in their leather seats and sipping miniature bottles of wine through straws: Diamond's idea.

"We forgot to toast," Linny said with a grin and held up her little bottle.

Diamond touched her minibottle to Linny's and gave a wicked grin. "To solving mysteries and freeing hardened criminals."

"And to smart women like you who save the day." Linny gave her a grateful look and took a sip.

Diamond bent her straw and took a long swallow, looking out the window as the plane taxied toward the runway. "Maybe I don't want to give up lawyerin' to become a housewife and organic gardener."

"What do you like most about practicing law?" Linny asked quietly. If she talked too fast or seemed too interested, Diamond would clam right up. Linny felt like she was sidling up to one of Jack's easily spooked rescue dogs: moving slowly, not making eye contact, and talking low and quiet.

Diamond scowled and fiddled with the handles of her bag. "This sounds sappy, but I remembered today how much I like helping people."

Linny paused for a moment. "That's not sappy. That's a fine thing to like."

Staring out the window, Diamond blew out a sigh. "I'm not sure being a housewife or sitting in a tiny house watching vegetables grow is going to cut it for me. I want a simpler life, but I may go out of my mind."

"True." Linny pictured a barefooted Diamond in a gingham sundress, her blond hair in pigtails like Daisy Duke and a basket of zucchini on her arm. She shuddered inwardly. "You can refine your plan," she said quietly.

Diamond gave a crooked smile and raised one shoulder. "I had one crazy idea. Even if Butch does propose I could still do retreats, maybe for attorneys thinking about career change or women going through life change or getting out of a marriage. One of my friends who quit practicing started a Save Your Marriage Boot Camp. Maybe I could house those folks. Maybe I could do getaways for people with autism."

Linny nodded. Diamond's nephew was on the autism spectrum, and because of him, she did fund-raising for autism advocacy groups.

Diamond tapped a long sparkly fingernail on her chin and looked thoughtful. "Maybe a retreat for the parents of kids with special needs. Now those folks could use a getaway."

"Interesting ideas," Linny said neutrally, trying to curb her enthusiasm.

"Hmmm," Diamond said as she leaned her head back in the seat and shut her eyes.

Discussion was over. Her moment of realness had passed.

Linny thought about some lonely years when she'd been single and then a widow. She'd study Facebook posts from girlfriends from college: the ones who'd met their husbands junior year, married after graduation, had tow-headed kids, posted recipes for gluten-free lunchbox snacks, and pics of Disney cruises with their families. They looked harried but happy, and Linny had envied them.

But then came the miracle of Jack. Linny glanced at Diamond and crossed her fingers that things worked out for her and Butch. Her mouth turned up as she saw the swoopy eyeliner and the slightly wacky streak of glittering blue eye shadow, but she also saw the fine lines around her eyes. They all were getting older. She felt like patting her friend but knew Diamond would hate it if she did. Instead, Linny closed her own eyes and sent up a prayer for her friend to get her heart's desire.

At the Worth County Regional Airport, Linny hugged Diamond good-bye and thanked her again. She stretched and stood up straighter. With a spring in her step, Linny walked to her car. Though tired from the trip and the drama of bailing her mama out of jail, she was proud that she and Diamond had managed to save the day.

Flipping on the air conditioner, Linny let down the windows to release the saunalike air in the car and called Jack. "Hey, you," she said, happiness flooding in as she heard his voice. She'd called and texted updates to him, Kate, and Mary Catherine, but she couldn't wait to fill him in on every detail of the trip. "I'm on my way home from the airport and all is well."

"You did good, honey," he said, but he sounded distracted.

Linny heard the sound of a baby wailing. "Why is Ivy at the house? I thought Jerry said he was going to take a few days off this week and be on full-time daddy duty."

"He did. He and Kate are at home with Ivy," Jack said calmly. "When Neal and I got home about an hour ago we found a laundry basket on the front porch." He paused. "Lin, there was a baby in it."

Who would drop off a baby? What if Jack and Neal had been delayed and the baby had gotten dehydrated or eaten by coyotes or... Her mind racing, Linny breathed deeply in and out and made herself drive slowly to the farm. Using signals on every turn she came to on the nearly deserted country road, she drove under the speed limit with her hands gripping tight to the steering wheel.

Holding her breath, she stepped into the living room and felt a lump form in her throat at the tender sight. Jack and Neal sat on the couch side by side watching an old *Star Wars* movie with the sound off. A white plastic laundry basket was wedged between them and an angelic-looking baby lay sleeping in a nest of clean towels. Jack's hand was on the baby's head and Neal lightly held the baby's foot.

Linny smiled at the men. Jack's eyes lit up, and even Neal looked relieved to see her. She leaned over to see the child. He or she had plump, rosy cheeks, a perfect nose, and a shock of fine dark brown hair. Linny stared, transfixed. Between precious Ivy and this beautiful child, she felt such a deep stirring of longing for a baby that she felt weak.

Watching her as if he read her thoughts, Jack quietly rose and nodded at Neal as if to say, *You're in charge.* He took Linny's hand and led her to the kitchen.

Linny hugged his neck and he held her so tightly she couldn't breathe. After a moment he let her go. She whispered, "Whose baby is it and why would they leave it on our doorstep?"

Jack turned up his hands, looking mystified. "No clue. There was no note or anything else to identify the parents."

They stood there in silence for a moment, baffled.

"I was waiting for you to get home to help me come up with a game plan," Jack admitted. Rubbing the back of his neck, he looked rueful. "I called Ned and he ran to the store to pick up baby supplies."

Linny blew out a sigh of relief. Ned, their farm manager, was the father of four little ones and would know exactly what she and Jack needed to tide them over.

Jack rubbed his chin and looked thoughtful. "We can use Ivy's crib for tonight."

But Linny couldn't get past how the baby had arrived so mysteriously. "Do you think the baby was stolen or did a teenaged mother give it up or..." Linny trailed off. "Is it a boy or a girl?

"It's a boy. Just what you need: another man in the house," Jack said with a grin.

But Linny gazed at him searchingly. She'd heard the subtext. Jack was quietly thrilled to have another baby in the house. Maybe he wanted a baby more than he'd let on. Maybe he was being New Agey and supportive of her going back and forth on the baby question because he knew how much she'd had thrown at her over the past year. "Don't get too attached, sweets," she said softly. "He's not our little guy."

"I know." A resigned look flitted across his face. "It's just nice to be around so many babies lately."

Linny tapped a finger to her mouth thoughtfully. "He looks older than Ivy."

Jack pointed to the laptop on the counter. "I looked up the baby developmental milestones. He's sleeping a lot. He can roll from his back to his stomach and kind of slide around on the floor like that. If he works at it, he'll be able to sit up on his own soon. My guess is he's around six or seven months old." With an indulgent smile, Jack added, "He's a smart little guy."

"Aren't we supposed to call the police?" Linny said, but she shuddered inwardly at the thought of the baby being taken away by Social Services.

"I called Mary Catherine for advice. She should be calling back soon," Jack said. "She'll tell us what our options are."

Linny blew out a sigh of relief but was startled when she heard the clomping of heavy boots on the porch.

"It's Ned," Jack said knowingly and strode to the door to keep his farm manager from knocking and waking the baby. Linny just stood there, arms crossed, digesting the news.

Jack walked back toting three bulky white plastic bags and a curious expression on his face. He put down the bags and handed her a dirty white envelope with one edge gnawed off. "Ned found this in the driveway. Roy or one of the other dogs must have picked it up from beside the baby."

Linny stared at the envelope punctured with doggie teeth marks and felt a sense of dread, knowing instinctively that this missive would answer their questions about the identity of the baby. If they knew who the child was, they'd have to give him back or give him up, and she wasn't sure she wanted to do either. "You open it," she said in a thin voice and moved to stand beside him so she could read it.

His eyes met hers and he pulled out a note written in a loopy scrawl. It read:

> *I never wanted a baby, and now I can't take care of him. My new boyfriend already has kids and doesn't want any more. We are going away to start over. Lucas is a good boy, but he's your problem now.*
>
> *Kandice Lane*
>
> *P.S. If you don't already know, Buck is the baby daddy.*

CHAPTER 12

Juggling Act

Linny gasped and leaned against the doorframe for support. She did some quick math. Buck died last August. He'd been having the affair with Kandi for a long while. If she was two months along when he passed, Lucas could very well be Buck's baby. She put a hand to her mouth, the marvelous and terrifying weight of the news starting to sink in. "Good Lord," she murmured and stared at Jack.

He shook his head and said wonderingly, "We've just been given a baby."

As she mulled it over, Linny took a quick shower and changed into shorts while Jack and Neal kept an eye on Lucas. As she walked into the kitchen, Jack was examining the formula and jars of baby food Ned had delivered, while Neal wore an expression of rapt delight as he held Lucas in his arms and fed him a bottle. She eyed the baby but busied herself pulling together supper. For some reason a nice supper seemed important, like putting a stake in the ground of normal after the extraordinary events of the past few days.

"Lin, do you want to hold Lucas?" Jack offered after he'd expertly burped the baby. But Linny eyed the baby warily and kept her distance. If she touched the baby or held him, she might never want to let him go. She loved Baby Ivy, but she was so adored by Jerry and Kate that Linny didn't feel bereft when she handed her niece back to her parents after her shift was over. But there was something about this boy being unwanted, adrift, abandoned that just got to her.

When her beloved first husband Andy had died, she'd felt adrift, almost ephemeral, like a gust of wind could come and just blow her away. And between her frequently absent daddy and her hound dog of a late husband, she knew a thing or two about being abandoned. A lump in her throat, she busied herself scrubbing the already spotless counter with a sponge, and polishing it with a clean dishrag.

From the corner of her eye she watched Jack and Neal sit on the rug in the kitchen with Lucas and drive yellow toy earthmovers over the delighted boy's chubby legs. The dogs were even acting respectable. Roy snoozed on the periphery of the circle of men, blinking open an eye every now and then just to keep apprised of the situation. Wilbur and Orville sat on their haunches and, Sphinxlike, eyed the construction site.

Neal—who, for the last day or two had specialized in sulks, one-word answers, and baleful glances—was making vroom, vroom noises to simulate the thrum of a front-end loader engine, and Jack was grinning from ear to ear as he showed Lucas how the bucket on the dozer lifted.

Linny jumped when the phone rang and snatched it up when she saw Mary Catherine's number. "Hey," she said, for some reason breathless. "You heard?"

"Jack left a long voice mail," Mary Catherine said.

"The baby is Kandi's. We found a note. His name is Lucas." Linny heard the tremble in her own voice. "She says Buck is the father and she wants to give us the baby."

"You can't just give a baby away like pizza samples at Costco." Mary Catherine blew out a disgusted sigh. "The courts will be involved. They'll probably grant you temporary custody. We need to find Kandi to see if she's serious about giving up the baby and willing to voluntarily relinquish parental rights." She paused for a moment and then asked bluntly, "If no one else lays claim to the baby and Kandi wants to give him to you all, are you and Jack willing to adopt him?"

Linny thought about it. "Not sure yet," she said, rubbing her forehead. A wave of fatigue hit her and a second wave crashed in: pure panic. Her life was getting so complicated so fast. She felt like she was behind the wheel of a speeding car with iffy brakes. "Jack and I haven't had a chance to even talk. I just got back from South Dakota and the baby turned up." She paused and glanced over as Jack and Neal clambered up from the floor. Jack hoisted Lucas up into his arms and gazed at the baby, looking besotted.

Linny had to ask. "Can we keep the baby until we get this straightened out or do we have to turn him over to Social Services or the county?" She tensed as she waited for the answer, watching Jack's head swivel toward her and Neal's face pinch with anxiety.

"For now, technically, you're simply taking care of the baby for a... friend," Mary Catherine said. "But tomorrow I'll call Social Services and notify them about the situation."

She blew out a sigh of relief and gave the men a thumbs-up. Neal grinned and punched his father's arm. Jack stood and did a one-arm-raised, touchdown-scoring dance around the kitchen, bobbling a smiling Lucas in his arms.

Mary Catherine went on. "You all talk about what you want to do and call me late tomorrow. No matter what, I'll need to get in touch with the mother so get me any contact info you have on her." She paused for a moment. "Are you sure Buck's the father?"

"Probably." Her scalp prickling with anger, Linny wondered again how her rat of a late husband could promise to put more effort into their marriage while sleeping with Kandi. Busy guy.

"We'll need to confirm that. Birth records and such," Mary Catherine said.

Linny rubbed a spot on her forehead and thought about it. "His affair with Kandi started before he even met me. If Kandi was several months pregnant when she had her final rendezvous with Buck, and if she was one of those women who didn't show much until the final months, I'll bet money Buck was the father." She paused a beat. "After all he bought her a Camaro."

"So sweet. Kind of like a promise ring," Mary Catherine said dryly. "And any idea where Kandi might have gone?"

"None," Linny said. "I only met her once."

"Okay. I'll get on it," she said, blowing out a sigh. "Right now, just go enjoy that baby."

After she ended the call Linny followed the men into the den, where they were getting Lucas settled for the night in Ivy's loaned crib. Arms crossed, she leaned on the doorframe and watched. Neal pushed up his slipping glasses and studied the baby monitor while Jack expertly changed Lucas's diaper on the antique sideboard buffet they'd jerry-rigged with padding to use as a diaper changing station.

Linny swallowed the lump that had formed in her throat. Wilbur and Orville were watching the action, as absorbed as diehard Wolfpack football fans with fifty-yard-line seats at a bowl game. Roy cocked his handsome head and looked at her. He always sensed when she was worried.

She'd found her little Lab mix when the previous renters had moved out and not bothered to take the dog. Jack had found Wilbur and Orville abandoned at a county dump. Their owners had left the puppies, just like trash. She rubbed her forehead. How did people abandon puppies . . . or babies?

And the question of taking in this baby was exponentially more complicated than taking in a dog. She was too tired to sort it out. "Can you all handle getting this guy down for the night? I can't stay on my feet another minute," she said. Seeing the sleepy baby's sweetly drooping eyes, she determinedly averted her glance as quickly as she could, just like she did when she drove by the scene of a crash on the highway. Giving the baby a wide berth, she kissed Jack and Neal and trudged off to bed.

At 5:30 the next morning a bleary-eyed Linny sipped coffee and stared at the computer screen. She printed an article on North Carolina laws pertaining to abandoned or surrendered babies, flipped to a website on how to help teens learn to manage stress by doing one-minute mindfulness breathing exercises, an idea Neal would snicker at. She stayed a while at Mommy's Organic Infant, a site detailing developmental milestones, nap schedules, and recipes for homemade organic foods for babies around what they guessed to be Lucas's age.

The mothers in the embedded clips were limp-haired, earnest, and pretty, and their eyes glowed like zealots as they described the myriad of preservatives and toxins in the processed baby foods served by less conscientious mothers. They grew teary-eyed as they explained how little Camila or Jameson or Zed thrived on Mommy's homemade organic meals.

Just to be on the safe side, she and Jack probably needed to grow their own organic foods rather than buy them. Linny would wear a red kerchief and ride around at daybreak on a tractor that smelled of French fries because it ran on used cooking oil. She'd harvest their crop of broccoli or bananas that they'd misted with lemon juice or some other environmentally friendly but ineffective way to keep away bugs.

Linny rubbed her eyes with her fingers. She'd just add that item to her to-do list.

Sitting back in her chair, she stretched and tried to ease the tightness in her shoulders. She and Jack had talked briefly before she'd fallen into an exhausted sleep. If Mary Catherine gave them the okay from the county, they'd keep Lucas temporarily. But how would they manage adding a toddler to their already hectic lives? Though the baby looked cute from four feet away, she felt a flicker of resentment that she and Jack were cleaning up other peoples' messes instead of easing into their marriage and enjoying their still new love.

As she took a swallow of cooling coffee, she shook her head, aware of a big fear. What if they all fell in love with Lucas and Kandi changed her mind and wanted him back?

She was going to drive herself crazy. Fresh air would clear her head. She'd walk down to the end of the driveway to get the paper and maybe take a short walk up the road. Linny quietly slipped on clothes and sneakers and stepped outside. She stopped short. A baby fairy had left a crib and a high chair on the front porch. The note taped to the leg of the chair read:

We fervently hope we will never need these again! Keep as long as you need. Ned and Jilly

Linny grinned. Their farm manager and his wife both seemed to be blurs of perpetual motion with several small children always in tow.

The seven o'clock breakfast table planning meeting was as high powered and deliverable oriented as any corporate meeting Linny had ever attended. She figured the troops needed fuel so she'd whipped up a big bowl of steel-cut oatmeal and set out bowls of blueberries, sliced peaches, and pecans for toppings.

As the men dished up heaping bowls and sat, Linny tapped her pen on a pad of paper. "We just need to get through this week. We need to get Lucas on a good schedule, take care of Ivy, and get our work done."

"If I could get hold of them I'd like to tell my folks about the baby," Jack said with a boyish grin as he began feeding Lucas, who was propped in his high chair all bibbed up. "Mama would be over the moon."

Linny took a swallow of creamy coffee and thought about it. Her in-laws, Rush and Ceecee, were away on a cruise to the Galapagos Islands, a trip they'd wanted to take their whole lives. Afterward they were going to Fort Lauderdale to catch a ship for a repositioning cruise. Her mother-in-law was a devoted grammy to Neal and just a few weeks ago she had given Linny an arch look and asked, "Can we expect the pitter-patter of tiny feet anytime soon? It would be heaven to have a few more grandbabies to love on!" Rush and Ceecee would probably dive off the cruise ship and swim home from the Panama Canal if they knew a baby was afoot and they might be needed to help.

Linny picked at a cuticle, again noticed her ringless finger and felt a stab of insecurity. She and her mother-in-law had this new bond of caring for each other, but if she met Lucas, Linny would have to explain to her very proper mother-in-law the unsavory backstory of her late husband, including the part about his affair with Kandi. Did Ceecee's friends at Oakwood Hills Country Club have those kinds of skeletons in their family closets? Seemed unlikely. And what if they had to give Lucas back? With a wild card like Kandi, all bets could be off. "Let's not say anything until we hear more from Mary Catherine. I don't want them to abandon their trip just in time for us to have to give Lucas up." She swallowed hard as she thought of surrendering the baby.

"You're right." Jack nodded. "They'll be back soon enough; we'll tell them then." He ducked as Lucas tossed a spoonful of a brown rice, oatmeal, and pear concoction in his direction.

"I'll help wherever you need me," Neal said quietly. He laughed and pointed at the baby. "This guy gets more on his bib than he swallows."

Jack squeezed the baby's foot and reviewed his list. "Neal and I will make a run to Babyland to pick up supplies. I'll drop Neal back here, go to the office to rearrange some appointments, stop at the grocery store, and be back home by two. Neal and I can make a few simple meals for the next two weeks and stick them in the freezer. Would that help?" he asked, cocking his head at Linny.

"So much," she said with a grateful smile.

"Lucas needs clothes. All he has are the ones he wore when we found him," Neal pointed out as he wiped away a blob of food from Lucas's chin.

Jack scribbled that down. "Thanks, buddy. I missed that."

Linny read off her own to-do list. "I'll call Mary Catherine to see if she has any news and schedule an appointment with a pediatrician. I have a FaceTime meeting at eleven, and Jerry drops Ivy off at 1:30 so he can take Kate to physical therapy, but both you boys will be home shortly after that." She blew out a little sigh. She'd need the men. Keeping two small babies at once could be mayhem. Linny paused, trying to think whether she'd forgotten anything and felt a pang of longing for her mama. She couldn't wait for Dottie to come home. She didn't want to pester Kate with constant questions while she was recuperating, but Linny knew so little about babies. She needed advice from Dottie; more advice than she could get from hurried trips to the baby websites. And she was going to need Dottie's physical help. Even with Jack and Neal's pitching in, she needed more hands, especially with two babies around.

Linny watched Jack as his big hands tenderly made soothing circles on the baby's back. So far she'd avoided physical contact with the baby, but that wouldn't be possible any longer. "I need to finish planning the class I have next week." She rubbed her forehead, feeling overwhelmed.

"You can work and I can watch the babies," Neal offered.

Linny paused and raised a brow at Jack. Where was the argumentative boy who shot death-ray glares at them when asked to pitch in with household chores? "That would be great if you could help me. I'll be in the next room at the computer, but I need just one hour of concentration." She'd be constantly supervising Neal, but she could be surreptitious about it.

"I can do it," Neal said firmly.

"Well, I'm going to give you a crash course on babies. I'll tell you everything I know and you're going to go online and watch all the babysitter and safety clips you can," Jack said.

Neal bobbed his head, looking serious.

If Neal studied up on babies he'd know more than she did. Linny had basically been winging it with Ivy, but she needed to get serious about this job. Leaning her elbow on the table, Linny put her chin in her hand and looked at the boy. "Neal, you decide which clips are the best ones and I'll watch them, too. I've picked up some tips, but I'm still new at this myself."

"Okay," Neal said with a quick nod, but the smile that played at his lips told Linny that he liked the idea of instructing her.

She watched him patiently trying to get Lucas to drink from a sippy cup and felt a thrum of anxiety. Wouldn't do for him to get too attached to the baby either. "Remember, guys, Lucas isn't ours. We may have to give him back today or tomorrow. Think of him as a kind of a loaner baby," she said nervously.

Neal's brows were drawn in confusion. "A loaner baby?"

"You know. Like bowling shoes. You get to keep them for a while, but then you have to give them back." Linny was babbling now and she knew it. Jumping up, she began clearing breakfast dishes from the table.

Jack arched a brow at her. "No ambivalence about this baby, right, Lin?"

She stopped rinsing bowls and gave him a chagrined smile. "A little," she admitted.

Later that week Linny sat at the kitchen table, her hands resting on the keyboard, stuck. She glanced again at the few sentences she'd managed to eke out on the proposal for training at a medical device company called Wanazak Sciences. Why was writing this taking so long? Linny thought about the meeting she'd had with the client just a few months ago—before Neal became a full-timer and before the house was full of babies.

The human resources director had introduced herself using the full name and title on the nameplate on her door: Dr. Eleanor Huffsteader. She'd smoothed back her sleek auburn bob and assured Linny that she'd be offering her own extensive expertise and monitoring to whomever delivered the training. Linny had to fake a coughing spell to hide her shudder. After the meeting she'd Googled Dr. Eleanor and found she had a doctorate in sociology from a college that was rumored to be a diploma mill.

Linny pushed back a stray lock of hair and thought about it. It wasn't just the idea of working closely with Dr. Eleanor that bugged her. Wanazak Sciences was huge and had been in the news lately for falsely claiming the parts they used in their manufacturing process were made in America when they were made in China. She had an uneasy feeling about the whole project.

Linny groaned softly. She'd committed herself so she'd have to force herself to write this proposal. But after tapping out a few more words she blew out a sigh and closed the document. She was just too tired to do good writing.

The schedule she and Jack—and Neal—had cobbled together was frenetic, but it was working. She took a swallow of coffee and stared unseeing out the window. She thought about her to-do list for the day and rubbed her eyes with her fingers.

She couldn't believe how much time babies took. Between feeding, changing, getting him up and down for naps, and the laundry Lucas generated, Linny was on the go all the time. Supper the last few nights had been hastily slapped-together meals: odd combinations like frozen burritos and Italian mixed vegetables, corn chowder she'd found in the bottom of the freezer served over ninety-second rice. The food pyramid was in shambles.

Linny pushed back her hair and realized it was messy and poofed up on one side from the way she'd slept. Her FaceTime meeting with Chanel Green was just ten minutes away. She needed to quickly fix her hair and slap on some makeup. Darned video calls.

As the Skype tone rang, Linny sat at her desk and found she was actually excited about her coaching meeting with the young CEO. Chanel Green needed help writing the speech she was going to give her employees at an all-hands meeting.

"Good morning." Linny smiled as the call connected, noting that the young woman looked professional in a full-coverage, non-jogging-bra-type blouse with what looked like red fire trucks on it.

"Hey there." Chanel smiled wanly, but she looked tense, spring-loaded. Her eyes darted around the room as though she might bolt for the exit.

Linny studied her and her mouth quirked up. "Don't tell me. You hate public speaking."

"Despise it." Chanel grimaced and raked her fingers through her short hair. "I'd rather do anything: go a few rounds with one of those women wrestlers on TV, go to a sorority pledge party . . ." She trailed off, looking defeated.

Linny nodded sympathetically. "I understand. The first year I spoke in front of groups I learned never to hold papers because my hands shook so badly. It gets easier with practice," she assured her. "You're going to get more comfortable with speaking, though. You have to. You're the leader."

"All right, all right." Chanel gave a resigned sigh. "Now what am I supposed to say?"

"Your talk is about how you want the company to move into the future." Linny looked at Chanel searchingly. "Why is improved professionalism and customer service important to you?"

Chanel froze, opened her mouth, and closed it again. "Can I look at my notes?" she croaked out.

"You can, but you don't need to," Linny said. "Just don't think too much and tell me why you want these changes."

Chanel drew a deep shuddering breath, blew it out, and closed her eyes for a moment. "Because we're better than this," she finally said.

"Go on," Linny said, smiling encouragingly.

"Because we need to portray who we are: not a group of merry pranksters but a smart, talented, and capable group of professionals who offer amazing products and services." Chanel still sounded tentative, but her voice grew more confident as she went on. "Because our business is going to double within the next two years and we need to be ready. We're moving onward and upward, and that means we need to be a seamless, grown-up team with superb relationships with our customers. No I'm-with-stupid arrows. No almost running off smart colleagues because we're playing the boys against the girls. No sports bras," she said, finishing with a rueful grin.

Linny beamed and held her hands palms up. "Excellent. You just gave me the basis for your speech. Your onward-and-upward speech."

"Huh. Onward and upward," Chanel mused, looking slightly less like a flight risk. "I like that."

"Now you came up with a list of what you all are doing well, right?" Linny asked.

"I did." Chanel bobbed her head and held up a piece of paper.

"And you came up with areas in which you'd like improvement," Linny said.

"I did." Chanel held up three sheets of paper and made a face. "Slightly longer list."

"Don't worry. You'll fix that," Linny said. "Put those two lists together and your speech writes itself." She gave Chanel a crooked smile. "Oh, and add a mea culpa."

Chanel flushed, looking chagrined. "How about *I'm sorry for micromanaging you and breathing down your necks instead of leading* you. My bad for never holding staff meetings or performance reviews. I'm a dolt for not communicating about expected conduct, professional work environment, and relationships with customers."

"Something like that, but don't beat yourself up that much. Just explain this is a learning process for you, too, and focus on the future," Linny suggested.

The young woman nodded and they started to work.

Chanel was rehearsing her last run of the much-improved speech when Linny heard the office door open and glanced behind her. Neal raced in one door, sliding on the wood floors on his fuzzy socks—his arms outspread like a surfer catching a big wave—and surfed right out the other door. This sock-surfing routine was another one of his new things, like the corny science jokes.

Linny felt the heat rise in her face. Bad timing given her preaching about professionalism. "I'm sorry, Chanel."

But the young woman was smiling broadly. "Tell your surfer buddy I said *cowabunga*."

"I will." Linny smiled, relieved, but shot a glance at the clock, knowing a hungry baby might start crying at any moment. If that happened on top of Neal's surf-by she'd really look unprofessional. "Let's schedule the employee training courses you decided on . . ." she began and paused as it hit her. This was a huge project, one she'd be excited to lead. She was really good at these types of programs, too. But she would *have* to farm out some of the work to colleagues if she was planning on staying sane.

Linny sat up straighter in her chair and her eyes met Chanel's. "I'll do the customer service segments for you, but I'm going to recommend a colleague for delivery of the program on professionalism in the workplace. She does an Employee Blooper of the Week segment and a What Not to Wear at Work Fashion Show. Participants love her." As she read Chanel the contact number from her phone, Linny felt lighter. With all that she had on her plate, she had to be realistic about what she could and couldn't do or risk failing her family or her clients. And surprisingly—even though she was saying no to the kind of work she loved—it felt good to let part of it go.

CHAPTER 13

The New Normal

Later in the week Linny lay on a yoga mat and groaned as she tried stretching to one side and then the other. Turning over, she eased into a child's pose. The muscles in her back were so tight that she might freeze in place, like Lot's wife. The stretching felt good, though the snaps and cracks she heard were slightly alarming. Linny reveled in the absolute silence in her house. She was keeping Ivy, but by some miracle both babies were asleep at the same time and Neal was spending the day at his mom's house.

Linny's phone vibrated on the floor beside her, and she smiled as Mary Catherine's name came up. Scrambling to get up, she stepped out to the front porch to take the call. "Hey," she said softly, glancing toward the window of the den and fretting about the sound-muffling qualities of the old farmhouse windows and walls.

"Hey, yourself." *Crick, crick.*

Linny held the phone away from her ear. Mary Catherine's eating pistachios while talking on the phone was irritating; not as bad as her soup sipping or slurping melting frozen yogurt bars but right up there. When laser-focused on work her friend wasn't big on social niceties.

"Any news?" Linny asked. She realized she was holding her breath and made herself draw in fresh air, anxious to hear the update on efforts to track down Kandi. "How did your meeting with Kandi's mother go?"

"She's a lovely woman," Mary Catherine said dryly. "Says she hasn't spoken to her daughter in five years, doesn't know or care where she is, and didn't know anything about baby Lucas. In fact, she said, *Lady, if you're lookin' at me to take care of that child, you can fergit it. And if you find my daughter, tell her she still owes me two hundred bucks.*"

Linny had to smile. Mary Catherine's imitation of a mean country woman was so spot on it was almost scary. But her smile faded as she realized the woman had probably sounded a lot like Mary Catherine's own beer-breathed mother, who tended bar down on the coast at Morehead City, married to no-account husband number five. "Yikes."

"Yup," Mary Catherine went on. "The good news is, she's Kandi's closest living relative and probably won't make a claim for Lucas if you and Jack decide you want to adopt him."

Linny was quiet for a moment. She and Jack hadn't had a chance to talk about it yet, or maybe she'd just been avoiding that conversation with him. "Any clues on where Kandi is?"

"Not yet. I did track down Buck's old fishing buddies. You said they knew her," Mary Catherine said.

Linny flushed, remembering that old mortification. After a fishing tournament Buck and his carousing crew had all stayed at a hotel down on the coast. That was the night he'd died—while he was in his room with Kandi.

"They all claim that night was the last they saw of Kandi. They did tell me one thing, though. She always talked about the Bahamas," Mary Catherine said. "That may be where she's gone, but there are thirty inhabited islands in that chain. Could take time to track her down."

Something niggled at Linny's memory. In her brain fog from the influx of babies she'd forgotten information that could help Mary Catherine. "When Diamond tried to find the money Buck stole from me, she learned Kandi had a police record."

"I'll check it out," Mary Catherine said. "Any other clues you've neglected to give me?"

Linny paused, racking her brain. "Remember that time Kandi showed up at my place demanding money? She said she was going to take me to court and threw a lawyer's business card at me. I didn't keep the card and can't remember his name, but Diamond will know. She called him."

"Excellent. I'll call her," Mary Catherine promised. "You still keeping the baby at arm's length?"

"Not really," Linny admitted. "The men can't do all the childcare, and he's just so cute. He smiles a lot, and when I raise my eyebrows up and down, he gives this belly laugh. I fed him this morning and he just kept his eyes locked on mine the whole time." Linny heard herself prattling and groaned. "Sorry, girl. I used to secretly roll my eyes at Kate when she went on about some clever new thing Ivy had done. I sound the same way."

"Well, as long as you're keeping him at an arm's length," Mary Catherine said, a smile in her voice.

The next morning the baby started whimpering for his bottle at 5:00 a.m. He usually took his bottle later, but when the little guy was hungry, he was hungry. The whimpers could escalate into earsplitting screams in no time. Hurriedly, she turned down the monitor. Jack was as beat as she was so she'd let him sleep a while longer. Slipping from the bed, she pulled on a robe and padded in to pick up Lucas, who blinked at her and smiled a gummy smile. He looked natty in his sock monkey pajamas.

After flipping on the coffeemaker and warming a bottle Linny sat on the porch swing with Lucas nestled in her arms and fed him. She sighed happily, breathing in the cool morning air and the scent of newly mown grass. After he'd finished most of the bottle Lucas began to hiccup. Linny smiled. His eyes grew wide each time the hic sounds came from his mouth. She slipped a cloth diaper on her shoulder, shifted him up into place, and gently patted his back in small circular motion. He gave a gusty burp.

Linny remembered a dash to the store to pick up formula and baby food earlier in the week. In the baby aisle she'd stood beside a woman wearing gray sweats with her hair falling out of a messy ponytail. Dressed in an almost identical outfit, Linny saw the faint spit-up marks on the woman's shoulder and the two exchanged tired smiles. She was part of that sisterhood now.

Lowering him, Linny just looked at him: his sturdy arms, his precious tiny hands, his tiny shell-pink fingernails. She stuck out her finger and Lucas looked at her gravely as he latched his fingers on to it. Linny breathed that intoxicating baby smell of milk, clean baby skin, and a trace of almond diaper cream. Before she fell, Kate had told her that when she was out with Ivy, perfect strangers approached her and asked to kiss or smell the baby. "Someone should bottle that new baby smell," one woman had gushed. Kate had put a stop to the baby kissing and sniffing. "No telling who has a cold," she'd said indignantly. But someone *should* bottle that smell.

As he leaned into her drowsily, she felt the warm heft of him and felt besotted. Just what she didn't want to feel. But there love was, despite her best efforts to dodge it.

The hamster wheel of worried thought started to spin. What if Kandi changed her mind? What if her rough mother claimed him, thinking there might be money to be made by demanding the baby back? What if Buck wasn't the biological father and the real father showed up to take Lucas from them?

She made herself take a long, deep breath and gaze out at the horses grazing, the morning mist around the red barn, and the fields that rolled in front of her. Things would turn out like they turned out, she reminded herself. As much as she wanted to control outcomes, she wasn't driving.

At the Memphis airport Dottie had kissed her good-bye and pressed in Linny's hand a small book of daily inspirational passages. Linny remembered one she'd particularly liked: *He directs your course as surely as rivers run to the sea.* She closed her eyes picturing that and felt a sense of serenity steal over her. Settling back into the cushion, she pushed off on the floor with her toes and started to gently swing. Sighing, she simply let herself enjoy the miracle of a baby.

Gently, she shook Jack awake, gave him a kiss, and handed Lucas to him. "I'm getting us coffee. I'll be right back," she said. When she came back bearing two fragrant mugs she set them on the bedside table, took off her robe, and slipped in beside Jack. She shivered. He felt so warm and lovely. Watching her stubble-cheeked husband gently holding a dozing baby on his chest, Linny knew her heart was melting.

She propped herself on her elbow, met his eyes, and said softly, "Let's do whatever it takes to adopt Lucas."

He snaked an arm around her, pulled her close, and said in his gruff, early morning voice, "I'd already decided that, darlin', but I knew you'd come around."

While the boys ate their peanut butter and banana toast, Linny spooned in yogurt and thought through her day. After his morning nap Linny would drop the baby off at Jack's office while she went to her meetings. Ruthie, Jack's office manager, had threatened to quit unless she got to do some babysitting.

Linny would present her proposal to Dr. Eleanor Huffsteader and then give moral support to Chanel Green by sitting in on her onward and upward meeting with her employees. She'd swing back by the vet clinic at 11:00, pick up Lucas and Neal, and run by to check on Kate and Ivy. Then she'd buy Neal lunch—anything he wanted at Chick-fil-A, including fries—and head home. Jerry would drop Ivy off at 1:30.

Neal took a long gulp of orange juice and looked poised for an extended burp, but Jack shot him a warning look. The boy shrugged and took another bite of toast.

Neal seemed happier these days, but she and Jack hadn't been able to spend much alone time with him since Lucas arrived. Neal liked helping out with both babies. He carried them around in a casual but careful way. He wrote shopping lists, helped pack lunches for him and Jack to take to the office, and did online research about the highest-rated organic baby foods. He'd been an excellent sport about the baby, but he didn't need to be overlooked either. Linny took a last bite of yogurt and made a mental note to talk with Jack about it.

After a shower, Linny slipped on earrings, smoothed on makeup, and dusted her face with powder. For her meeting she wore her blue silk wraparound blouse: her best blouse and the only clean one she owned at the moment. She hurried in to change Lucas. Knowing it was dicey to change him when she was dressed up, she plowed on. She needed to leave in a half hour.

With Lucas on the changing table, Linny held her breath as she cleaned him up. Did fighting the urge to gag mean she was bad mother material? She'd have to look that up. While she smoothed on the almond diaper cream—the one Neal's research said was the highest rated by the Jessica Alba baby crowd—she kept up a patter of small talk with Lucas.

"So, little man, we have a busy day. It's sunshiny out, though, and I saw a bluebird this morning. That's good luck, you know." He waved his arms and made a bubble so he seemed to enjoy it, but was this the right way to talk to babies? Should she be trying to use bigger words or more complex thoughts to help him excel academically later on? Another question she'd Google as soon as she found the time.

After dropping Lucas at the vet clinic Linny pulled into the parking lot of the glinting office building of Wanazak Sciences. Releasing her seat belt, Linny took deep breaths and tried to get psyched for her meeting. She opened the car door . . . and shut it again. She didn't want to work with Dr. Eleanor Huffsteader or her company. So why was she going in to try to win the business?

Here she was, cheerleading Diamond and Mama and everybody else in the world to go for what made them happy, but she wouldn't do the same for herself. And Mama's words came back to her: *I hope I raised a daughter who pays attention to what she wants.* She remembered what she'd said to Chanel Green about making time for love, family, and enjoying life.

Linny rested her head on the wheel. Life was going too fast. She was careening around, not even taking the time to properly kiss Jack or look at the stars with Neal. She'd treated Lucas more like a problem that needed to be solved than a child to be enjoyed.

After all she'd been through she had finally gotten the life she'd always wanted. So why was she rushing through it, and taking on new things she didn't even want to do?

Linny picked up her phone and glanced at the clock. Seven minutes before the meeting. Praying for voice mail, Linny entered the numbers with a trembling finger.

"Dr. Eleanor Huffsteader," the woman said, sounding irritated.

Hearing the sociologist's tone confirmed her decision. Firmly, Linny said, "Eleanor, I'm sorry, but I need to cancel this morning's meeting, and I'm going to need to withdraw my name from consideration for your project. . . ."

As she steered the Volvo sedately from the parking lot of Wanazak Sciences, she resisted the urge to roll down the window, stick her arm out, and wave it madly as she yelled, *yahoo!* When she turned the car back on the main road Linny felt bubbling elation and grinned from ear to ear.

With extra time, Linny swung by Jumpin' Joe's Bean House and got a skinny latte and two lemon raspberry muffins for takeout. She'd enjoy them as she checked out one of the local parks a Bodacious Bonus Mom had raved about in a post she'd read last night: *Historic Pullen Park is the family friendliest park in the area! It sits on sixty-six wooded acres right in the middle of Raleigh and features a refurbished historic carousel with beautifully carved animals. The carousel works, and a train rides you and the kiddies around the park.*

Linny sat on a dock in Pullen Park, her bare feet dangling in the lake as she finished off the last of the amazing muffins. Brushing the crumbs from her lap, Linny sipped her latte and held her face up to the sun.

Later Linny arrived at Green Sage. Unlike the dread that had filled her before her last scheduled meeting, she felt a flutter of excitement to be there for Chanel at her onward and upward speech.

The young CEO beamed at Linny when she walked into the large room they had set up for the meeting. Hurrying over, she put a hand on Linny's arm that felt like a vise grip. "I can't tell you how glad I am that you're here," she murmured. She gave her an imploring look. "Tell me again why I can do this?"

"You can do this because it's important to you, and to Green Sage." Linny gave her a little nod. "You know this talk backward and forward. You've got your notes on the screen so you can remember everything. If you need a break just stop talking and collect your thoughts. People don't mind you stopping to think."

Chanel nodded, as if memorizing every word Linny said. "If I forget anything you said I should just speak from my heart, right?"

"That's right." Linny said.

Chanel spun away and began greeting employees.

Linny watched her and saw that Chanel's lips kept sticking to her teeth. Dry mouthed from nerves probably. She slipped off and got a bottle of cold water from the refreshment table and casually handed it to her. Chanel sent her a grateful look, twisted off the cap, and took a long swallow.

Linny took a seat at the small table set up catty-corner to the podium. As she slid her feet under the tablecloth, she felt a warm, furry body. She hid a smile. Sage was attending the meeting.

Chanel caught her eye and gave her a rueful smile. *For good luck,* she mouthed silently.

Linny nodded and glanced around, trying to gauge the mood of the employees as they traipsed into the rows of chairs they'd set up in the middle of the common area. Some looked like they'd been sent to the principal's office, while others had the buoyant look of kids who'd just flown out the door for recess. Many simply stared down at their devices, their fingers flying.

Linny recognized some of the employees she'd interviewed. Afro-bearded Vaya, who called his female co-workers *chicks*, gave her a wary nod. In deference to the occasion, Jax hadn't worn his I'm-with-stupid hat to the meeting. Jarrett wore a loud Hawaiian shirt and his hair was disheveled, like he'd just crawled out of that hammock he'd requested. Grinning, he held up his hand, curled his three middle fingers, and rotated his hand back and forth in a hang-loose sign.

Linny couldn't help but smile.

Chanel cleared her throat and rose to stand behind a small podium, looking like a gazelle catching wind of a tiger in one of those awful cycle-of-life nature documentaries. She shot Linny a desperate glance, then began. "Welcome," she said in a small voice.

Linny watched as employees kept talking and joking with one another, possibly not noticing that Chanel was trying to start the meeting. Linny met Chanel's eyes and gave her an encouraging nod, willing the employees to be quiet and listen.

Chanel glanced around the room for a moment, and then a look of irritation crossed her face. Standing up straighter, she squared her shoulders and, too loudly, boomed out, "Welcome."

Instantly, the room fell quiet.

Chanel met the eyes of her employees and seemed to grow in stature from her place at the podium. "Good morning and welcome. I've brought you here today to share good news about Green Sage, and to paint a picture for you of what will be our very bright future." She cocked her head. "Take a look at the person to your right and the one to your left. Look at the person behind you and the one in front of you."

Laughing nervously, employees glanced at one another.

Chanel paused for a moment. "You are looking at some of the most talented IT professionals in the consulting world. I'm very proud of each and every one of you."

The nervous laughs turned into looks of relief, back-slapping, and fist bumps.

Now looking poised, Chanel leaned away from the podium, took a sip of her water, and smiled as she let them be silly. She queued up a PowerPoint slide and, after a moment, went on. "Let me show you where we are currently with profits, earnings, and market share. Next, we'll look at projections on the same for the next two to five years. Finally, I'm going to talk about what we need to do to take us from here to there. Specifically, we are going to talk about improvements we need to make in teamwork, professionalism, and customer service."

Linny breathed out, relieved. Chanel looked nothing like a nervous speaker. Instead, she looked and sounded like the confident, practically charismatic owner of a small business. Linny's shoulders dropped. She'd been unaware she'd hunched them in nervousness. Leaning back in her chair, she watched Chanel, feeling proud of the young woman. The speechmaking practice Linny had insisted she do had paid off. Leaning down, she gave Sage a quick scratch behind the ears. He was a splendid good-luck charm.

Feeling fizzy optimism about life itself, Linny wheeled into the parking lot of Jack's vet clinic and walked with a light step as she went in to pick up Neal and the baby.

Ruthie greeted her, laughing as she gently disentangled Lucas's fingers from the sparkly reading glasses she kept on a chain around her neck. "He's just fascinated with these glasses. Good thing they only cost a dollar." Handing the baby to Linny, Ruthie shook her head, grinning. "He is just the sweetest little pea and his big brother was so good with him."

"I'll bet he was." Linny shifted Lucas's heft to her hip and kissed his head. She saw Neal behind Ruthie, busily packing games and his iPad into his backpack. "Hey, buddy," she called, then spoke to Ruthie in a voice loud enough for him to hear. "Not only has Neal been gentle and helpful with the baby, he's been a tremendous help in other ways. I don't know how we could have done it without him."

Ruthie laced her fingers together and turned to gaze admiringly at Neal. "Neal, you are just the best young man."

Neal flushed and pretended to adjust the straps on his backpack. "Thanks," he mumbled.

Linny gave Ruthie a grateful look and a quick hug. She, Neal, and Lucas walked to the car.

Neal was already seat-belted in the Volvo and engrossed in a game on his phone as Linny double-checked the security of Lucas's car seat. The buckles were tricky, and she worried she'd get it wrong and somehow catapult the baby out when she slowed to stop at a light. She was getting good at imagining unlikely catastrophes: tooling down 1-40 with Lucas in his baby seat teetering precariously on top of the car, getting Lucas mixed up with another baby at the pediatrician's office and taking home another woman's much less bright child, or baby snatchers dressed as rural postwomen putting him in a sack and screeching off in an undersized mail truck.

She gave the buckle a pat, satisfied she'd gotten it right, and slipped into the driver's seat. Looking toward the other side of the parking lot, her heart skipped a beat as she spied a familiar black Mercedes—and the petite blonde standing beside it, gesticulating as she talked earnestly to Jack. Linny gasped quietly as she watched Vera throw her arms around Jack's neck and hug him fervently. She darted a glance at Neal to see if he'd witnessed the happy reunion, but he was engrossed in his game. Was her husband out of his mind? Glancing behind her, she slowly backed up, her hands icy on the wheel. Linny's thoughts careened around wildly as she pulled out of the parking lot.

Jack couldn't still be romantically interested in Vera, she reasoned. He just couldn't. He was so exasperated by her, and angry at her for allowing drama in her personal life to come before parenting. She racked her brain, trying to think of any other excuse for the embrace she'd witnessed. More kindly, listening-ear TV preacher moments, she guessed, but the thought made the blood pulse in her ear. What would it take for Jack to stop being so close to Vera? Linny was still fuming as she pulled into the driveway at the farm, but Jerry was waiting for her on the porch to drop off Ivy and the rest of the afternoon passed in a blur.

At five thirty, Linny was trying to figure out what to cook for supper when Jack breezed into the kitchen, all smiles.

"Hey, darlin' girl,' he said softly as he reached around her waist to give her a hug. But Linny spun away and stood in front of the oven, arms crossed. She gazed at him coldly. "Anything interesting happen at work today? Any visitors?" she said in an icy voice.

He met her gaze unflinchingly. "You saw Vera when you stopped by the office?"

"I did," she said.

He put his canvas briefcase down and leaned against the counter.

His eyes met hers and he said in an even tone, "I was going to tell you, Lin, as soon as supper was over and we had some time alone."

She gave him a flinty look. "You can tell me now."

Jack blew out a sigh and rubbed the back of his neck. "Vera stopped by, all broken up. Chaz served her with divorce papers. She was crying so hard she couldn't breathe. So I walked her outside to move the dramatics out of the office. I didn't want Neal or the staff to see her upset," he said, looking grim. "So at the car she said that divorcing me was the biggest mistake of her life and just launched herself at me. She kept hugging my neck and wouldn't let go." He shook his head, looking embarrassed, and met her eyes. "That's the moment you saw."

Linny felt her face flame with anger and tried to decide who she wanted to strangle first: Vera or Jack. Probably Jack.

He looked at her gravely. "You don't for one minute think I'm in love with anyone but you? You know that, Linny."

She thought about it and nodded slowly. She did know that. But she wasn't letting him off the hook so easily. "When are you going to set better boundaries with her?"

He held up a hand. "I will, I promise, but today wasn't the day to do that."

She waited.

He leaned forward and held her eyes. "I told her you were the best thing that ever happened to me, and that there was zero chance that she and I would ever get back together."

"You should have had that conversation with her a good while back," Linny said, not ready to forgive him yet.

"Agreed," Jack said sheepishly.

"How did she react?" Linny asked.

"Angry, hurt, pitiful. Her usual," Jack said and rubbed his forehead with his fingers. "Next time I get run by guilt about failing Neal and try to fix Vera so his life with her is stable, will you hit me in the head with a board?"

"A two-by-four," Linny promised, softening. Since she'd met him she'd had a crash course in just how powerful a force guilt was for divorced parents. "You can't fix Vera. The only thing we can do is to give Neal as much stability and love as we can in our little family."

He raised a brow at her, a determined glint in his eye. "And exes can't be best pals. This listening-ear foolishness has got to end."

Linny felt giddy with relief. Jack Avery was finally *getting* what she'd been trying to tell him. Vera's insistence on staying too close for comfort eroded her and Jack's bond and kept him from holding his ex-wife accountable for her behavior. She cocked her head and gave him a cheeky grin. "You're sounding a little like John Wayne and I like it."

"Come here, little lady," he said in a not bad imitation of the Duke. He pulled her into a long hug.

Linny shivered, feeling deliciously safe, loved, and, finally, understood. After a long moment she pulled back and gazed at him. "I had my own epiphany today. I quit on a client."

Jack's eyes twinkled. "You look cheerful about that."

"I am," Linny said. "If you'll pour me a glass of wine I'll get this delicious frozen meal cooked up and tell you what else I've been thinking about."

Jack opened a bottle of Sauvignon blanc and poured them each a glass.

Linny checked the cooking time on the package. As Mama Alessia's Frozen Lasagna began to twirl around in the microwave, they sat at the kitchen table and raised their glasses to each other in a silent toast. Linny took a sip of wine. "I'm overwhelmed," she said, gazing at him.

"I know," Jack said simply and took her hand. "I've been worried about you."

Linny paused to think about it, reassured by the warmth of his strong hand holding hers. "We've taken on all these new roles but not put down any others. I can't just keep trying to go faster. I want to pay attention to what I want to do, not just do what I've always done."

He nodded slowly.

"When I worked at my old job and new mothers came back after having a baby and seemed overwhelmed, I didn't get it." She winced, not proud of what she was admitting. "I secretly thought they were wimps. I remember a staff meeting when a woman just back from maternity leave said she couldn't work overtime because of family obligations. A single girlfriend and I went out for a beer after work and rolled our eyes about that woman. We said things like, *How hard could it be?* and *How could a fast-tracker like her want to go that route?* Now I know the answer to both those questions." She gazed at Jack.

"If we can afford it, instead of ramping up my business I'm cutting back—at least for the time being. I'll do the work I've already committed to but not take on anything new and try to phase out the business for the time being. It'll take a little while to wind it all down so things will be crazy until then. But I'm needed at home right now, and that's exactly where I want to be."

"That's a big decision for you and it's fine by me." Jack picked up her hand and kissed it. "I made a decision today, too. For now I'm stopping my volunteer work at the spay and neuter clinic."

She studied him a moment, knowing how strongly he felt about the importance of the program. "You sure?"

He nodded firmly and squeezed her fingers. "I'll work with them again when our lives are more settled. Family comes first now. It has to. You need me, Neal needs me, and Lucas needs me."

And that's when Linny just had to kiss him.

CHAPTER 14
The Duke Finally Arrives

The next morning Linny leaned against the counter and took a sip of her coffee. She grimaced. It tasted funny, almost metallic. Like pennies had been dropped in it. She opened the refrigerator and sniffed the half-and-half. The cream still smelled okay, but she dumped the quart down the sink just to be safe.

A rumple-haired, stubbly-cheeked Jack gave her a sleepy smile. In his terry bathrobe he stood at the stove, dropping slices of turkey bacon in a frying pan. Turning on the burner, he padded toward Neal's room to wake him up.

As the bacon began to sizzle, Linny covered her mouth and ran for the bathroom. She emerged a few wretched minutes later.

Jack was whistling as he flipped bacon and punched toast down in the toaster.

Trying to breathe through her mouth so she wouldn't get another whiff of bacon, Linny poured herself a glass of ice water and took a long swallow. She turned to Jack. "Did your stomach do okay with that lasagna last night?"

"Fine. I was hoping there were leftovers for me to take to work today," Jack said as he pulled strawberry jam from the refrigerator and put it on the table. "Why?" he asked.

"My stomach . . ." she began.

But Neal walked in and Jack turned to him and smiled. "Morning, buddy. How'd you sleep?"

Neal mumbled something, slipped into his chair, and rubbed his eyes. He picked up his phone and scrolled through it.

Linny eyed him. The boy's lower lip stuck out and his brow was furrowed. But today was going to be a good day, she assured herself. She'd promised Neal an outing. Taking him to a Carolina Hurricanes players' Meet the Fans event this afternoon was one of her better stepmother ideas, she decided, and gave herself an imaginary pat on the back.

After Jack left for the office Linny caught a quick shower. As she toweled herself dry and slipped on a robe, Lucas began wailing. She hurried to his room, scooped him up, and did the little bouncing dance that seemed to soothe him. Lucas quit crying, but Linny caught a whiff of his diaper and fought to keep herself from gagging.

Breathing through her mouth again, Linny reached in the drawer of the dresser they used for baby supplies and with her free hand felt for a diaper. She came up empty. She rummaged through the other drawers. No diapers. How could they have let themselves run out? Feeling panicky, she riffled through a towering stack of baby supply bags they'd piled on the floor of the closet and spied a promisingly large one. Feeling a flash of relief, she reached for it but paused when she heard a cacophony of barking dogs. Gravel crunched as a car pulled up to the house. Peering out the window, she saw Diamond's white Range Rover with the spinning wheels and relaxed. Their pack of dogs surrounded the car, wagging their tails. They knew the good guys from the bad guys.

Draping a towel over Lucas, Linny scurried to the door, holding the naked baby to her chest and knowing at any moment Lucas could decide to pee—or worse. She pulled open the door and grinned at her friend. "Morning, Diamond."

Diamond stopped tapping at her phone and glanced at her. "Kitten, you're not answering calls, texts, or emails." She raised a brow and glanced at Lucas. "Mary Catherine told me about the new baby."

"Things have gotten lively around here," Linny admitted and turned the baby so Diamond could admire his perfect cherub face. "This is Lucas."

Diamond patted his head like she would a dog. "Good boy," she said absently.

Linny took a good look at her friend and jiggled the baby to hide her surprise. Instead of looking like her usual glamorous self, Diamond wore a drawstring linen skirt and a cornflower blue tank with sandals that looked like the pretty new Birkenstocks. No swoopy eyeliner today. No crimson lips. She wore light makeup, and instead of her towering updo, her hair was pulled back in a loose braid. Diamond was a beautiful woman, but she usually was intimidating: always in full makeup, perfectly color-coordinated, and wearing her expensive St. John-knit meets Victoria's Secret–looking outfits. Today she was lovely in a fresh faced, wholesome way. "You look so pretty, like Jennifer Aniston when she's in her casual mode."

"Thanks," Diamond said, ducking her head. "It's the new, simpler-me look."

"Is everything okay?" Linny asked, feeling a flutter of worry. Despite knowing she probably had been hard to reach, Diamond never just stopped by.

Diamond pointed to two L.L.Bean tote bags on the porch behind her and said airily, "Four weeks' worth of casseroles. Healthy stuff."

Linny blinked disbelievingly. Diamond was the type of woman who might use an oven strictly for storing her cashmere sweaters, if she didn't already have a huge, cedar-lined megacloset for that. "You cooked for us?"

Diamond gave a whoop of laughter. "Mother of pearl no! I had my housekeeper, Jean, whip them up. Since I've moved to the tiny house she doesn't know what to do with herself." She leaned forward and spoke in a confidential tone. "She's originally from California, and you know how those women are. They all need *meaning* in their lives. You have *got* to keep them busy or you know what they do," Diamond said darkly.

Linny found herself nodding knowingly and made herself stop. She had no idea what a California woman with too much time on her hands might do. Orchestrate a ceasefire? Reverse global warming? Realizing Diamond was doing her brilliant distractor shtick because she was embarrassed to be caught doing something thoughtful, Linny just smiled at her. "You gave us the perfect, thoughtful gift."

Diamond frowned and fiddled with her braid. "I was going to send over a pitcher of Bloody Marys and some Xanax, but I'm trying to be more practical."

Linny put a hand to her chest, so relieved not to have to try to scrounge up meals on the fly for the next month. "I am so grateful."

"You did me a favor," Diamond insisted. "I've been throwing flour on the kitchen floor and upending flowerpots to keep Jean busy. Cooking for you all gave her meaning."

Linny shook her head and smiled. Diamond's housekeeper wasn't the only one who was looking for more meaning. "Thank you, Diamond."

Diamond shrugged. "I must fly, pumpkin. I'm going to look at a piece of land. Big plans," she said, looking mysterious.

Linny cocked her head, intrigued. "I can't wait to hear all about it."

"I'll spill once I get the deal done." She nodded in the direction of Lucas. "Good luck with the tyke. Learning to like small children is on my new improved-me list. Maybe Auntie Diamond can babysit him after I do the reading." She whirled off.

Linny shook her head, bemused. Diamond was growing up. But she felt a spreading warmth on her chest and drew in her breath. "Hey, little man," she said, grinning at the baby. "That's your mama you're peeing on." As she turned to go back inside, she thought of what she'd said and felt a pang of longing. *Your mama.* She hoped with all her heart that she'd get to be this baby's mama forever.

"Neal, Neal," she called softly and rapped on his door. Sometimes she swore the boy just pretended not to hear her. No response. She rapped again, wincing, and hoped she wasn't making enough racket to wake Lucas, whom she'd just put down for his morning nap. "Let's get going, buddy. You need to get your chores done. I'm even going to help you."

Neal mumbled something she decided to take as an assent. Poking her head in the other room to check on the baby, she paused for a moment and smiled, just taking him in. Hard to say whether he looked more adorable when he was sleeping or when he was awake. Making a mental note to check in with Mary Catherine later to see how the Kandi hunt was going, she gave a little shudder as she imagined a petulant Kandi demanding Lucas's return. She pushed the thought out of her mind, something she'd had to practice more and more since she'd fallen in love with the baby.

Closing the door softly, Linny grabbed the baby monitor and checked to make sure it was working. Grinning, she heard the cute little whistling sound Lucas made when he slept. She slipped the monitor in a backpack, along with two stainless-steel glasses of ice water. In the mud room she pulled on her barn boots. Still no Neal. With a sigh of exasperation, she knocked on his door again. "Neal, if you want to go to meet the Hurricanes, I need you at the barn now."

As she strode down toward the pastures, she'd glanced surreptitiously behind her to make sure Neal was following her, and he was. Good.

Was she crazy taking baby Lucas along to the Meet the Fans event? Nah, she could do it. Maybe she could find him a darling little jersey. Linny thought about all the rigmarole involved in taking a baby anywhere and began to make a mental list. She shook her head wryly. Just a few weeks ago—before Lucas arrived—she'd stared at her sister uncomprehendingly as she detailed how much planning it took to take the baby with her to the grocery store. Now she knew Kate wasn't exaggerating.

The big bay named Reggie stuck his head in the window of his stall from where he stood outside the barn. He nickered and watched as Linny used a pitchfork to rake up a pile of soiled bedding made of wood pellets and shavings. "Hey, big guy," Linny called, and he blinked his chocolate brown eyes at her. Pulling up her T-shirt to dab the perspiration from her forehead, Linny thought about Neal. It was two steps up, one step back with her stepson. He could act loving and cooperative one minute and revert back to negative and snappy the next.

Helping out with Neal took time, but she'd soon start to have more. They needed to shop for school clothes and she'd promised to take him to the IMAX to meet his best friend, Tyler, for a movie about humpback whales. She'd also agreed to oversee Neal doing a list of chores Jack had created to help him earn his allowance. Jack wanted his son to have a good work ethic, but supervising the young man when he was in a balky mood was the hardest work of all. *She* should get an allowance, she decided.

Linny glanced out the barn door and blew out a sigh of exasperation. Where was Neal? He'd been gone ten minutes and all he'd had to do was pull the full manure cart around the barn to the composting bins and dump it. Ned would later activate a blowing system, cook the waste, cure it, and then sell it. But Neal was dawdling like he had been all morning. The sun was climbing in the sky and it was going to be a steamy August morning. They were almost finished, but Linny wanted this chore done before it got much hotter. She strode off to find him.

Neal was leaning against a fence post beside the empty manure cart, studying his phone. He glanced up when he saw her, shook his head wonderingly, and pointed to his cell. "Do you know that a horse produces almost fifty pounds of manure in a day? So our six horses produce three hundred fifty pounds of manure every day."

"I didn't know that," Linny said, trying to tamp down her annoyance. "But I do know this job is taking twice as long as it should because you've been stopping every five minutes to look up a fact on your phone. This is the last time I'm going to ask you to put it away." She was nervous at the implied *or else* because she hadn't thought through what would happen if he didn't.

He gave a martyred sigh but shoved the phone in his pocket. Grabbing the handle of the cart, he tromped back toward the front of the barn. Over his shoulder, the boy sent her a baleful look. "All I've done since I came to stay with you two is clean up poop."

Linny closed the gate and tried not to roll her eyes. "You mean other than going camping in Arizona, seeing famous planetariums, going to the museum, and meeting the Hurricanes?"

"I mean it," he insisted. "This is like when the pirates shanghaied people and forced them to work as crew on their ships."

Linny nodded as they walked through the open doors of the barn. No point in debating.

But even without her speaking, the boy continued. "And why do I have to work? This is my summer vacation. I'm supposed to be relaxing."

As she put away the pitchfork and shovel, Linny's patience was thinning. He groused harder than he worked. She said firmly, "We all have chores in this family. Your dad and I give you an allowance for helping out."

"I get an allowance but no chores at home," he said sullenly. "And I need a raise."

The boy was just spoiled. Linny tried to tamp down her irritation. "Neal, you and your dad talked about this last night, and the last thing he said to you before he left for work this morning was that you were to do as I asked."

He whirled around and gazed at her defiantly, his fists clenched at his sides. In a voice hot with anger, he said, "You're always bossing me around."

Flashing on all the juggling and honeymoon curtailing they'd done over the past few weeks to suddenly make room for him in their lives full-time, Linny struggled not to counter his resentment with a little dose of her own. Willing herself to calm down, Linny gave him a level look. "Neal, your dad left me in charge with a very clear plan for what we were doing today. If you have trouble with that plan let's get your dad on the phone and you two can clear that up." Linny held up her phone, her hand shaking a little. She didn't want to have to call Jack. She knew how busy he always was at work.

But Neal just stared at her defiantly.

Linny gave him a level look and hit Jack's number. One of the Bodacious Bonus Moms' cardinal rules was to never make threats you weren't prepared to back up.

Jack took the call after the first ring. "Hey. What's up?"

"Neal is bucking me on chores," she said, hearing the faint echo that meant he was on his cell.

"Put him on the phone," Jack said brusquely.

But the boy had a hand up to his forehead to shield his eyes from the sun as he gazed at a car turning into the gravel road to the farm. He smirked at Linny and trotted toward the approaching car.

As a cold knot of dread formed in her stomach, she watched Vera's black Mercedes rocket up the driveway, kicking up a storm cloud of gray dust and gravel. "His mom is pulling up," she said, watching the car fishtail and Vera correct it. "She's speeding up the driveway. Let me go see what's going on."

"I'm only a few miles away. Left a thumb drive I need at the house," he said. "Leave the phone on so I can hear what's going on. I'll be there in a few minutes."

"Good," Linny said, blowing out a sigh of relief as she slipped the phone into the pocket of her T-shirt without ending the call. Drawing in a deep breath, she walked over to greet Vera and what she knew could only be trouble.

Vera wheeled in to the parking area and jerked the car into park so fast that the Mercedes rocked. Flinging open the door, she stepped out, her hair smooth, her makeup perfect, and her mouth a hard, thin line. Looking like she stepped straight out of *Town & Country* magazine, she wore a white linen dress with black piping and black and white houndstooth check high heels.

Vera stalked up to Linny and scowled, hands on hips. "My son called and told me you'd been making him work all day in this heat doing manual labor. What is wrong with you? Don't you know anything about kids?" she demanded.

Linny heard the blood pounding in her ears. The mother who had screaming matches with her husband in front of her son was questioning Linny's judgment. She drew herself up and made herself speak calmly, "Neal exaggerated." She shot a glance at the boy, who flushed and studied his sneakers.

"My son does not lie to me," Vera said. She walked over to Neal, put a hand on his forehead, and glared at Linny. "He's burning up."

"It's summer in the South, Vera." Linny tried to hide her exasperation. "I'm not sure what he's said, but Neal's hardly being mistreated. He and I just spent forty-five minutes feeding the horses and mucking out stalls. We've finished. He's done with chores for the day. He drank water to stay hydrated." She'd never been so direct with the woman and it felt good.

"He says you have him doing housework all day long," Vera tilted her head and shot back, "Did he exaggerate that?"

"He does chores to earn his allowance," Linny said, trying to keep her voice even. "Jack's talked with you about that."

Vera's eyes glittered. "He's doing a lot of free babysitting for you, too, I hear. Is that why you wanted him to stay with you: free babysitting?"

Linny felt the heat rise in her face at this twisting of the truth. She did feel some guilt about how much Neal helped with Lucas, but they'd all been in overdrive since the baby arrived on their doorstep. Just as she opened her mouth to explain, the baby monitor in her backpack erupted with the sound of Lucas's crying. Rummaging inside, Linny grabbed the monitor and looked at the screen. He looked fine, and his cries sounded like the ones he made when he needed a diaper change.

She studied Vera, who stood rigid with anger, and wondered why she was explaining herself to this woman who was determined to find fault with her. "I'll be back in a few minutes," she said curtly and strode toward the house.

In a steely-voiced drawl, Vera said to Neal, "Honey, get your things. You're coming home with me."

Linny stopped abruptly, turned, and gazed at Vera. She pushed back her shoulders. "I thought we'd all decided that it was best if Neal stayed full-time with his dad and me until things got . . . sorted out."

"He's coming home with me," Vera said with a stubborn tilt to her jaw. "It's not good for a boy to be away from his mama so long."

The giant diamond in her ring glittered as she put a hand on her hip and glanced at Neal impatiently. "Son, let's go."

Neal looked at his mother and then gave Linny an imploring look.

"We need to discuss this with Jack," Linny said, working hard at an in-charge tone. "He should be here any minute."

Jack's voice sounded from her pocket. She held the phone to her ear. He said grimly, "Put Vera on the phone."

"Vera, Jack wants to speak to you," Linny said, proffering her phone.

"I don't want to speak to him," Vera snapped. She marched toward Neal, the in-charge effect marred by the fact that the heels of her stylish shoes kept catching in the grass. Grabbing his arm, she pulled him toward the Mercedes. "Neal, *now*. We are going home *now*."

But Neal jerked his arm away from his mother and whirled on her, his eyes flashing. He shouted at her, "Get away from me."

Vera gaped at him. "Why are you talking to me like that?"

Neal threw up his arms and shouted, "Don't you get it, Mama? I don't want to come with you. All you and Chaz do is scream at each other. I can't stand to be around you." He threw his work gloves on the ground and stomped to the house. He stopped, turned around, and screamed, "I hate you!" He threw open the door to the house and slammed it thunderously.

Vera stood stock-still, put her hands up to her face, and began to cry.

The baby wailed louder through the monitor, and miracle of miracles, Linny saw Jack turn into the driveway.

Jack stepped down from his truck and strolled toward them, looking like he had all the time in the world. But he had a Clint Eastwood squint to his eye and his jaw was set. He stared at Vera as he walked toward them, looking like a quietly angry man you didn't want to cross.

Linny shivered. He looked slightly menacing, like the sheriff who rode into town to straighten out lawless cowboys running amuck.

He fixed Vera with a look and said in a steely voice, "You are going to sit your little self down." He pointed to the chairs on the front porch. "And we are going to get this straightened out right now. This kind of scene will never happen again. Are we clear?"

Braced for a confrontation, Linny tried not to gape as Vera began to cry, nodding meekly as she walked toward the chairs on the porch.

Her face blotchy and her shoulder hunched, Vera looked fragile and defeated. Linny found herself almost feeling sorry for the woman.

Jack looked at Linny. "You can go on inside. I've got this handled."

Relieved, Linny nodded and gave him a look full of gratitude. About time this guy showed up. She drifted into the house, feeling light and buoyant.

After checking on Lucas and changing his diaper, Linny slipped him in his Balboa sling, sighing at his warm bulk and sweet baby smell. As he grasped at her hair, she tapped on Neal's door.

He opened it, eyes red with tears. "Sorry I was a jerk," he mumbled.

The baby reached out, grabbed Neal's ear, and gave it a long, determined pull. Lucas looked delighted with himself.

Linny smiled at him. "Apology accepted. Dad is going to work things out with your mom so you just chill out for a while. We're still on to see the Hurricanes."

His eyes brightening, he nodded and went back into his room.

Filling two glasses with iced tea, she grabbed a box of tissues and walked out to the porch where Vera and Jack sat in the two Adirondack chairs, talking. Wordlessly, she handed each of them a glass, gave Vera the tissues, and went back into the house.

She slipped the drowsy-looking baby back in the crib. Not feeling remotely like taking the high road and giving Jack and Vera some privacy, Linny fixed herself a glass of tea, grabbed a bag of Flamin' Hot Cheetos she kept in the bedside table drawer for emergencies, and sat on the floor beside the window closest to the front porch to eavesdrop. She chewed quietly so she could hear their conversation over the crunching.

"Don't let Neal saying he hated you upset you. He doesn't mean it. He said that to me and Linny twice last week," Jack was saying.

"No," Vera said shakily. "My friends with teens tell me they hear this. It just hurt when he said he couldn't stand being around me. We used to be so close."

"It's the fighting," Jack said, stating the obvious. "He's also upset that you're unhappy and that he might lose Chaz." He went on, his voice firm. "Do you understand that if you don't get things settled down in your household, we're going to need to renegotiate the custody arrangement?"

"You can't do that to me. Neal is my world." Vera cried harder, a feminine, tragic weeping that for all of her life had probably caused people to rush around trying to fix things for her.

Linny frowned and chomped on a big cheese puff, willing Jack to be strong and not go into appeasing mode.

"If he's your world you need to get hold of yourself and start acting like a normal mother. If you can't or won't you're leaving me no choice," Jack went on calmly, seemingly unaffected by the waterworks. "You can't put your own needs and problems before Neal's."

"I would never do that," she said indignantly. She sniffled and said in that breathy, little-girl voice that probably caused men to fall all over themselves, "But things with Chaz have been so . . . complicated."

"So uncomplicate them. You need to fish or cut bait," Jack said bluntly. "Are you in counseling?"

"You know how I feel about counselors . . ." she trailed off, as wispy-voiced as a consumptive.

He said gruffly, "Your feelings about counselors aren't important. You just need to find one and go. Our son's happiness is at stake."

"It helps when I can talk to you and my friends about it . . ." she began in a beseeching tone.

But he wasn't having any of it. "I don't want to talk to you about your marriage problems again, ever. You're a grown woman. You need to fix this problem with a professional counselor." He paused for a moment. "Linny mentioned that a friend of a friend is an attorney who runs a Save Your Marriage Boot Camp. May be worth checking out."

Vera said, "I really don't think . . ."

He cut her off. "I'll take you to court unless you get your act together."

She started to cry again, now in earnest.

His voice softened. "You've been an excellent mother to Neal up until this mess with Chaz. You need to get back to that kind of mothering and not let your marriage problems get in the way of giving Neal a loving and stable home."

Vera murmured something Linny couldn't quite make out, but she had heard enough to know that Jack was handling himself beautifully, perfectly, manfully. Grinning, Linny punched the air and did a quiet happy dance with her feet. Thank goodness the cards were on the table, everybody knew what the stakes were, and Jack had finally put the kibosh on their cozy TV preacher phone sessions.

She heard a little yip from Lucas and checked the monitor. He was awake and waving his arms at the World War II airplanes flying around in the mobile above his head. He was probably ready for his bottle. She rose, stashed the cheese puffs, rinsed the orange Cheeto dust from her fingers, and went to feed her young man.

When Jack walked in the door she launched herself at him, throwing her arms around his neck and murmuring, "Thank you, thank you, thank you," as she kissed him.

CHAPTER 15

The Jig Is Up

The next day Linny tried to be quiet as she peeled shrimp and chopped vegetables for a salad. Tonight she was determined to cook a healthy meal that didn't come with directions about pulling back the corner to vent. Roy trotted into the kitchen, his toenails clicking on the wood floor, and gave a loud groan as he stretched. Linny whispered, "Shhh, buddy." Studiously ignoring her, he curled around twice on his bed in the corner and lay down with a sigh.

Jerry had dropped off Ivy and driven Kate to a follow-up appointment with her orthopedic doctor. Linny glanced at the monitor on the counter. Both babies were sleeping quietly as lambs and she wanted to keep it that way.

But Jack and Neal clattered in the door at almost the same time, bumping shoulders and guffawing about something. Linny hushed them, pointing to the babies' room.

Looking apologetic, they began an exaggerated tiptoe, straight from the reruns of the old Bugs Bunny cartoons they sometimes watched together on Saturday morning. She couldn't help but smile at them.

Jack leaned over and kissed her cheek, eyeing the monitor. "Hey there," he whispered. "How long have they been sleeping?"

She held up crossed fingers. "Forty-five minutes. It's been heavenly," she said quietly and shot a smile at Neal. "Mama and her friends are supposed to FaceTime me in just a few minutes. Remember, she doesn't know about Lucas, or about Kate's fall."

Neal nodded solemnly and touched the side of his nose with his forefinger, a move he'd picked up in an old Humphrey Bogart movie Linny had dragged him to at the library.

Linny hid her smile and scraped the carrots she'd sliced into the bowl of lettuce. The FaceTime ringtone sounded. She shot the two men a panicky glance. Grabbing the monitor, she scurried away, calling softly over her shoulder, "Will you try to keep the babies quiet?"

Jack nodded and Neal looked cheerful as they walked softly into the living room.

In the little home office she slid into her chair in front of the laptop and took the call. "Hey, everybody." She smiled cheerfully and waved at the three women gathered around the screen.

"Hey, honey bun," Dottie called.

"Are you all staying out of trouble?" Linny asked, grinning.

"Hey, Linny." Mack's head bobbed up behind the girls and smiled. "Perry and I are keeping them on the straight and narrow." He gave a two-finger salute and disappeared.

Dessie leaned in, grinning. "Those men claim they love sleeping under the stars on their air mattresses, but in the morning both of them walk crooked and smell like Bengay."

"Tonight they're staying at a hotel right down the road that's shaped like a wigwam," Ruby added.

"How was Mount Rushmore?" Linny asked.

"Inspiring and majestic. They do a ceremony and light it up at night," Dottie said.

"It makes you proud to be an American," Dessie added. "Yesterday we piled in the boys' SUV and drove the Loop Road all through the Badlands."

"We saw prairie dogs and rock outcroppings out the kazoo," Ruby said, and then spoke in a confidential tone. "You'll never guess who's been texting me like crazy. Hal."

"What about Letty?" Linny asked, hoping Ruby wasn't setting herself up for heartache.

Ruby bounced in her chair, looking elated. "She's his sister. She's got some mental health–type issues, and he and his two sisters take turns having her stay with them. Five years ago his wife left him for her podiatrist. Isn't that fabulous?"

Well, not exactly *fabulous*, Linny thought but edited, "So he's single and you're keeping in touch. That's great. I thought he seemed like a steady, good guy."

"He is," Ruby said, beaming and giving a quiet hand clap.

"Guess what else?" Dessie asked. "Ruby and I have promising

new clues on the ring heist. I can't say much now, but let's just say we have a person of interest." She gave Linny a professional PI-type nod and pulled on Ruby's arm. "Come on, honey girl. Let's take a walk and let Linny and her mama talk without us hogging the screen." Both women waved and strolled off.

"How is every little thing, sugar?" Dottie asked, peering at her. "You have circles under your eyes and you look worn out."

"Oh, I'm fine," Linny said and sat up straighter, trying to look peppy. "Things are fine. Jack and Neal are doing great. Work is fine. The dogs are great." Did she know words other than *great* or *fine*?

But Mama moved closer to the screen to examine her better. "Are you sure you aren't getting worn out? Is Jack helping around the house? Sometimes men need to be encouraged in that department."

"Jack does more than his share. Everything is fine. Just quiet and calm around here," Linny assured her.

As soon as the words left her mouth, earsplitting wails erupted from the baby monitor she'd put on the desk. Why had she brought it? Sheer habit. But now she hurriedly turned it off and smiled brightly. "Just keeping Ivy for Kate. She went . . . to get her nails done."

Her mother arched a brow and looked skeptical. "Sister hates getting her nails done and that was two babies crying, not one. Why do you have two babies there?" her mother demanded. "And where's your sister?"

Linny glanced over her shoulder as Jack and Neal hurried by the open door to the office, bobbling screaming babies in their arms and looking helpless. Trying to duck out of camera range and only lining up better with the camera, they slipped out the back door.

"I saw that," Mama said loudly.

From the other open door Jerry bellowed out, "Hello, hell-o-oh?" as he pushed a transport chair containing the beaming Kate into the house and toward the office. Despite her boot and her blue sling, her sister looked thrilled to be out and about. "How's that new baby boy?" she called as Jerry maneuvered her chair right into view of the screen.

The jig was officially up. Linny glanced at the screen. Her mother's eyebrows had shot up and her mouth was a perfect O. "Well, Mama, we didn't want you to worry, but there have been a few new developments here. . . ."

So Jerry rolled Kate up to the laptop and the sisters told the tale of the fall, the found baby, and Neal's coming to stay. Linny brushed away brimming tears as Mama clucked and fussed and said, *Oh my goodness*, *Bless your heart*, and *You poor little things* about twenty times.

Mama shook her head and looked at Kate. "I was wondering why every time I FaceTimed you Jerry claimed you were running an errand. You seemed to have a lot of errands all of a sudden."

Jack and Neal came back in the house with the now-quiet babies. Holding Lucas up to the screen, Jack said, "Hey, Dottie. Meet the new guy."

Mama cooed at him, "Hello, sweet baby."

Jerry picked up Ivy's hand and waved it at Dottie and Kate showed off her hurt arm and boot.

"May I talk with Neal a minute?" Dottie asked.

The boy ducked his head, causing his glasses to droop down his nose, but he smiled at the screen. "Hey, Gramma."

"Neal, honey, Linny says you've been real helpful with the baby. I'm so proud of you." Dottie shook her head, looking impressed.

"Thanks," Neal said quietly.

Kate was getting emotional. "We sure have missed you, Mama."

"Well, it's plain to see you all need a mama around. Why didn't you call me?" Dottie asked.

"We didn't want to have you miss one minute of your trip," Linny said and glanced over at Kate, who was nodding her agreement.

"You still should have called. This is what mamas are for—to help out when their kids need them." Dottie gave them a stern look. "I love all of you so much. I can't wait to see every single one of you." She swallowed hard and seemed to be collecting herself. "Now can you all pull up the websites for the airlines and help me figure out the best way to fly home pronto?"

"I've got it," Neal said, stepped up with his iPad in hand and clicked a few screens. "The closest major airport to the Badlands region is Rapid City." He rattled off flight options, but Linny stared over his shoulder at the calendar on the website, looked at the dates, and felt the blood drain from her face. She stopped listening and started doing the math in her head.

* * *

After the call with Mama ended and Jerry, Kate, and Ivy rolled off toward home, Linny muttered something about needing more diapers, slung her purse on her shoulder, and scurried to the car.

In the drugstore she approached the family planning aisle and, heart thundering, hurriedly rerouted herself. She dropped a jumbo-size bag of Peanut M&M's in her basket, tossed in bottles of instant tanner and nail polish remover, and added a pair of sparkly flip-flops. Edging back toward the aisle where she'd find what she needed, her thoughts careened around. How in the world could she and Jack manage a new baby with everything else they had going on in their lives? Though her legs and arms turned to water, she made herself grab the box and put it in the basket.

Jack took both boys to work on Thursday morning. In the reception area of Green Sage Linny shifted nervously in her seat as she waited to go into what she hoped was her final meeting with Chanel. In the car on the drive over Linny had thought about it, feeling wistful. She'd helped the young woman identify the problems in her company, but last night after she'd seen the pink line, she'd made the decision to hand off all the rest of the training to a trusted colleague.

Her palms were clammy as she walked beside Chanel toward her office. Linny felt a thrum of anxiety in the pit of her stomach. She was nervous about bowing out.

After she patted Sage and told him how handsome he was Linny settled into the guest rocking chair. "How are you?" she asked.

"Married." Chanel gave her a one-sided grin and held up her hand. "I listened to you and decided to finally get a life."

"Congratulations." Linny grinned, delighted. She stood and leaned over to examine the slim braided gold band nestled beside the ring with the small square-cut yellow stone. "Just beautiful," she said and felt a pang of longing for her old rings. Once things settled down they'd find replacements.

"We went to the courthouse Friday." Chanel shook her head, looking bemused. "Can't believe it myself, but we're official now."

"Good for you." Linny remembered almost floating with a quiet euphoria as she and Jack said their *I do*s just a few short months ago. "I'm thrilled for you."

"It makes work so much easier when I've got someone to come home to," Chanel said and flushed, looking embarrassed at revealing such a personal thought. "Anyhow, the staff got wind of it and called in the food trucks. We had a big old celebration after work."

"Great," Linny said, leaning forward. "How is work? How did things go with the employees after the meeting?"

Chanel shook her head, looking amazed. "It's starting to turn into a new place—a place where grown-ups work."

"Tell me," Linny said, noticing the hunched shoulders and tense look Chanel often wore were gone.

"We still have work to do," Chanel said cautiously. "I had to pull aside a few employees who were still stuck in the past and say something like, *The train's pulling away from the station and everybody's on board. Are you coming with us or not?*"

"That was a great thing to say," Linny said admiringly.

"I read it in a leadership book," Chanel admitted, looking sheepish. A troubled look flitted across her face. "I may need to let one or two folks go; the ones who don't pull their weight and seem to be trying to undermine all the changes I want us to make."

"You might wait until after the training to size that up," Linny suggested.

"Good," Chanel said, looking relieved. "I'm holding regular meetings and trying to be more of a leader." She gave Linny a baffled look. "Can you believe I had to tell someone they needed to bathe more regularly and use deodorant?"

"I can," Linny said, nodding.

Chanel grinned ruefully and leaned back in her chair. "We're looking forward to you coming in and starting the customer service training at the end of the month." She paused for a moment. "Well, most of us are. I still have a few employees I need to talk with you about."

Linny paused for a moment, gathering her courage. "Chanel, I've got some news. I've had big changes in my family circumstances and I'm going to need to scale way back on work for a while."

Chanel's face fell. "Oh snap," she said, frowning. "I liked working with you."

"I've liked working with you, too," Linny said, feeling a wave of guilt as she saw how crestfallen the young woman looked. "I've got a colleague I'm going to suggest take over, with your approval of course."

Chanel looked doubtful, but then nodded slowly. "At least you aren't going to leave me out there alone, twisting in the wind."

"Never," Linny said. "The woman I'm referring you to is named Amy Sanders. She's smart, participants love her, and she knows the IT industry inside and out." Linny looked away for a moment, tapping a finger on her chin. "I would describe her as . . . crusty."

Chanel burst out laughing. "Crusty might be perfect for my folks."

Afterwards, Linny walked to the car feeling lighter. She thought about it. Chanel was a dream client: incredibly bright, courageous, and willing to learn. Even with trickier clients, Linny had loved her work. If someone had asked her a year ago if she'd ever give up working even on a temporary basis, she would have said they were crazy. But she thought about all her men, her sister and her brood, and Mama. She smiled and knew she was making the right decision.

As she pulled into their driveway, Linny drew in her breath sharply. Jack's parents' tan Tahoe with the red NC State *Go Wolfpack* plate on the front was parked in the driveway. They weren't due back from their trip for days, maybe weeks. Her heart began to race and she hurried toward the front door. Was someone sick?

As she pushed open the door, her father-in-law, Rush, beamed at her and put down the silver cocktail shaker he'd been vigorously jiggling. "Hello, Miss Linny," he boomed, collecting her into a hearty hug.

"Everybody okay?" she asked anxiously.

"Right as rain," he said.

Linny breathed out a sigh and let herself relax for a moment on the big man's shoulder. He felt safe and reminded her of her own father.

Releasing her, he ran his hand across his bald pate. "Your mama called Ceecee, though, and spilled the beans about the baby and Neal being here full-time. Dottie said we needed to hightail it home." He gave her a sly grin. "I was getting bored anyhow. One Galapagos turtle started to look like the next, and then all that ocean with not a golf course in sight." He shook his head, feigning disbelief.

Linny grinned at him.

He shoved his hands into the pockets of his baggy khakis and rocked back and forth on his heels, his boat shoes squeaking. "How are you, sugar?" He gave her a concerned glance. "Things have picked up steam around here since we left. Y'all doing okay?"

"It's been hectic," Linny admitted, her eyes prickling because she knew he genuinely cared about her. "Lucas was a big surprise, but we're all enjoying him. He's a sunny-natured guy and we've all pitched in."

"I can't get any time with him. Mother has been hogging him since we walked in the door," he groused. "Now how about my boy Neal? I was real sorry to hear the way Vera's been acting."

"Everything is settling down in that department," Linny said, hoping what she was saying was true.

"Good," Rush said briskly. "Can I fix you a little restorative drink?" He pointed to the cocktail shaker. "Brought my own equipment and ingredients. I'm still working my magic with the old-timey drinks in the *Mr. Boston* guide."

Linny grinned. Rush took his mixology seriously.

"I can whip you up your favorite," he coaxed with a mischievous grin and reached for the crème de menthe bottle.

The Grasshopper he thought she loved tasted like spearmint mouthwash, but she always drank it because she didn't want to hurt his feelings. She was quitting that say-yes-when-you-mean-no habit. "I'm going to pass tonight. Sometimes those fancy drinks are a little too sweet for me."

"Sure, sweetheart," he said, looking not the least bit offended. He nodded toward his shaker. "I'm fixing Ceecee one of my newest. It's called a Battery Charger and it's a crowd pleaser," he said with a canny nod. "She and the boys are in the kitchen. If you change your mind, just holler."

Linny smiled. Turning down one of his concoctions was easier than she'd thought it would be. She poked her head into the kitchen. With Lucas in the baby sling resting on her chest, Ceecee sat at the kitchen table facing Neal. Each stared at their hand of cards, looking as flat-eyed and serious as the people on the poker TV shows.

With a triumphant grin, Neal laid down his hand and called, "Gin!"

Laughing, Ceecee glanced up, saw Linny, and smiled with delight. "Hello, sugar. Come give me a kiss."

"Welcome home!" Linny stepped over and hugged her mother-in-law, genuinely glad to see her. Kissing Lucas's head, Linny put her hands on Neal's shoulders to give them a squeeze. "Hey, buddy."

"I just showed this little so-and-so how to play the game not long ago and now he's beating me!" Ceecee pretended to complain, looking flushed and girlish despite her snowy white hair.

"You turning into a card shark?" Linny asked Neal.

"Yeah," he admitted, grinning. He hopped up to open the refrigerator door and stare inside.

"Supper in about half an hour," Linny said. "There are apples on the counter."

He closed the door and gave her an as-if look as he sauntered away.

Linny slid into a chair and fought another pang of possessiveness as she watched Ceecee jingle her charm bracelet for a fascinated Lucas and gaze at him cooing something about *precious wescious* and *Gwammy's good boy*.

Ceecee glanced at her and flushed. "I'm being greedy with this darling boy. Let me let him say hello to you." She unwrapped the baby and gently handed him over.

Linny started to say, *Oh, no, you go ahead*, but she really did want to hold Lucas. "Thanks," she said and hugged her boy, feeling an almost overwhelming rush of love.

Rush stepped into the room, handed Ceecee her green frothy drink, and sat down with them, sipping his Rob Roy and looking as affable and unflappable as ever.

Ceecee took a bracing sip of her Battery Charger and gave Linny a steely look. Doting Grammy had morphed into General MacArthur. "So what do we need to do to keep this precious child and get him away from his trashy mama?"

Linny broke into a smile and updated them both on Lucas's status. Though she'd expected shocked looks and pursed lips from her mother-in-law, all she got was kindness and determination. Rush would contact one of his old colleagues who'd worked with a private investigator on a custody case in the Bahamas. A bridge partner friend of Ceecee's from the club had adopted a baby from her crack-addict granddaughter and might have some advice. Linny's eyes widened at this last bit of news, though she knew that money couldn't insulate people from addictions or evil or sadness.

"Jack will be back from the barn in a few minutes and I need to get supper going. We'd love for you all to stay and eat with us," Linny said, meaning it.

"'Course we'll stay." Rush smiled and shook his head knowingly. "I wouldn't want to be the one who tried to pry Mama away from her grandbabies."

Feeling lighter than she had in weeks, Linny rose and handed Lucas to a delighted Rush. "Do you two mind getting this guy fed for me? The bottle is in the fridge and the warmer is on the counter."

Ceecee hopped up and began to bustle around the kitchen, her kitten heels clacking on the hard wood.

"We're having chicken enchiladas that a friend brought by," Linny said, grateful she could offer them more than a family-size pack of frozen mac and cheese.

Neal had wandered back in and stood in the doorway. "Linny's not that good a cook. She's just learning. My mom makes excellent enchiladas."

Ceecee turned from the bottle warmer and walked over to Neal. She put her hands on his shoulders and waited until he looked at her. She smiled sweetly, but her voice was steely as she said, "Darlin', that's no kind of talk I want to hear from you again. We need to be grateful for all the many things Linny does for you, your daddy, and the baby."

Neal flushed and met Linny's eyes. "Sorry."

Linny gave him a quick nod and tried to hide her shock. Ceecee had caught the dig and stood up for her. Hallelujah!

Rush met her eyes and said quietly, "Mama and I talked about it and we're going to walk beside you and Jack every step of the way. No matter how things turn out with this young man, you all need us, and we need family."

CHAPTER 16

Happily Ever Afters

Linny dragged an Adirondack chair into the yard and pulled it up next to Kate in her wheelchair. Handing her sister a cup of her favorite peppermint tea, Linny sat beside Kate, sipping her own tea and marveling at the peace of the morning. Lucas and Ivy lay dozing side by side in the playpen she'd positioned just a few feet away from them in the shade of the white oak tree. They looked so adorable that Linny had been compelled to take fifteen or so photos of them. Roy had forgiven her for her inattention over the past two months and was sleeping at their feet, his feet twitching as he chased a rabbit in his dreams.

"How's it feel to be a stay-at-home mom?" Kate asked, a smile playing at the corners of her mouth.

Linny grinned and glanced at her watch. "Well, I've only officially been at it three hours, but so far it's been great. No frantic juggling of schedules, no packing poor Jack off to the clinic with kids in tow. I actually made us all breakfast this morning." She decided not to mention that she'd lost her meal shortly after she'd eaten it. Linny studied her sister, sloe-eyed, creamy skinned, and remarkably lithe for a newish mama. She looked charming in her vintage pink floral sundress. "You look so rested and pretty," Linny said.

"I showered this morning, too," Kate said. "Mostly on my own. Washed my hair and everything," she said proudly. "Soon I'll be able to get around my house on the scooter instead of this bulky chair. Yesterday Jerry got a cleaning service to come scrub the house from top to bottom. Everything smells good. The clutter is put away. Life is finally getting back to normal." Kate smiled, stretched luxuriously, and tucked curls behind her ears. Her face had lost the pallid, pinched look of a woman carrying too much worry on her shoulders. She turned her head and smiled at Linny. "So Mama and Mack made it home safely from South Dakota late last night?"

"They did," Linny said. "And I talked with Ruby this morning. After the girls and Perry drop the RV off in Omaha, the three of them will catch a flight back to Raleigh."

"Good. I've missed those women." Kate stuck a finger inside her walking boot to scratch her leg. "Mama can be a handful, but I'm so glad she's home. It's not just the practical help I know she'll give us. Somehow I feel safer having her back home."

Linny thought about it. "Me too."

Kate gave her a sideways glance. "So she says she's treating us all to a kind of welcome home to the SWAT Team supper at Marnie's Café on Saturday night. She's splashing out."

"Yup," Linny said. "Sounds like fun. It will be the SWAT girls, their beaus, and family and friends. She even booked the private room so we won't bother other diners with the babies."

Kate grinned. "I like the way she's eased into having money. If I ever win a bucket of money on the nickel slots remind me to be as gracious." She pointed to Neal, who was in the saddle atop his favorite horse, Reggie, and chatting away to the big bay as they made slow circles around the paddock. "How is that young man doing?"

"Better. All sorts of good news on that front. The grandparents are back and Neal loves all of them. He played golf with Rush yesterday, Ceecee's taking him to the pool at the club, and as soon as Mama recovers from her trip and gets caught up on her smooching with Curtis, she'll go full bore into spoiling him."

"How about his mama and Chaz?" Kate asked as she kicked off her sandal and rubbed Roy's back with her good foot.

"We're guardedly optimistic. Since Jack's come-to-Jesus meeting with Vera, things have calmed down on that front. She and Chaz are doing the Save Your Marriage Boot Camp this weekend and she sounds determined to get her life straightened out." Linny held up crossed fingers and leaned her head back in the chair.

"Maybe the boot camp will work. Calm things down in that household." Kate glanced over at Linny. "Is it ten o'clock?"

Linny picked up the phone on the arm of her chair. "It's 9:59. Thanks for being with me for the Kandi update. I need the moral support." She grimaced. Mary Catherine's text had come early that morning and read: *IN COURT NOW BUT CALL ME AT 10. NEWS!!*

Mary Catherine never used large caps or exclamation points. Add a bad-gut feeling to those aberrations and Linny was plain scared. "What if she tells me Kandi's coming for the baby? What if she says Buck's not the father?" Her heart lurched. "I don't think I could take either one."

Kate patted her arm and got that faraway Zen look in her eyes. "Things are going to work out according to God's plan."

Linny gazed at her sister, willing herself to try to believe her. Picking up the phone, her hand trembled as she dialed her friend's office. When chirpy Shania put her through Linny said, "Hey, just calling to..."

But Mary Catherine interrupted. "I found her."

Linny froze and her heart and breathing stopped. The next words out of her friend's mouth would change the course of her and Jack's life forever.

"Kandi and her prince charming are living in Eleuthera. He's running a dive shop and she's waitressing. She has zero interest in taking that baby back. Not a real domestic-type woman," Mary Catherine said dryly.

"Thank God." Linny gave her sister a radiant smile.

Wide-eyed and grinning, Kate grabbed Linny's free hand and squeezed it until it hurt.

"I thought she'd try to shake you down for money but sounds like she'd pay you to take the baby. She's ready to relinquish parental rights and transfer custody of the baby to you and Jack," Mary Catherine said, sounding exultant. "I finally tracked down Buck's family members, too, and none of them have any interest in the baby. If all goes well Lucas is going to be yours."

Barely able to contain her joy, Linny thrust the phone at Kate, put her face in her hands, and burst into tears.

Saturday evening Linny stood on the brick sidewalk outside the restaurant and gazed up at the soaring windows of the deep pink Victorian home that housed the restaurant. She breathed out, happy, and shifted Lucas in his sling while the boys unloaded baby gear from the truck. Linny loved Marnie's Café. Housed on the outskirts of one of Raleigh's oldest neighborhoods, the home had once been crumbling and ready for the wrecking ball. Her friend Marnie, the proprietress, had seen the home's potential and lovingly restored it, bringing it back from the brink of oblivion.

With a rotating menu of farm-fresh but not fancy Southern cuisine, Marnie's had been discovered by the restaurant critics and the foodies and was now a five-star restaurant. Greeting her guests warmly from the door, slim, lovely Marnie was looking very Ava Gardner in a vintage scarlet dress, her glossy black hair pulled back in her usual high ponytail. "Welcome, Linny, Jack, and baby." She gave them both a quick hug and smiled at Neal. "You must be Neal. I've heard so many nice things about you."

Neal blushed and mumbled, "Nice to meet you."

Linny watched, grinning. Hard for a twelve-year-old boy to take in all that glamour. "Where is Mama's little party going to be?"

"We have you out back. It's nice and private," Marnie said.

"Is it in the garden?" Linny asked hopefully. She'd heard Marnie had just finished adding a walled garden for private parties but had never seen it.

"I'm afraid another party has reserved that for this evening," Marnie said regretfully. "But we have you all in another charming space we've just added for private parties. We took the original kitchen house and added to it a good-sized banquet room." With Jack trying not to bump diners with the portable playpen he carried and Neal being equally careful with the giant diaper bag he lugged, Marnie led them through the crowded restaurant and into a sunny, high-ceilinged room lined with French doors that framed a Monet-inspired view. The flowerbeds outside were filled with a riot of colorful delphiniums, hollyhocks, and lavender. The inside of the room was equally appealing. Tall ivory candles flickered softly and the tables were adorned with sumptuous bouquets of flowers. "Have a lovely evening," the proprietress called and swayed gracefully away.

Linny leaned into Jack, admiring a tall vase overflowing with lush pink roses and peonies. She leaned over, closed her eyes, and breathed in the sweet scent. "Beautiful," she murmured and smiled up at Jack.

But he was studying her. "You're beautiful," he said quietly.

"Gross." Neal pretended to stick a finger down his throat and gag.

Jack put a hand on the top of Neal's head and grinned at him. "Come on, buddy. Let's get things set up for Lucas and Ivy." The two walked off, glancing around appraisingly and discussing where would be the best spot for the playpen.

Mama bustled in, wearing a deep violet number with cute espadrilles. Thank goodness not the white Velcro sandals she usually wore with dresses. Maybe Linny could root them out one day while Mama was at church and burn them. Dottie's hair was pushed softly back from her face and her eyes sparkled. Linny raised a brow. "Mama, you look so pretty."

"Thanks, honey." Mama colored at the compliment. "Must be all that fresh air, sunshine, and adventure."

Mack stepped into the room, looking spiffy in a blue blazer and a white button-down shirt. With an arm linked companionably through his was a woman who looked to be in her midthirties with smoky dark eyes, a smattering of freckles, and a shining sweep of chestnut hair.

Linny watched her mother's face light up when she saw Mack. Love was why her mother looked so incandescent.

"Here's Mack, and that's his daughter. I want to introduce the two of you," Mama said and beckoned them with a wave.

Mack kissed Mama's cheek and leaned in to give Linny a peck. With a flourish, he held his hands out to the young woman at his side. "Linny, this is my daughter, Callie. You two might have quite a bit in common. She runs a small business, just like you do."

Her eyes bright with interest, Callie shot out a hand and Linny shook it, liking the woman's firm handshake and direct gaze. "Who is this guy?" the woman asked, tilting her head toward Lucas.

"One of my many men," Linny said, grinning at Callie. "This is Lucas."

"Looking sharp, Mack." Jack strode up and gave the older man a one-armed man hug.

Mack broke into a grin. "Hey, Jack. Meet my daughter, Callie. I think you and Linny might be seeing more of her in the future," he said mysteriously, looking like he had a happy secret.

Dessie and Perry arrived and Ruby stepped into the room, wearing a pink sheath with a plum-colored feathered pashmina swathed dramatically around her shoulders. Then Marnie ushered in another familiar figure. Looking dapper in a seersucker jacket, Hal stood in the doorway, blushing and jingling the change in his pants pockets as his eyes swept the room. He saw Ruby, broke into a smile, and hurried to her side.

Linny glanced at her own skirt and flats and whispered to Jack, "Everybody looks so nice. Maybe we should have dressed up more."

"You look fine, Lin," Jack reassured her and gave her shoulder a squeeze. As guests greeted each other, Linny glanced outside. With clear skies, low humidity, and a slight breeze, whoever had booked the private party in the garden had gotten lucky and landed one of the prettiest nights of the entire summer.

With Ivy swaddled in her arms Jerry rolled Kate in and expertly wheeled her into a spot beside Linny's chair. The two held their babies in their laps while Jack and Jerry caught up. Lucas and Ivy were guest magnets, charming everyone who came to meet them as they burbled, waved, and reached for noses, hair, and earrings. Linny knew this run of charm could go south fast and devolve into cranky, tired crying, but she jiggled Lucas on her knees and smiled proudly, enjoying every moment of his and Ivy's happy mood while she could.

Dessie, Perry, Ruby, and Hal greeted the sisters and cooed their hellos to the babies. Hal cleared his throat, looking nervous, and gazed at Linny. "My dear, I have an apology to make." He reached into his jacket pocket, pulled out a box, and pressed it into her hand.

Linny cocked her head at him, searching her mind for any reason why Hal would feel the need to apologize. As she pulled open the box and lifted the tissue paper, she put a hand to her mouth and blinked back tears. She looked at him wonderingly. "How did you find my rings?"

He shook his head, looking pained. "My sister had them. She had your ceramic cat, too." Ruby gave his shoulder an encouraging little squeeze. "Letty has a mood disorder, and when she gets off her medication she does impulsive things she'd never do if she was in her right mind," he explained. "We have Dessie to thank for finding these items."

Linny slipped the rings on her finger and just sat there for a moment, gazing at them and not quite believing they were back on her hand. She looked at Dessie. "How did you find these?"

Dessie explained. "I told you I went snap happy with my new cell. The editing features on that phone are amazing. So I zoomed in on each shot and examined them with a magnifying glass. I came upon an interesting photo of Letty on the day of the break in."

Ruby jumped in, the feathers on her shawl bobbling gracefully as she jumped animatedly into the storytelling. "She did that little expand thing and recognized the ring on Letty's hand. She was wearing it, plain as day. So she gave word to Hal and he talked to Letty and got it back. He checked her dresser and there was the ceramic kitty, every dollar bill still inside."

Jack and Neal came back, looking curious about the small crowd gathered around her and Kate. Linny held up her hand and showed them. "My rings are back."

Neal broke into a grin and Jack beamed and said, "That's great."

But Hal still looked abject. "Can you forgive me . . . and Letty?"

"Of course," Linny said, patting his hand. "I'm so happy I could just kiss you, but I don't want to rile up Ruby."

Ruby chuckled. "You do not," she assured her. "I've got my man and I'm going to hold on to him." She grasped Hal's arm and looked up at him, her eyes merry.

Kate nudged Linny and pointed to the door as Diamond and her big handsome beau, Butch, walked in. Well over six feet tall, he towered above the petite Diamond the same way Jerry towered above Tinker Bell–size Kate.

Linny handed Lucas to Jack and waved her over. Diamond flashed a smile at her, held open her arms, and called to the group, "Hello, cuddle bunnies." She gave Linny an extravagant hug. "Your mama been in any more brawls?"

"Not a one." Linny shook her head in mock disappointment.

"Dang it." Diamond snapped her fingers. "That was fun." Taking Butch's arm, she gazed up and batted her eyes at him. "Tell him our big news, puddin'."

"You tell her, honey," Butch drawled.

The big man didn't flinch at being called puddin'. Must happen a lot, Linny decided, trying not to smile.

Diamond said, "I bought a piece of land that abuts Butch's farm and I'm going to build a fancy camp or a retreat center. We'll have a lodge and a cluster of tiny houses or cabins."

"*Real* tiny houses," Butch clarified with a knowing grin. "She's going to set up a ropes course, an archery range, and bring in horses.

There's a good-size lake on the property, so she'll have canoeing and swimming."

"I want to come," Linny said firmly and Jack nodded in agreement.

She wagged a finger at them. "You can't come now because you're happily married and I'm starting out housing fighting couples for my friend doing the Save Your Marriage Boot Camp. Later, though, I might do a fun, pampering-couples camp, or a getaway fun-and-mingling week for young adults with autism. The sky's the limit," Diamond said confidently and twinkled up at her beau.

Butch said proudly, "We talked about partnering up to do corporate retreats, too."

"Ah. A family business." Linny eyed the two of them. "I love the idea. You two will build something marvelous."

"We will," Diamond said and winked at Linny as the two drifted off.

"Butch's bachelor days are numbered," Linny whispered to Jack.

Marnie glided over to Dottie and Mack and leaned her head in for a quick word with them. Afterward, she clinked a knife on the side of a glass and smiled pleasantly at the group as they quieted. "Ms. Dottie and Mr. Mack have an announcement."

Dottie's cheeks were flushed with pleasure. Mack slid an arm around her waist, gave her a quick glance, and said, "We'd like for you to follow us. We've planned something special." He took Dottie's hand, opened the French doors, and led them outside.

Delighted, Linny smiled at Jack. "We finally get to see the garden."

They followed Mama and Mack through a wrought-iron gate and Linny gasped. Yellow Carolina jasmine and purple wisteria draped gracefully on trellises lining the pink stucco walls and the air was redolent with their delicate scents. A fountain sprayed into the air and shoots of water danced in the early evening light. Pink, yellow, and orange Chinese paper lanterns made the garden softly glow. The place looked like a fairy garden.

"They even got musicians. Mama knows how to throw a party." Linny pointed to a garden nook where a quintet of scrawny-looking young people looked bored as they tuned up their instruments. The men wore ill-fitting black tuxes and tugged at their bow ties and the woman with the violin wore a black number with rows and rows of pearls and a Holly Golightly updo.

Jack nudged her. "It's more than a party, Lin." He tipped his head toward several rows of folding white chairs and a beaming man in an indigo blue robe holding a Bible. The man stood under a trellis covered with yellow roses.

Linny put a hand to her mouth and swallowed hard, scanning the crowd for her mother.

"We're getting married," Dottie announced to the group with a tremulous smile. Mack caught her hand and dabbed at his eyes with a handkerchief.

Jerry wheeled Kate over and with Linny and her men, they all surrounded the couple, hugging and kissing them. "I'm thrilled for you, Mama. You deserve every bit of this happiness," Linny whispered fiercely in her mother's ear.

Jerry positioned the transport chair in the middle of the front row. Linny slipped into a chair bedside her sister and they held their babies, bookended by Jack, Jerry and Neil. The musicians launched into an instrumental version of "Here Comes the Sun". Tears brimmed in Linny's eyes and she squeezed her sister's hand. Mama and Mack smiled radiantly as they walked down the aisle.

The ceremony was short but moving. When the minister came to the part about to love and to cherish; from this day forward until death do us part, the sniffing of tears in the small crowd was audible.

As the new bride and groom turned to face the small crowd, the musicians came to life again. A young man with an odd coif that listed to one side of his head grabbed the mike with authority and, pausing for a moment, broke into an achingly beautiful version of Elvis Presley's "Can't Help Falling in Love." Linny felt herself choke up and squeezed Jack's hand.

Afterwards, waiters poured sparkling wine and they all raised glasses to Dottie and Mack. The band struck up Etta James's "At Last," and the couple moved onto the small wooden dance floor. Guests smiled and Linny felt her eyes well again as she watched her mother dance gracefully with Mack, who was gazing at her adoringly. The band moved seamlessly into a set of classics—"Crazy Love," "It Had to be You," "Unforgettable," "Mack the Knife"—and more and more guests moved onto the dance floor.

The musicians launched into livelier, more modern songs and more guests joined in the dancing. Jack bobbed around on the dance floor with Lucas and Linny held Ivy while Jerry spun her laughing sister around the dance floor in her wheelchair. As the band eased into another up-tempo song, Linny watched delightedly as Callie tapped Neal on the shoulder and led him onto the dance floor. He looked rigid with embarrassment until she steered him into a loopy, fast waltz. After a few moments she dropped his hands and, eyes sparkling, began a wild, uninhibited freestyle that Neal soon joined in, grinning like mad. She led and Neal mimicked her as she did raise-the-roof hands, Egyptian arms, a lassoing Pony, and a bouncing Pogo. Other dancers smiled indulgently and a few of the kids joined in. After the song ended Neal tried to leave the dance floor, but Callie made a dramatic down on one knee show of begging him to come back for another dance, and he did.

Ivy fell asleep on Linny's shoulder and she hugged the sweet girl. She smiled, feeling a wave of contented happiness. Most everyone she loved was here, Mama and Mack had found each other, and Neal was letting himself be silly. All was right with her world.

The newlyweds rounded up Linny and Callie and circled around Kate. Mack said, "Dottie and I had such a good time on our adventure trip that we're planning to travel more over the coming year."

Mama gave them a twinkling smile. "We're going to get our kicks on Route 66, tour more national parks, and take a train ride through the Canadian Mounties."

"Rockies. Canadian Rockies." Looking amused, Mack raised his eyes heavenward. "So the point is, we won't be able to give you girls as much help with the kids as you'll probably need, at least for a while." Looking proud, he turned Callie to face them and rested his hands on her shoulders. "So, Linny and Kate, we're giving you a gift."

"You're giving us Callie?" Linny teased.

"Goody! We like her!" Kate added, doing a miniature hand clap.

Mack chuckled and looked at his daughter. "Tell them, honey."

Still flushed from her wild dancing, Callie pushed back her bangs and explained. "My company is called Callie's Caregivers. We provide home health aid and companion services to older people who need it. One of my smartest colleagues, Liza, owns a nanny service." She broke into a smile and pointed to Mack and Dottie. "These two asked me to ask Liza to hand pick two excellent part-time nannies for you new mamas. Their treat."

Linny's hands flew to her face and she gazed wonderingly at

Mama and Mack. They'd somehow divined the perfect gift: the extra set of hands she'd so desperately need during the coming year. And that gift had arrived without them even knowing about the pink line on the stick.

Kate shook her head slowly, looking incredulous. "We've been trying to stay positive, but I've still got a long way to go before I'm back to my old, spry self. This will make life so much easier." Eyes brimming with unshed tears, she looked gratefully at Dottie and Mack and held up her arms. They beamed and leaned down to hug her. Linny joined in the thank-you group hug. Kate glanced up and held out an arm for Callie. "You too, missy. I need a hug from you, too." Callie broke into a grin and joined in.

And that's when Linny finally decided to tell Jack. For several days after she'd purchased the test, she'd made a wide berth around the second drawer of her dresser, eyeing it as if it contained a coiled-up snake. She'd finally drummed up the courage to take the test and was waiting for the right time to tell him the news.

As the afterglow of the sunset faded, a full moon hung low in the sky. The paper lanterns glowed luminously and the fairy lights shimmered. In a tender Sinatra-inspired voice, the odd-haired young man crooned "Someone to Watch Over Me" as Linny danced with Jack, leaning her head against his chest feeling the beating of his heart and breathing in his familiar cedar, clean-man scent. "Are you happy?" she murmured.

He pulled her closer and kissed the top of his head. "Very."

She cocked her head and looked up at him, lacing her fingers behind his neck. "Is our family life full enough for you?"

He pretended to think about it. "It's full all right, but I love it."

Linny fixed him with a gaze and smiled slowly. "You'd better hold on tight because it's about to get even fuller." She stretched up to whisper in his ear. "I'm having a baby."

Jack stood still, his eyes widening. He broke into a radiant smile, lifted her up, and spun her around in circles.

Closing her eyes as she whirled around, Linny laughed and did what she'd been doing ever since she married Jack Avery: she just hung on tight, let herself feel the love, and enjoyed the ride.

ABOUT THE AUTHOR

Susan Schild writes wholesome and sunny Southern fiction. She likes stories about charming men, missing money, adventuresome women, sweet dogs, and happily ever afters at any age.

Susan is a wife and stepmother. She enjoys rummaging through thrift stores for treasures like four-dollar cashmere sweaters and amateur watercolor paintings. She likes taking walks with her Lab mix, Tucker, and his buddies. She and her family live in North Carolina.

Susan has used her professional background as a psychotherapist and management consultant to add authenticity to her characters.

Readers can visit Susan's website at www.susanschild.com and sign up for her quarterly newsletters at www.susanschild.com/newsletter.html. Follow Susan on Facebook at her Susan Schild Author page.

Dear Readers,

Thank you for reading *Sweet Southern Hearts* and for spending time with me in Willow Hill.

I'd like to ask for your help. Readers' reviews are the most powerful way to get the word out about my books. While the book is fresh on your mind, would you please take a few minutes and write a review about *Sweet Southern Hearts* on your retail book site or Goodreads?

I am so grateful for your support and always look forward to hearing from my readers.

My best wishes to you all,

Susan Schild

susan schild

Linny's Sweet Dream List

Starting over, one wish at a time...

A WILLOW HILL NOVEL

susan schild

Every day is a chance to start anew...

Sweet Carolina Morning

A WILLOW HILL NOVEL

CPSIA information can be obtained
at www.ICGtesting.com
Printed in the USA
BVHW031148050620
580969BV00001B/16